"I knew t... dead,"

Cass said. "Everything in me rose up and said that I loved you and you could not be dead, and here you are."

He wrapped her in his arms and pulled her up against his chest, into the deepest security she had ever been offered. Vere pressed her free arm up around his neck and closed her eyes, feeling his strong, confident heartbeat, and wished for a moment that things were as he believed they were.

Then she struggled gently and said, "I'm sorry. My name is Vere Bourne. And I'm afraid the woman you love really is...must be dead."

He let her go then. "All right," he said calmly. "Of course you don't trust me yet. But you will. I'll give you all the time you need. Meantime, when you need me, and you *will*, I'll be here."

Dear Reader,

The weather's hot, and here at Intimate Moments, so is the reading. Our leadoff title this month is a surefire winner: Judith Duncan's *That Same Old Feeling*. It's the second of her Wide Open Spaces trilogy, featuring the McCall family of Western Canada. It's also an American Hero title. After all, Canada is part of North America—and you'll be glad of that, once you fall in love with Chase McCall!

Our Romantic Traditions miniseries continues with *Desert Man,* by Barbara Faith, an Intimate Moments-style take on the ever-popular sheikh story line. And the rest of the month features irresistible reading from Alexandra Sellers, Kim Cates (with a sequel to *Uncertain Angels,* her first book for the line) and two new authors: Anita Meyer and Lauren Shelley.

In months to come, look for more fabulous reading from authors like Marilyn Pappano (starting a new miniseries called Southern Knights), Dallas Schulze and Kathleen Eagle—to name only a few. Whatever you do, don't miss these and all the Intimate Moments titles coming your way throughout the year.

Yours,

Leslie J. Wainger
Senior Editor and Editorial Coordinator

Please address questions and book requests to:
Silhouette Reader Service
U.S.: 3010 Walden Ave., P.O. Box 1325, Buffalo, NY 14269
Canadian: P.O. Box 609, Fort Erie, Ont. L2A 5X3

THE
VAGABOND

Alexandra
Sellers

INTIMATE MOMENTS®

Published by Silhouette Books

America's Publisher of Contemporary Romance

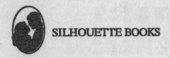 SILHOUETTE BOOKS

ISBN 0-373-07579-0

THE VAGABOND

Copyright © 1994 by Alexandra Sellers

Books by Alexandra Sellers

Silhouette Intimate Moments

ALEXANDRA SELLERS

used to force her mother to read to her for hours. She wrote her first short story at ten, but as an adult got sidetracked and didn't get published until she was twenty-seven. She also loves travel; she wrote one book in Israel, and began another in Greece. She is currently living in London, but that could change at any time.

for Nick

Prologue

Don't think of sharks. They said night was when predatory creatures came into the bay—when they were most dangerous, unseen but seeing in the dark. But she must keep her mind resolutely away from the thought of what might be fanning its sinister way toward her in the depths. It would do her no good to panic. She shivered. She was cold, though the water and the night air were warm.

Her progress seemed slow. Every minute was increasing the chances of discovery. She swam with her head above the water. It slowed her down, but an engine propeller would kill her more surely than a shark.

There were so many lights, so many boats, and so much darkness in between. She had no landmark, only the line of moored boats she must follow, chosen for their easy recognition in the dark. If she lost her bearings she might not find her way again.

At last she saw the shape she was looking for—the green catamaran. Behind its mast the huge bulk of the yacht appeared. She struck out in a wide arc and came at the yacht amidships. At a distance of a few yards, inside the yacht's shadow, she rested, treading water. From here she could see the night watch in the wheelhouse above. He sat in the captain's chair, working at something on the table in front of him, intermittently watching a screen. Twice, as his idle glance strayed out over the water, she ducked her head.

Another figure appeared on the bridge. She sighed in relief—it was a woman, carrying a tray. She watched as the woman set down the tray, handed the watchman a glass, took one herself, bent and kissed him, and then, as he pulled her down, settled onto his lap. She watched as they drank and nestled in each other's embrace, kissing and talking.

Her inactivity became gradually more terrible, her courage and confidence draining away. What she was doing was stupid and very dangerous, but she had been able to ignore that fact as long as she was moving. The waiting was giving her time to think about the consequences of discovery—and the chances. Until this moment she had believed in success. But if the couple did not move soon ... There! The woman was standing up, holding out her hand. The man set down his glass and stood up. After a moment they disappeared from view. A light went on behind the drawn curtains of the captain's cabin, farther aft.

Keeping her eyes on that light, she swam slowly to the stern. When the light went out, she pulled the flippers off her feet and laid them on the swimming platform, then as quietly as possible pulled herself out of the water to sit beside them. Here she was still in shadow, but above her head the stern light threw a gloomy half light over everything, and she would be exposed as she climbed to the deck. She must step confidently. More important, she must walk softly. The noise of footsteps carried on a boat.

She skirted the Jacuzzi. Now the aft camera would be picking her up, but the night watch wasn't there to see. She climbed the ladder to the next deck.

Here the glassed-in deck, with all its greenery, was sinister in the gloom. She slipped gratefully into the relative protection of the side deck and crept forward to the crew entrance.

It was unlocked. The second hurdle passed. Inside, she paused, breathing heavily, and waited for her heart to still. Then she moved down the steps and along the carpeted hallway.

Small deck-level lights outlined her way now—but she would have known it in the dark. At the end of the short corridor she pulled a latch and with terrible slowness slid open a metal door.

She carried a small, powerful flashlight, and here, in the dark heart of the ship, she could use it without fear. She turned its glow upward, slowly playing it along the ceiling with its bare, exposed metalwork as she stepped awkwardly around the equipment at her feet.

After a few moments, she moved to the doorway, doused her light, and slid the door open again. She crept down a short corridor and into the darkened lower-deck saloon. Taking a deep breath, she turned on her flash again.

She moved to a drawer behind the room's luxurious wet bar and lifted out a pointed tool, then reached up as if at random to prise out one of the leather-covered panels lining the ceiling over her head.

After a struggle to work loose the first, she pulled down three in quick succession. Time was passing. She played the flash briefly on her watch, then moved forward, pulling down the panels as quickly as she could and laying them softly at her feet.

Suddenly her mouth opened in a soundless gasp as she gazed up toward the area of ceiling bared by her exertions. Now she began working more quickly, as if inspired, leaving a trail of panels as she crossed the room in a straight line.

It happened without warning. A panel slipped from her grasp, and in her convulsive attempt to catch it, the ice pick flew from her hand and landed on a bronze tray in the middle of a glass-topped table. The noise was horrible in the silence—a ringing clangour from the tray and a loud, echoing thump from the dropped panel. She might as well have brought a brass band aboard with her. She killed the flash and stood unmoving, listening for movement from above.

The sound of a shout from *behind* her, on the same deck, made her gasp in dismay. Who besides the watchman was aboard? There was a noise overhead, too, of the night watchman on the deck above. Would he go into the saloon above and down the stairs into this saloon? Or would he go straight down the forward companionway? Which way should she run?

In the shadowy glow that filled the room, she saw the ice pick on the carpet a few yards away and instinctively snatched it up before running on tiptoe up the carpeted staircase to the next deck, through the saloon and into the glass-enclosed aft deck. She paused to pick up a potted hibiscus from a table just inside and threw it back down the stairwell, where it landed with helpful thunder, then ran to the sliding-glass door.

The key was in the lock. She turned it as quietly as she could and opened the door. An onshore breeze blew against her face. She slipped out onto the small, open section of the deck and closed and locked the door behind her. After a second's hesitation she sent the key overboard.

Behind her she saw light in the stairwell—they had reached the lower-deck saloon. Too late, she realized the plant had been a mistake, for it would tell them exactly where she was.

She flung the ice pick in a high arc toward the bows of the upper deck, but it did not land with any noise. Behind her, in the saloon, she could see a head coming up through the stairwell. There was only one way out now. She climbed over the side rail, clinging high above the water with one hand, and leapt off into darkness.

She sank deep beneath the surface, with scarcely enough breath to let her claw her way back up. Fear was using up too much of the oxygen in her blood. Had they seen her? Had they heard the splash? Would she come up to find a searchlight blinding her?

She surfaced in darkness and gratefully heaved in oxygen. She had, perhaps, moments. She dived under and began to swim in long, powerful strokes. No time to think of other dangers now.

When she surfaced for the third time, she heard the sound of an engine. They were in the dinghy. Her heart sank; she had a long way to go. She could play hide and seek among the boats for a while, but she would be worn out before they were.

Suddenly, ahead of her, there loomed the shape of the green catamaran. She drew a breath in the first hope she had felt since dropping the panel. She dived under and kicked powerfully toward the blessed blackness between the two small hulls of the boat riding lightly on the swell.

Please God, let her make the protection before they came in this direction. If only they hadn't seen where she jumped.

She felt the shadows fall on her, felt the protection envelop her as she came between the cat's green hulls. She surfaced and then slipped as close as she could beside one of the hulls, at its centre point. When her eyes grew accustomed to the darkness, she saw that the hatch in the hull opposite was open. Someone was aboard. God help her if he looked out and saw her.

The harsh sound of the dinghy motor was getting closer. They had gone the length of the big yacht, but now they were coming around the bow and directly toward the cat.

In the second before the fierce searchlight pierced her cocoon of darkness between the hulls, she pulled herself under the water, clinging to the cat's smooth side. When she surfaced again, she was calmer. She could wait here now until they had gone—the bay was big and it would be impossible for them to search it systematically. They would give up soon.

In the distance, the motor slowed almost to idle, and over the muted roar she heard the words, "Under the cat." Then the noise kicked up again, and grew louder as they returned to her refuge.

She almost lost control then. They would find her now, unless—unless . . .

On the other hull the open hatch beckoned. Out on the water beyond the cat's hull, the bright glow of the searchlight glinted brokenly on the tiny wavelets. If she stayed where she was, they would get her. She swam toward the open hatch, reached up to grab the lower rim and drew herself out of the water and into the depths of blackness inside. There were only seconds now. She leaned over the edge of the hatch and fell through.

She landed on the softness of a smoothly made bed, leapt up and reached out to pull the hatch cover closed. It clicked into place as the blinding rays of the searchlight pierced the gloom between the cat's hulls, and she opened her mouth in a sigh of relief. She turned then, and her sigh became a gasp of surprise.

A man was standing in the darkness beside the bed, silent and unmoving.

Suddenly the searchlight's rays streamed in through the hatch, falling on his face, and her whole being was swept with a shudder. *"You!"* she whispered in horror.

Chapter 1

"I dreamt about Cilla last night," said Vere.

"Again?" Alexa bit her lip as she poured coffee into a cup and pushed it to Vere across the worn oilcloth covering the pine table. Vere picked it up gratefully.

The morning sunshine slanting onto the verandah was warm, and a soft breeze blew across the lake. Another day of Indian summer. What Cilla used to call, "A day torn from the clutches of winter."

She had dreamed about Cilla for the past five nights. Vere took a mouthful of coffee. It was hot and burned her mouth, bringing tears to her eyes. She set down the cup and fanned at her mouth; it was not a serious scald, but the tears, once started, spilled over.

Her aunt reached across the table and covered Vere's hand with her own. "Well, it's the anniversary," she said, her own eyes abruptly wet. The two women sat in silence as tears dampened their cheeks. "We've got each other," said the older woman gently after a moment. "Funny how things turn out, isn't it?" She meant that Vere had lost her mother,

and she had lost her daughter, and now aunt and niece were
left together. They smiled at each other through their tears.

Vere said, "She's trying to tell me something, Aunt Alexa. I know they're not just dreams."

Alexa said firmly, "Vere, you have your own life to lead.
Cilla has been dead for a year. However it happened, nothing can change that fact."

"What life am I leading?" asked Vere with a shrug. She
looked out over the lake. "I've been sitting here doing
nothing for nearly two months now."

Come to the cottage for a while, her uncle and aunt had
said, when her life had fallen to pieces. *You need a rest, and
then you can think and plan what to do next.* But she hadn't
wanted to think, and planning what to do, while her life lay
in ruins around her, seemed to be beyond her.

Her aunt said, "You still have a lot of recovering to do.
Of course, what Rory and Marta did—" Alexa prided herself on never judging people, but she could not keep the in-
dignation she felt out of her tone "—has taken the lid off
other feelings, too. I always thought you didn't grieve
properly when Cilla died. You can't escape grief, Vere. But
it's a lot harder to get through it when you've saved it up."

Maybe she was right. Vere blinked up at the sky, where a
hawk was coasting on an updraft, the sun glinting from his
bright feathers. She wished her aunt wouldn't keep saying
their names. Rory and Marta. It was like being stabbed. She
said, "I know I didn't think enough about Cilla when it
happened. There was no time for it. I was working so hard
to try and keep the business from going under." And what
a waste it had all been, in the end. She looked at her aunt.
"But that doesn't mean my dreams of Cilla are about grief.
You know we were always linked, like you and Mother."

Her aunt smiled mistily. "I know you were," she said
softly.

"Well, the dream is like that. It's like our old link.' *It's not right,* the dream Cilla had told her urgently. *It's not right.*

"I believe you," said Alexa. "It must make you feel lonely and rather helpless." Alexa had been a therapist before taking a sabbatical after her daughter's death to write; she slipped easily into clinical technique. "Of course, in Jungian terms, Cilla is your shadow," her aunt went on. "You were so different in character. You each could adopt extremes because the other was always there to show you what your alternative path was. Cilla always knew what her life would have been like if she'd settled down, and you always knew what would have happened if you'd kicked over the traces. Now you have to explore that side of your personality for yourself. She's not here to do it for you. The dream Cilla is your shadow, reminding you you will have to explore that other side of yourself in order to be a full human being."

"She wants me to do something about it," said Vere stubbornly, resisting the pull of that therapeutic, self-centred logic. If she listened to it, she would lose what she knew—this was only grief up to a point. Behind the dreams there was some reality, some truth. Cilla was trying to tell her something, trying to urge her to action.

"What action can you possibly take?" asked her aunt, abruptly losing her grip on therapeutic technique. "Don't you think the insurance company has investigated the accident down to the ground? Do you think they're going to pay out millions if there's the smallest possibility they aren't legally bound to do so?"

"They haven't paid yet, though, have they?" Vere pointed out.

Alexa sighed. "The announcement that they are going to pay the claim is proof enough to me that they're satisfied."

"They're only losing money. We've lost Cilla," Vere said.

"A year ago," her aunt pointed out. "Even if you're right, I don't see... Do you have any doubt that Cilla is dead?"

"No," said Vere. "Not...no."

"Then what is the point?"

Vere watched the hawk beat its wings into lazy flight and disappear over the top of the yellow forest, then stood up. "I want to show you something," she said.

They had always had a link, Vere and Cilla. As small children, they would sit in a silence broken by the occasional exchange, incomprehensible to an outsider, "Ice cream!" "Raspberry!" "No, Silly, butterscotch!'" or "Dog!" "Collie!" "Yes!" interspersed with long bouts of giggles. When people asked what they were playing, they sometimes said "the listening game," sometimes "the thinking game."

Fortunately, no one bothered to attend very closely to the cousins' explanations of how exactly the game was played, and so no one ever told them it was impossible. By the time they understood that their telepathic link was considered unusual, even suspect, it was too well-established to be damaged by hostile opinion. After the age of ten they rarely mentioned it to outsiders.

Their mothers were identical twins, and physically both their daughters, only six weeks apart in age, took after them. Met singly, Vere and Cilla might sometimes be mistaken for one another, but when they were together, everyone knew which was which. It was a curious phenomenon, and no one ever quite understood the reason for it.

When she was twelve, Vere's mother and father died in a road accident, from which Vere herself miraculously escaped. The car had concertinaed, leaving a small pocket of safety where she was sitting in the back seat. She had gone to live with her aunt and uncle, sharing a room with Cilla. Their bond had only been strengthened by this proximity.

Curiously, in spite of their physical resemblance and their mental link, temperamentally the two cousins were very different. Cilla had always been "the wild one," refusing to worry about the future, to think about settling down, refusing to knuckle under to other people's ideas of what was right. Vere lived a much more prosaic life, thinking of the future from the beginning. While Vere was in university slogging over a design degree, Cilla had traveled the world on a shoestring. When Vere got engaged to Rory, whom she had met in her last year of university, Cilla was maintaining a string of boyfriends, and had no intention, she told her mother, of settling down with any of them. While Vere started a business with Rory and her friend Marta on her inheritance and a loan from her uncle, Cilla was working as a stewardess on yachts in the Mediterranean and Caribbean, coming home for vacations looking carefree, brown and vital. For the first time, then, she was not mistaken for Vere, because Vere was pale and thin and working too hard.

"It's not worth it," Cilla had told Vere on her last trip home, after Vere had described what the recession was doing to her business. "Why don't you toss all this to the winds, where it belongs, and come back with me to Bequia? I know of a yacht with a couple of jobs going. We'd have a fabulous time."

"I'm building something that's going to last. You could stay here and come to work with us," Vere had countered.

"With winter coming?" Cilla had simply laughed. She hated Canadian winters. "Never again."

She was right. She never saw another winter. A few weeks after her return to the Caribbean, she had taken a new job on *Incitatus*, a fabulous megayacht. Not long afterward, *Incitatus*, setting off across the Atlantic to the Mediterranean, had caught fire at sea. The captain had radioed for help, but before help could arrive the fire had gone out of control. Everyone in the engine room fighting the fire had been seriously wounded. The yacht had had to be aban-

doned. They said Cilla had panicked and that it had been
impossible to get her to board the lifeboat. They had had to
leave her aboard the yacht as they fled, though they had
taken the bodies of two of the crew. Cilla was still aboard
the yacht, screaming, when it exploded and sank.

Thousands of miles to the north, Vere had awakened from
deep sleep, sweating and shaking, and refusing to accept
that she had just heard Cilla say goodbye.

Vere stood in the doorway for a moment. The cottage
bedroom had remained unchanged for years. It still had the
twin beds that had been bought when the girls were twelve
and the decoration on the walls that had built up during
their teenage years. In this room Cilla was still alive. Vere
crossed to the wall above Cilla's bed, where an imperfectly
framed old newspaper clipping was yellowing behind its
glass. She lifted the frame from its place, exposing a rec-
tangle of paler pine wallboard behind it, and returned to the
verandah. She set it down in front of her aunt.

"Oh, that," said Alexa, obediently glancing over it. *Stu-
dent Heroine Saves Lives in School Fire,* read the headline.
The heroine had been Cilla Fairweather. There had been a
gas explosion in the chemistry lab, and the fire had blocked
the way to the door. Chemistry labs by law had two doors,
so panic had not set in until the class had discovered that the
second door was unaccountably locked. It was Cilla whose
calm command had stemmed the panic, Cilla who had
climbed up to smash the tall windows, Cilla who had forced
her fellow students and the teacher to jump one by one into
the garden ten feet below, and then, with the fire breathing
on her skin, had been the last to leap to safety.

"I'm a fire sign," she had lightly told the journalist from
her hospital bed. "Fire doesn't frighten me."

"They said she panicked," Vere told her aunt now, in the
way people do repeat things they know their audience
knows.

Alexa, her elbows on the table, put her face into her hands and then lifted her eyes to look out over the lake to a neighbouring island. "Yes, I know," she said softly.

"The only element that scared Cilla was earth," Vere pursued. "Fire wouldn't have scared her, and she loved water. The only thing I ever saw her scared of was 'getting rooted.' If Cilla was caught in a fire at sea she didn't go down screaming."

"No," agreed her aunt.

"She said goodbye to me in my sleep. She wasn't panicked then. I'd have felt it."

"Yes, I understand that."

"And she would *hate* to be branded a coward like this."

"Yes," said Alexa. She sniffed and wiped her nose on the back of her hand.

"I'm sorry, Aunt Alexa."

"No, don't be sorry, Vere. I've always known this. So has Robert. But there didn't seem to be anything we could do. If they were lying, there didn't seem to be any reason for it. And she was dead, so what good would it do to stir things up? Whatever really happened, finding it out won't bring Cilla back."

Vere recognized her uncle's calm voice in that, and realized suddenly that her aunt had suffered more over this than Vere had known. She had a vision of long bedroom conversations, her aunt in tears and her uncle saying, "It won't bring her back."

"It won't bring her back, but it'll set the record straight," Vere said stubbornly. "I think Cilla has a right to the truth, and so do we. I think it makes a difference."

Suddenly her aunt's face was wet with tears. "So do I," she whispered. "What shall we do, Vere? What are you thinking?"

"I'm going down to the Caribbean to find out what really happened," she said, as the cloudy ideas that had been roiling in her head for days past abruptly cohered.

Alexa sobbed once in a quickly repressed relief that told Vere all she needed to know. "We don't have a lot of money at the moment, Vere."

"I won't need money. I can do what Cilla did," she said quietly. "I'll get a job on the yachts. I'll be a stewardess."

Chapter 2

As the sun set beyond its starboard wing and darkness enclosed the jet, the drone of its engines seemed to change into a deeper, more intimate sound.

"That's quite a boat," said the voice of her seat partner near her ear. "Is that the one you're going to join?"

Vere looked up from the photograph of the yacht and the tiny figure whose vitality was unmistakable, even at such a distance. Cilla had sent her the picture just before the accident—herself on the deck of *Incitatus,* a tiny brown-and-blond figure against a majestic white hull. Vere must have been gazing at it for minutes without realizing it, her brain almost at a standstill. She had been looking for her passport. They were almost ready to land.

"No," she said. "This is a megayacht. *Brigadoon* is a smaller yacht. It's lovely, isn't it?" They had chatted casually during the flight, enough for him to learn that she was going to work as a stewardess on a yacht and for her to learn that he "worked in security."

"What's her name?" asked her seat partner.

He was young and attractive in a stocky, Saskatchewan-farm-boy way, and he was making it clear that he found her blond looks a draw. "June," said Vere, pulling a name out of the air. She hadn't told him anything about Cilla. If people knew she was investigating her cousin's death, there was always the possibility they might not talk to her.

He smiled. "I meant the yacht."

Vere laughed lightly. "Oh—I don't know that. She didn't say."

"It's written on it, isn't it?" said the farm boy, casually plucking the photo out of her fingers and bending to examine it.

"If you can read it," Vere said, resisting the impulse to snatch it back. The name was half obscured, and anyway, what did it matter? This man was too ordinary, too much of a type to be part of the yachting crowd. He looked like exactly what he said he was—a security guard. Short, but not fashionably short, clean-cut hair, square, bland face with thick skin, his shirt perfectly pressed even after nearly three hours in the air. The wrinkles at the corners of his eyes were not from smiling, but from watching. Probably he felt naked without a gun on his hip.

"*Tatus,*" he read at last. "Funny name for a boat."

She resisted the urge to point out that it was only part of the name; the rest had been cut off by shadow. "Boats do have funny names, I guess," she said.

He flipped the photo over as he handed it back to her, briefly, but a second was all it took to read what was written there.

"See what you're missing?" Cilla had scrawled. "Why don't you give it up? It's not worth the grind!"

She had been right about that. It hadn't been worth the grind. Three years of hard work and determination had not saved the business once Rory and Marta had privately agreed the fight wasn't worth it; and four years of loving trust had not counted for anything when her fiancé and her best friend decided they loved each other better than they loved her. So much for building for the future.

"Are you joining your friend?" asked the farm boy, tacitly admitting to having read the scrawl.

"No," said Vere, her heart clenching in sudden pain. "No, she—she's in the Mediterranean at the moment. Maybe we'll meet up later. I might try to find a job on a yacht going over there." That much was true, anyway. If she found out nothing in the Caribbean, Antibes would be her next target, if she could manage it.

"I guess the grind, whatever it was, got to you," he said, a curious lack of real sympathy in his tone, as though he had learned the ritual but did not understand the reality behind it.

Vere shrugged dismissively. There was no question that she was still not fully recovered. Vere had always had resources, always been resilient, and she was surprised at how long her physical recovery had taken. But of course she had been suffering from exhaustion even before they told her. The last eighteen months of devoted energy and insane working hours culminating in failure had made the terrible, subsequent blow of Marta and Rory's betrayal simply impossible to stand up to.

She glanced at Cilla's figure again as she put the photo back into her bag. Cilla had been right about something else, too, something she had said more than once—what had Vere been building that couldn't be destroyed in a single night? That was what Cilla had believed—that nothing was permanent, anyway, so what was the use of trying to keep a wave on the sand?

Vere's tide had gone out pretty brutally, nonetheless.

"What kind of business did you have?" asked her seat partner.

"We were in design," she said. "I'm a designer. Rory did the accounting and Marta did sales."

He made a face. "The recession was tough on businesses like design, I guess."

"But not on the security business," said Vere with a smile. She had told him enough about herself, and she wasn't sure why she had been so open when all he did was ask questions. "Have you ever worked as a personal bodyguard?"

"Sometimes," he said.

"What's that like?"

"Not like the movie," he assured her with a grin.

"Ladies and gentlemen, we'll be landing at Saint Lucia in a few minutes," the stewardess's voice began. Their conversation died, and in the business of getting ready to disembark was not revived.

Vere wasn't sorry. In retrospect, she felt she had talked too much. She was not naturally secretive, and she would have to learn quickly to keep things to herself. If she were right about Cilla's death, someone must have had good and sufficient reason for lying about it.

"Welcome to Saint Lucia!" exclaimed a voice, and a middle-aged woman hugged her warmly and stood back to look at her. "I'm Jill, and you're Vere, all grown up since I last saw you! My, aren't you a beauty! Just the living spit of Cilla!"

Vere laughed and eyed the darkly tanned woman in perplexity. "When did we meet? Alexa thought we had, but I don't remember at all."

"Oh, I guess about thirteen or fourteen years ago. Before we left on our great adventure. You and Cilla were running around like young colts that summer before we left."

Vere shook her head. "I just don't remember."

"Cilla remembered us, but then we saw a lot more of Cilla than we did you in the old days. We ran into her quite a bit down here."

"Oh," said Vere.

"It was terrible, what happened. A terrible piece of luck. If she'd been able to get in the lifeboat, she'd be alive today. We were really upset about it."

"Yes," said Vere.

"Well, let's not think about it!" said Jill brightly, bending to pick up one of Vere's bags and then shepherding her towards the airport parking lot in the warm twilight. "Are you looking forward to your new job? Alexa says you've never done anything like it before."

"No, I went into design. But I'm a quick learner."

"Oh, yes, you'll have no problems. In this business, the right attitude to work is more important than experience."

She opened the door of a van and tossed Vere's bags inside. "Climb in," she said.

"Hi," said a voice beside them.

Vere turned to see her seat partner from the plane. "Hi," she said.

"Sorry to impose on such short acquaintance, but my taxi doesn't seem to be here, and I'm in a bit of a hurry. I was wondering if I could catch a lift with you, if you're going in my direction."

"We're going to Rodney Bay," said Jill.

"Ah, too bad," he said. He smiled ruefully at Vere. "Maybe we'll meet again somewhere."

As he melted off into the darkness, they got into the van. "Rodney Bay Marina," said Jill to the driver, and then, as he started the engine, she asked Vere, "Who was that?"

"He sat beside me in the plane. We didn't exchange names."

"Well, he can always find it out. The Caribbean is a small world."

"What do you mean?" asked Vere.

"I mean, if he's interested enough, and he sure looks it."

"Interested in what?"

Jill turned and pointed out the back window of the van as it waited to pull out of the airport onto the main road.

"He's right over there getting into a car, so that story about his taxi not showing was a crock," she said. "All he wanted was to find out where you were going."

Vere shivered as she looked toward the car. Even in the darkness of a Caribbean night the stocky shape climbing inside was clearly that of the man who had sat beside her.

"But not for the reasons you're thinking," she observed quietly, suppressing a chill that said something was wrong here. "He wasn't attracted to me. But he wanted me to think he was."

Her sleeping cabin was the smallest room Vere had seen in her entire life. Right at the bow, it was triangular in shape, and so were the two bunk beds along the side. The pillow was at the wide end, and she noticed that her feet would thus have about a foot of space to move in. There was a tiny cupboard, and the space beneath the lower bunk was her locker. There was no porthole. It was going to be a little like sleeping in a coffin.

"Believe me, you'll be too tired to notice where you sleep most of the time," Jill said apologetically. "Luckily you don't have to share it. We don't carry a deckhand anymore."

"Is this how Cilla lived?" Vere asked in surprise, as she obediently stowed her luggage under the bed. She had always got the impression from Cilla that her on-board accommodation was rather sumptuous.

Jill smiled and shrugged. "Oh, well, you know Cilla. The owner's stateroom is always pretty plush on motoryachts, and that's usually where Cilla ended up."

"Oh" was all Vere could say.

"And don't frown like that. If you're thinking Cilla was being sexually exploited, you should know better. Cilla always knew exactly what she wanted, and she took it. I know of at least two owners who proposed to her over the past few years, but Cilla wasn't having any of it. She never took men seriously."

"I've got three rules around men," Cilla had told Vere once. "One—never be in love longer than a month. Two—always leave them wanting more. Three—never trust 'em."

Oh, if only Vere had listened to rule number three. Suddenly, she began to laugh. How wonderful to have been able to carry off such an attitude! To go through life utterly heart-whole, bending a finger when you wanted someone!

"Oh, she'd have made mincemeat out of Rory!" Vere exclaimed. "He wouldn't have known what to do with himself!" She began to laugh at the mental image of Rory's probable fate at Cilla's hands, and she felt the first real lifting of the burden of pain she had been carrying since she had learned about Rory and Marta. "Oh, I wish she could have taken my place when he told me! She'd have laughed at him and wished him good riddance!"

"Was he the one who was in business with you?" asked Jill. "She met him a couple of times before she died?"

"Yup."

"Well, if it's any comfort, she always said it would happen. 'No balls' was how she saw him."

Vere stared. "Really?"

"She figured on you coming down here for a month or two when it all went bad. And here you are, you see. Cilla always did get her own way."

Brigadoon was a handsome boat, without being in the megayacht class. It generally carried between four and six people on a charter, and between them, Jill and Vere would do all the cooking, cleaning and catering.

"And shopping," Jill told her next morning over breakfast on deck, outlining their routine as Vere yawned and stretched in the morning sun. The bay was full of a variety of boats, mostly small and medium sailboats, with the flags of a dozen different countries visible on their sterns. They were encircled by dusty green-covered hills; the sun was already warm at nine o'clock; and the sky was utterly without a cloud. It would be impossible, Vere reflected, to feel urgency in such a setting. After a few moments she picked up her cup of coffee, padded over to the rail and looked appreciatively down into the turquoise sea.

"We'll leave in about half an hour to go ashore and load up," Jill continued. "Sorry to drop you in at the deep end, but we've got charter guests coming in this afternoon and there's a lot of work first. The last lot left last night, but with picking you up there wasn't time to get much cleaning done."

"That's fine," said Vere. She didn't mind work. She leaned out over the railing, staring down. "There are about a million tiny silver fish down there," she observed.

"Yes, they seem to like the boat's shadow. It always happens," said Jill. "Do you want more coffee?"

Vere crossed to the table again and held out her cup gratefully. She was already wearing her "uniform"—a pair of knee-length white cotton shorts and a short-sleeved turquoise cotton polo shirt with the name *Brigadoon* printed above the left breast in white letters that matched the script on the bow. Her feet were bare, her long hair loose around her shoulders. A breeze was blowing across the deck. She felt the unfamiliar sensation of freedom. As Jill poured the last of the coffee, Vere slipped into a chair and heaved a satisfied sigh. "I think I'm beginning to understand what Cilla saw in this life," she said.

For the trip into town she slipped into a pair of white rubber-soled shoes, tucked her hair up under the hat that went with her uniform—a white baseball cap with the yacht's name in turquoise—and put on a pair of sunglasses, very necessary in the bright tropical sun.

Ron and Jill wore the same outfit, and there was no mistaking them as "boat people" as they rode to the dock in the yacht's dinghy and scrambled ashore. Ron disappeared on his own errands, and the two women made their way to the supermarket.

It was hotter ashore than aboard the boat, and the streets were dusty. "This is a pretty good supermarket," Jill said, as they moved up and down the aisles in a dark shop that deserved more the name "general store." "We'll get everything we can here, and then I'll take you to the bank."

"Everything we can" turned out to be three shopping-cart loads of everything from frozen meats to chips, wine and beer. When they had paid, they loaded as many bags as possible into two carts, and then, each carrying a bag, they pushed the carts over the bumpy road and between two low buildings towards the dock.

They had unloaded all the bags onto the dock by the time Ron arrived. "Right," he said, "let's get this stuff into the dinghy." He jumped down into it, and Jill began passing him the bags.

Jill and Ron were practised at the art, and Vere felt useless just watching as the shopping passed into the dinghy. "Shall I take these back to the supermarket?" she asked, after a minute. She pushed the three carts together and drove them clanking and banging back across the grass toward the supermarket.

By the time she had delivered them, she was covered in a fine sweat. Crossing back toward the dock again, Vere paused in some shade to look around at a scene familiar from a hundred postcards and advertisements. Wiping a hand across her forehead, she slipped off her cap and sunglasses to feel the breeze on her face. Her hair, carelessly tucked up under the cap, fell heavily down around her neck and shoulders, and she clicked her tongue. Next time she would wear a ponytail.

She hooked her glasses into the neckline of her shirt and lifted her hands to her hair.

"Cilla!" cried a voice, in wonder and surprise. "Cilla!"

Vere was still as her eyes moved to the man who was standing a few feet from her, staring and immobile.

But only for a moment. Abruptly he came toward her, his hand outstretched as though he were going to take her arm. "Where have you been?" he demanded hoarsely. "Where did you go? They said you were dead!"

As though coming to his senses, he dropped his hand before he reached her, but the look in his dark, almost anguished eyes was gripping enough. One glance into those passionate depths was enough to tell Vere that she was looking at a man whom Cilla had left "wanting more."

Chapter 3

He was extremely attractive and very masculine. He was tall and well-proportioned, his chest broad, his hips slim, his legs powerful. His curling hair, heavy, well-shaped eyebrows and thick lashes were all lustrous black; his eyes were black as the night sky, and as easy to get lost in. His nose was strong, his mouth beautifully curved, his lower lip full, his forehead and the corners of his eyes lined. His skin was sun- and windburned, and he looked virile and vibrant with health. He was wearing a shirt, shorts and deck shoes, but even without these clues, it was clear he was from a boat.

The look in his eyes was piercing and rather moody as he gazed at her. Vere's heart was beating uncomfortably fast: she had the feeling that he was an eagle and she was a rabbit the eagle very, very badly wanted to eat. She could see that he wanted to touch her, grab her, kiss her...whatever, and the fact that he didn't could only mean that with Cilla he just didn't have the right. Just for a moment she allowed herself the luxury of thinking that Cilla had been an idiot.

She smiled rather distantly. "I'm sorry," she said. "You're mistaken; you must have the wrong person."

At that he did take her wrist, but it was an involuntary movement. For a reason she didn't understand, Vere did not pull away. "No, I'm not," he said. "You're Cilla. Cilla Fairweather. You were reported dead. I knew you couldn't be dead. Look, I'm—" he paused, and she saw that he was swallowing against a powerful emotion. How he must have loved her cousin. Vere wanted to tell him to stop hoping, but she bit her lip and was firm with herself. It would be foolish to blow her cover with the first contact she made.

"My name is Vere Brown," she said gently. "I'm afraid you really do have the wrong person. I've never seen you before in my life."

"No," he said. "I know it's you. You were on *Incitatus*, weren't you? It went down at sea after a fire. You were one of four who were said to have died in the fire. How did you escape? What happened?"

It was extremely difficult to maintain her air of ignorance through all this. She wanted to say, "You think there was something wrong about her death, and so do I. Tell me what you know." But until she knew exactly who he was, it would be a foolish course to adopt. Even someone who knew for certain that Cilla was dead might react this way to seeing her double, after all. Someone who knew exactly how and why she had died would be poleaxed to see Cilla alive.

So she said, instead, "I really am not the person you think I am. I'm very sorry. I think—I think you...were you in love with her?"

He was still holding her wrist, and he lifted his other hand and gently brushed her palm open, looking down into it. A shiver ran through Vere's arm at the touch. "Yes," he said softly, and suddenly his grip on her hand was so strong it hurt. He looked at her face as though he wanted to drink the sight in. "Yes, I was in love with her," he said, with passionate urgency. "I *am* in love with her. And there is noth-

ing she could have done that would have changed that. She
could always have turned to me, though I don't think she
knew it...knows it." And then he bent and kissed her palm.
The pressure of his lips was light, but so hungry it was almost desperation, and a rocket of feeling shot through Vere
as his desire called up an almost overwhelming answer in
her.

Sweat broke out on her upper lip again, and he raised his
head and looked at her, into her, as deep as her soul; and for
five long seconds he held her gaze, and she knew that if he
moved to embrace her now, she would not be able to draw
back. For one terrible moment she felt, like an ocean within
her, the urge to pretend to be Cilla, to experience the passion she knew he could offer.

He did not embrace her. "Do you understand?" he asked
roughly, gripping her wrist more tightly in his urgency, his
dark eyes still piercing her. She knew he still did not believe
her denial. He believed she was Cilla. And he suspected Cilla
of something underhand.

The thought a little chilled the heat he had raised in her,
so that her brain began to function. She was suddenly sure
it was crucial to convince him *now* that she had no connection with Cilla or *Incitatus*. What he believed, others might
believe. And suppose there *was* reason to suspect Cilla of
something...not quite right? It had not occurred to her
before what a two-edged sword her resemblance to Cilla
might be. Until this moment she had not even asked herself
whether something that Cilla had been involved in had led
to her death.

It was an effort to open her mouth, with his touch still on
her hand and his eyes burning her—a double source of
electricity that seemed to meet in the centre of her chest,
making her heart ache. Vere licked her lips and swallowed
against the dryness in her mouth and throat. "I understand, but do you? I really am not the woman you think I
am. I'm Vere Brown." She thought abruptly that she should

not lose all contact with him. He might know something valuable, something important about Cilla. "What's your name?" she added.

"Cass," he said quickly. "Cass Conway. I'm on *Vagabond*. Will you remember that? *Vagabond*. She's just over there. Burgundy hull, white trim."

He pointed just behind her, and Vere turned. Out in the water she suddenly saw Ron in the laden dinghy, heading for *Brigadoon*. Twenty yards away, Jill was standing waiting, a quizzical look on her face.

"Oh, I've got to go!" she said guiltily. "Someone's waiting for me!"

"*Vagabond*," he repeated. "If you ever need anything."

"All right," she said. "I've got to go now." At last he let go of her hand. The flesh felt unfamiliar, as though it had gone to sleep. Vere awkwardly clenched and unclenched her fist, trying to bring normal sensation back, as she jogged lightly over the grass away from him to where Jill stood.

"Have you met a friend?" asked Jill.

"No. A friend of Cilla's. He thought I was her, come back from the dead," Vere said, trying to keep it matter-of-fact. "I don't suppose you know who he is?"

"I didn't recognize him. What boat is he on?"

"*Vagabond*, he said." Vere turned to look out into the bay again. Ron had reached *Brigadoon* and was beginning to unload. Closer in, off to the right and behind a couple of smaller craft, she saw a wine-coloured sailing yacht with sharp white trim. "That's her there," she said.

"Oh, yes. We've seen her around for the past few months, but I've never met the owner. What did he say his name was?"

For one moment of horror she thought she'd forgotten. Vere's heart gave a kick she felt in her temples. "Cass," she said a little breathlessly as the name returned to her. "Cass Conway. Did Cilla ever mention him?"

"Cilla never talked about men. They weren't important enough to her," said Jill matter-of-factly. "It's a very handsome boat, though. Looks about forty feet. Shall we go to the bank? Ron'll be back for us when he's unloaded. We've got a lot of work to do before our guests come aboard."

She was not exaggerating. Vere was used to long and dedicated hours, but she had little experience of hard physical work, and aboard *Brigadoon* she was expected to be chambermaid, cleaner, laundrywoman and waitress. Six beds had to be made, and six sets of towels had to be laid out. There was a load of clean laundry to fold, including things that had to be ironed. Brass and chrome and mirrors were polished, floors vacuumed, bathrooms cleaned. Wood paneling was rubbed up. The huge aft lounge, where, Jill informed her, their paying guests would spend much of their time, had to be spick-and-span, and the bar restocked.

Vere worked as hard as she had ever worked in her life, but it was work that left her imagination free. And as she scrubbed and polished and plumped and dusted, her mind kept returning to the man who loved her cousin with a love so strong it had withstood even death. And when, involuntarily, she compared that to Rory's kind of loving, she knew that she had been fooled all along. It had been comfortable, it had seemed secure, but it had been a very pale love. Cass Conway might one day learn to love another woman, she thought, but she knew as surely as she had been born that he would never love anyone as he loved Cilla even now, an entire year after her death.

What had Cilla had that, for all their similarity in looks, Vere did not have? What was the quality that made a man so crazy for a woman? In that one moment of feeling Cass Conway's lips on her hand she had sensed more concentrated passion than she had felt in Rory in four years of be-

ing engaged. A feeling so powerful it had forced her own
desire to answer it.

For a moment Vere let herself imagine Cass in love with
her, making love to *her*, and all the blood seemed to rush
from her head to the pit of her stomach. She felt faint, but
her body was singing. In spite of the air-conditioning in the
galley, sweat beaded her brow. Vere bent her head and
closed her eyes, forcing the images from her mind.

"Are you all right?" asked Jill, on the other side of her
worktable.

Vere opened her eyes. "I'm fine," she said.

"There's a bit of a swell today," said Jill. "Not surprising if you feel a little queasy. But you'll get your sea legs
soon enough."

"I guess so," said Vere. "I've finished these. What can I
do now?"

"Ron'll be here with the customers pretty soon. Why
don't you go, have a quick shower and change your uniform? I'm going to change, too, and then start getting dinner ready. After that the dining table needs to be set."

Ron had taken the yacht in to the marina and filled up
with water and fuel while the two women had been working
inside, and from now on water use, particularly by the crew,
was somewhat restricted. Vere took a cooling thirty-second
shower, rubbed herself dry and changed into a repeat of her
earlier uniform.

As she combed her hair, standing in front of the mirror,
she wondered again what special quality Cilla had had, so
that millionaires had proposed and a man such as Cass
Conway had fallen so powerfully and passionately in love
with her.

For the first time in her life she envied her cousin.

The charter group was a business deal in the making.
There were three men who apparently intended to talk a
certain amount of business between the swimming and eat-

ing and fishing, and three women who were simply decoration. They all came aboard and settled down in the saloon with the slightly manic joy that marks Canadians who are escaping winter briefly to a warmer climate. Vere managed to get their attention long enough to take their drink orders.

Then she went to the galley, where Jill was laying a tray with snacks. "Catastrophe," Vere announced. "Two of them have ordered banana daiquiris. How the heck do you make a banana daiquiri?"

Jill looked up with a smile. "The captain always pours the first round of drinks," she said. "Don't worry for the moment, he's just making sure the baggage gets aboard. For the future, there's a book inside the bar cupboard, and the instructions are easy to follow."

The galley door opened, and one of the men stepped inside. "Hi there," he said, with casual enthusiasm. "Sorry to bust into the backstage area like this. Just want to have a word with you girls, if I may."

"Yes, of course," said Jill.

"See," he began, "I'm trying to close a deal with these guys. The yacht I normally charter down here was booked up the whole month. I just want to make sure that my friends get the best treatment on this trip, get put in a receptive frame of mind. And I'd like them to think you all know me, if you understand. So it'd be nice if you'd call me George and make it clear that I'm a regular customer. It's a good deal. It's got a good chance of going through, and if it does, there'll be a nice little tip for everybody at the end of the trip. What do you say?"

"Of course," said Jill.

"What are your names?"

"My name's Jill, and this is Vere. But Vere's new this year, you won't recognize her."

"That's fine," said George. "I'm glad you understand. Okay, Jill, Vere. I'll leave you girls to get on with your work."

"There, that's done," said Jill, as soon as he had gone, putting the last trimming on a beautiful tray of vegetables, cold meat, cheese and small, savoury pastries. "Will you take that up? Ron'll be up there by now."

Vere said, "Do you get a lot of that?"

"One way or another. The first thing you learn in this business is, there's a lot of ego around. If you just cater to it, you'll be all right."

Ron was behind the bar, which was by now surrounded by a cheerful group prepared to believe this was going to be a wonderful holiday. He was mixing the banana daiquiris and delivering a lecture on the careful use of fresh water on a yacht. Cheers greeted the appearance of the savoury tray. All the women exclaimed at how famished they were, but Vere noticed, as the hour progressed, that, of the three, two of them ate only enough for a mouse's breakfast, and both of them skillfully disguised that fact.

They allowed themselves a greater calorie consumption in alcohol, though after the first round of banana daiquiris, white wine became the same two women's drink of preference. "Could you mix that with a little water, please?" one said at her second order, with a certain look in her eye, and the other nodded agreement. After that Vere was careful to water their wine liberally.

The exception was the oldest woman, apparently George's live-in partner, if not actually his wife. She was thin, at least as thin as either of the others, Vere thought, but whatever this was due to, it wasn't lack of alcohol consumption. She ordered whiskey on the rocks as her first drink, and she continued with whiskey on the rocks throughout the evening.

By eleven o'clock most of the party were in bed, the dinner dishes were finished, the saloon had been tidied, and Jill sent Vere to bed. "Not a moment too soon," said Vere, who was by this time dropping with fatigue.

Jill laughed with her. "Yes, it's rough on you starting with such a large group, and with only a day to get used to things. But you'll be all right, you've done fine. You've got lots of stamina, just like Cilla."

Vere would have liked nothing so much as a long, hot bath, or failing that, a cooling swim. But the only bathtub on *Brigadoon* was the one in the master stateroom, and she would only have been allowed an inch or two of water in the bottom, anyway. And Ron had told her it might be dangerous to swim at night: it was possible that sharks and other less-attractive creatures of the sea might come into the bay at night, and they would be invisible.

But she could not just fall into bed. Vere took another brief shower—barely enough to make herself wet—and without drying slipped on briefs and the knee-length man's shirt that served as her nightdress. She brushed her hair and then went out onto the aft deck to look at the stars and the softly lapping black water for a few minutes.

There was a light breeze blowing, making her damp skin shiver pleasantly. Vere leaned back on the luxuriously padded seat, propped her bare feet up on the rail and gazed up at more stars than she had ever seen from the city.

The Big Dipper was almost directly overhead. She was trying to remember how to find the Little Dipper and the north star when she heard an unfamiliar brushing noise, and then a voice very softly called, "Cilla!"

A shiver of terror rushed through her. She jerked up, her heart kicking hard behind her breast. "Who's there?" she called, and it was only when her own voice came out as a subdued half whisper that she realized that to use the tone of a conspirator was to tell whoever had called that she, too, had something to hide.

"Who is that?" she called again, in a more normal voice. By this time she had realized that the voice came from the water at the stern, and she leaned over the rail and looked down.

He was recognizable in starlight, she wasn't sure why. Cass Conway sat in a small dinghy, holding onto the yacht's stern. "What do you want?" she demanded. Enough adrenaline was pumping into her system to prepare her for a run to China, making her feel giddy, almost sick.

"Can we talk? Will you come down for a minute?"

She said, "I am not Cilla, whoever she was. There's no reason for us to talk."

"Vere," he amended. "Whoever you are. Just come and talk to me for a minute."

The urgency in his voice moved her, reminding her that he had been Cilla's lover and that he loved her cousin deeply and passionately—and that Cilla had not loved him. Vere felt her eyes go damp. She wondered if Cilla had been as brutal to him, sending him away, as Rory had been to her.

"All right," she said. "But I don't see what good it can do." Holding her shirt down to prevent the wind blowing it up around her hips, Vere climbed over the rail and let herself down onto the yacht's swimming platform. He pulled the dinghy close in against the swell, his tanned hands dark against the shadowy white paint. She put one bare foot on the inflated side and stepped down into the dinghy.

It takes longer than a day to learn how to climb into a dinghy gracefully, or even competently, especially in darkness. Vere slipped and stumbled, and automatically she reached for him. And as quick as that, his arms were around her, catching her and pulling her down against him, burying his face in her flesh.

She landed with her back against his chest. His face was against the side of her neck, breathing her scent as a nearly anguished groan came from his throat. "Oh, God!" he said. "How I've waited for this! Kiss me. Oh, God, kiss me!"

It was impossible to remember that it was really Cilla he wanted. His arms encircled her, his hands gripped her, she could feel him trembling with barely containable need. Vere had never been on the receiving end of such passion, and animal response simply took over.

He felt her shivering response to the touch of his mouth against her neck, and firmly and deliberately turned her body till she lay facing upward, lying across his legs and gripped in his strong arms. He bent over her, and the starlight that had been reflected in those dark eyes went out as he did so, and there was only blackness burning into her soul.

"I love you," he said hoarsely. "Kiss me." And then his mouth found hers—not with any practised demand, but with the gentle, questing passion almost of a first kiss; and sweetness simply opened a gate inside her and flooded in, bathing her with a taste like honey.

She gasped. She could feel the fullness of his lips, soft and generous as they moved against her mouth, and then, slowly, to her cheek, her ear, her eyelids, the brow of her nose, and down again to her mouth. He didn't choose, but simply caressed with his lips everything that came in their way. One hand stroked her loose hair, and lifted it up, and he kissed that.

He said, pressing her up against him, "I could die happy just smelling you and knowing you're real. Will you come with me?"

Her hand rubbed against his hair, and it bristled in her palm. A few drops of sweat, or water from her shower, had collected in the hollow of her throat, and he kissed her there and trailed wet lips up her throat to her chin. "Come with me," he urged again.

She was filled with unfamiliar languor, so that she almost imagined she should do whatever he said. "Where?" she asked, and her body hummed with the thought that he would take her somewhere and make love to her.

His kiss moved the other way, down her breastbone into the vee of her shirt between her breasts. His hand gripped her ribs and ran up the side of her body to her arm, but did not touch her breast, not yet. He caught her hand and kissed the palm. "We'll disappear," he said. "We'll go somewhere and I'll sort everything out. Don't worry. Whatever's happened doesn't matter. I'll find a way. I'll fix it. But you shouldn't be around here. People will recognize you."

He touched her cheek and raised his head to look at her. Starlight returned to his eyes. "God, you're beautiful," he breathed. "Think of all the marvelous and beautiful creatures in the world, and then think that you are most beautiful of all. I knew that you couldn't be dead. Everything in me rose up and said that I loved you and you could not be dead. And here you are." He wrapped her in his arms and pulled her up against his chest into the deepest security she had ever been offered, and Vere pressed her free arm up around his neck and closed her eyes, feeling his strong, confident heartbeat, and wished for one moment that things were as he believed they were.

Then she struggled gently, and his hold loosened and he smiled down into her eyes. She said, "I'm sorry. My name is Vere Brown. And I'm afraid the woman you love really is . . . must be dead."

He let her go then, and helped her sit up. "All right," he said calmly. "Of course you don't trust me yet. But you will. I'll give you all the time you need. Meantime, when you need me, and you will need me, I'll be here."

The breeze was suddenly cold against her skin as he released her to pick up the oars. As he began to row, Vere looked around. They had drifted during the past five minutes. Dark water surrounded the little dinghy, and the few distant lights from the shore and the moored boats gave her no bearing whatsoever. She had no idea where *Brigadoon* was. She looked at Cass and the knowledge of her own vulnerability made his inherent power more visible. She realized that he could probably have made good on that promise to Cilla—if she were in trouble, he would have fixed it, whatever it was.... But she was not Cilla, and what she saw in the darkness was that he would make a dangerous and implacable enemy.

She was not Cilla. It was not Vere he loved. Cilla Fairweather would have been utterly safe with him, but Vere Brown... She had to force herself to the realization...it would be better for her if she were never in his power...and never allowed herself to get into a position where she was at his mercy.

Chapter 4

They had not drifted very far. Within a few minutes he had pulled up behind the large white hull of *Brigadoon* again, and Vere clambered onto the swimming platform. She turned.

"Were you waiting out here for me?" she asked.

"No. I was on deck and saw you come up. I got into the dinghy and rowed over." His voice was quiet, and she realized again that hers had been, too. She had the feeling that they sounded like conspirators, and yet there was a very good reason to speak softly: it was late, and voices carry across water.

"Where are you moored?" she asked in surprise, because he had arrived soon after she had come up on deck. He pointed over his shoulder with his thumb.

"Right there." Behind the yacht, its rigging clacking in the wind, a tall mast rose above a dark, smooth shape riding the swell. A light hung from the centre of the boom, but she couldn't identify *Vagabond* from the brief glance she had had of it earlier.

"Did you change your mooring today?" she asked suspiciously. "Weren't you moored closer in before?"

"You know I was."

She didn't, for sure, because she was no good at recognizing boats. Perhaps she would become so with practice. Jill and Ron seemed to be able to name a boat from an amazing distance.

"Why?"

"To be close to you," he said simply. "I told you, if you need me, I'll be there."

She stared down at him for a long moment. "Why are you so sure I'm going to need you?"

"Everybody needs somebody sometime," Cass said. "When you need someone, I'll be there. Then it'll be me that you need."

He spoke quietly still, and yet somehow the words burned in the night air, so that she felt them physically in her heart. They were an invitation to rest in the security of his love.

Three—never trust 'em. She heard Cilla's voice in her head, and reminded herself that whoever this man was, he was one of any number whom Cilla had refused to be in love with for longer than a month.

"I won't need you," she said levelly. The invitation was not for her, but for Cilla, and anyway, what proof had she even that this man really loved her cousin? For all she knew he was so angry over being rejected that he actually wished her harm. "And I am not Cilla. And I think you should stop following and watching me. I don't like it."

"Good night" was all he replied to that. "Would I were sleep and peace." Then his teeth flashed in the darkness, and there was only the sound of his oar against the water.

She stood for a moment gazing out after him as he silently made his way toward the boat behind. His progress was slow, and it was only when he paused halfway between the two boats and she heard the sound of a motor that she understood that he had deliberately not used the dinghy's outboard motor when he came.

What had made him think he ought to arrive silently? What had made him moor near *Brigadoon?* "Everybody needs somebody sometime," he had said, but she had the uncomfortable feeling it was not the whole answer. He knew something, she was sure. He knew something about Cilla that made him think that if she were alive, she would now be in danger; made him accept without question the idea that she was living under an assumed name.

What had Cilla been part of? What was it this stranger suspected her of? Perhaps he even *was* the danger she should run from. As she climbed up onto the afterdeck, Vere shivered in the night breeze. If Cilla had not died in the way they had been told, how—and why—had she died?

For the first time in a very long time, she slept soundly. Her first day of fetching and carrying had exhausted her more than two years of great mental stress; or perhaps it was just that mental exhaustion had not been conducive to sound sleep.

Her sleep was dreamless, too. If Vere had unconsciously been hoping for some guidance from Cilla on the subject of Cass Conway, she was disappointed. Cilla had ceased to trouble her dreams on the day that Vere had made her decision to come to the Caribbean, and apparently there was nothing in the appearance on the scene of an old lover to arouse her to new activity. Vere didn't know whether she was glad or sorry.

Jill woke her at seven. She awoke feeling more refreshed than she could remember feeling since college days, and by seven-fifteen she was at work, vacuuming and cleaning, then setting the table on the stern deck for breakfast while she listened to the news on the BBC World Service. The state of the world had not improved in the past twenty-four hours, and she was reaching to shut it off when George appeared, yawning and stretching.

"Leave that on for the market news, please," he said. "Is there any coffee going?"

Vere stopped what she was doing and made her way to the galley. "Make him some in the cafetiere and take it up," Jill said. "There's a coffeemaker on the bar in the deck saloon. If they're going to be drinking coffee all day, you'd better start that going first thing in the morning from now on."

When she returned to the deck with the coffee on a tray, several other guests were up, and each seemed to have their own individual way of starting the morning. Vere was rushed off her feet, eating her own breakfast in snatched mouthfuls, until breakfast was cleared and the dishes were done. She was cleaning the table and chairs on the aft deck when a hallooing from the stern made her heart leap. Imagining it was Cass again, she dashed over to the rail.

Two young black men sat in a rowboat full of bananas and other fruit. "Yes?" said Vere.

"You want bananas, Saint Lucia bananas?" one of the young men asked.

From the deck above her, Ron called down, "Go and ask Jill if she needs anything, Vere."

Jill came on deck at her summons, climbed down onto the shelf and haggled lightly in the fresh morning breeze over the quality and the price of the fruit. An unaccustomed pleasure suddenly descended on Vere, and so long was it since she had experienced it, it took her a moment to place: the simple pleasure in small things, in brief moments.

The sun was warm, the bay beautiful with the tall masts of its sailboats; the men in the fruit boat were slim and firmly muscled, their glowing, dark skin a bright contrast against the yellow of the bananas and the green and orange of the mangoes and papayas stacked in the brightly painted little boat. Jill stood barefoot and stocky in her neat turquoise-and-white uniform, her skin tanned to a deep orange, her hair bleached by the sun, one hand up to shade her eyes as she looked down at the fruit. It was like a picture on a postcard, and might have been entitled, "Caribbean market." In that moment a strand of the cable of tension that had been her constant companion for two years and more loosened and gave way, and Vere breathed in deeply and sighed.

Jill bought what Vere thought was a huge amount of fruit, and the fruit boat rowed away. The two women carried the purchases aboard, and then, without warning, Jill said, "Oh, look! There's *Vagabond!*"

Vere had been avoiding looking at it all morning, though she had been fully aware that it was there: in the sunlight the burgundy hull was unmistakable at such a distance. "Yes," she said, glancing over at it.

Cass Conway was on deck. He looked up as they glanced over at him, and waved. Jill waved back; after a brief hesitation Vere followed suit. "He changed his mooring," said Jill. She grinned at Vere. "I wonder why."

Vere shrugged. "It's not me he wants. It's Cilla. When he knows me better he'll recognize his mistake." She was gazing absently over to the deck of *Vagabond,* where Cass, wearing only dark swim trunks, was wiping down the paintwork. He was beautifully proportioned, with a body straight out of a steamy movie. The muscles of his calves and back flexed and relaxed hypnotically as he worked.

"You're going to be seeing him, are you?"

Vere came to with a start. "No... I don't know. Why?"

Jill smiled. "You said, 'When he knows me better.'"

Vere bit her lip and grinned. "Did I? Well, I don't know about that. He seems very... determined, for want of a better word. But he'll realize soon that I just am not Cilla. If he really loved her, that is. And if he didn't love her... what does he want from the woman he thinks is her?"

"Do you like him?"

"No," said Vere flatly, suddenly assailed by the memory of last night's encounter and that crazy desire she had felt for a stranger. "No. He scares me. He thinks Cilla did something . . . wrong or illegal . . . I'm not sure. And I keep wondering why he's so sure."

Jill was staring at her. "Thinks Cilla did something illegal? What? And when?"

"I don't know. He keeps saying he'll be there when I need him. He accepts without question the idea that Cilla would be using a false name. What does that tell you?"

Jill stared at her. "What could Cilla have been involved in? Drugs? Illegal immigrants? *Incitatus* did make a couple of trips to South America after she joined it, I think." She stood holding half a dozen mangoes against her breast, her eyes unhappy. "Does he think—was she smuggling?"

It was a thought that must easily occur. "I don't know," Vere said again. "I only know he thinks I am Cilla, and that means that in his mind it's not impossible she is alive. If he knew for sure she was dead, he'd know I wasn't her. I haven't so far told him I have any connection with Cilla, and I don't intend to."

"No, you'd better not. If he thinks she was smuggling, God knows what reason he has for thinking it. It would be absolutely *awful* if he started thinking Cilla had passed on anything to you." She paused. "Or that you still have possession of something, as Cilla. You know what I mean."

"Yes," said Vere, bending to pick up a huge bunch of bananas and turning to look toward *Vagabond* again. She was just in time to see Cass Conway—if that was his name—go off the stern in a quick dive. She watched till his head appeared above the water and he struck out in a slow, rhythmic crawl. "He didn't buy that boat with peanuts, did he? And what does he do for a living that lets him hang around the Caribbean for months at a time? I suppose he chose the name because that's what he is, but even vagabonds have to do something to get their money, don't they?"

"Vere, you look so much like Cilla," said Jill softly. "Please be careful."

Over the next few days, Vere was run off her feet. She woke at seven, and went to bed after eleven, and in between she was lucky to get any break at all. By tradition the stewardess should have had two hours each day, between the end of lunch and the cocktail hour, but in practice Vere's inexperience meant she generally had to work through those hours. And even when she had finished all her appointed tasks, she was often summoned by a guest to perform this or that errand during that time. She found that there was no time in the day when she could consider herself totally free.

In the morning she laid the table, served breakfast and cleared it, made beds and tidied the sleeping cabins; then she laid the table, served lunch and cleared it. Before dinner she served drinks and canapés, laid the table again, and then served and cleared dinner. She also loaded and unloaded the dishwasher after each meal. After dinner it was her job to turn down all the beds, leaving a chocolate rose on each pillow, and replace ice water in all the bedside drinking jugs. In addition to all this she had to find time to clean all the bathrooms, put out fresh towels, vacuum the entire yacht once a day, do the laundry and iron. The heavy laundry, such as sheets and towels, was generally sent to a laundry when they were visiting one of the larger ports, but that still left a great deal of washing to be done on board. The ironing seemed an endless task: along with the staff uniforms, there was a constant supply of tablecloths and napkins, as well as the fiddly, irritating task of ironing the top edge of every bed sheet.

"I don't know what the laundry does to make the top edges wrinkle like that, but they always do," Jill observed sympathetically one day when Vere was cursing a recalcitrant bed sheet. Vere did the ironing in the crew mess, which adjoined the galley, so the two women spent many hours chatting while Jill cooked and Vere did the laundry. "I was a stewardess for a few years before I met Ron, and ironing was the job I hated most. The stewardess works harder than anyone else in this business. It's the killer job on any boat. We used to have a deckhand, but since the recession, we make do with just ourselves and a stewardess." She smiled ruefully, but she had warned Vere how hard the job was before she came. "They say a change is as good as a rest."

"It better be," Vere said, because it was clear there wasn't going to be much in the way of actual rest. But she was laughing as she said it, because in spite of the hard work and the rather unpleasant sense of never having a real moment of time off, she was enjoying herself. Some combination of the heat, the light and the island air was revivifying her, in spite of the hard physical labour and long hours.

Her thoughts, at least, were freer than they had been for a long time. She was not weighed down by the constant grind of fearing the business would go under, nor the horror of feeling her creativity dwindle with each new care. And somehow Rory and Marta's betrayal seemed distant here, small and unconnected to reality. At least it did not plague her as it had once done.

And she enjoyed the conversations with Jill. Woman-to-woman chat built her strength, she found. She began to realize, by contrast with the far-ranging, no-holds-barred nature of her talks with Jill, that for the past eighteen months she and Marta had had a friendship in name only. Their conversations had become stilted, limited to business and an exchange of personal-health reports; and the excuse Vere had made for this state of affairs when it was happening— that of pressure of work—was, she saw now, not the real answer to the distance that had grown up between them. If she had not been so worn down by stress Vere would have known long before Rory and Marta confessed the truth that there was something wrong.

"How did Rory act through all this?" asked Jill, when she had expressed this thought one day.

"You know, Rory never changed. I used to find that comforting—he seemed so solid. But when I look back on it, I see that he was no different during the time that he and Marta were—were—"

"Cheating on you," Jill supplied, with the air of one unafraid to name the crime.

"Yeah—well, he was exactly the same through it all. Sometimes I wonder what that says about him. Didn't he have a conscience about it? Or was he just a very good actor?"

Jill put the finishing touches on a beautiful tray of canapés and crossed the galley to slip it into the fridge. "Some people are happy as long as they're doing just what they want to," she observed. "Other people's happiness doesn't trouble them. What made Marta change toward you was guilt. Maybe Rory just didn't feel guilty."

Vere shrugged. It seemed a long way away now, and in some ways she was glad it was all over. It had been a terrible grind, and although it had broken her heart to let the business go, perhaps Marta and Rory had been right to force her to do it. Cilla had used to say, not very originally, that "life was too short," and by her own death she had shown how right she was. It would be a long time before Vere thought of trying to build for the future again. She was going to enjoy herself.

They sailed leisurely down the Windward Islands, from Saint Lucia to Saint Vincent, and then to Bequia, which everyone pronounced "Beck-we." Vere had her sea legs now, and was gradually learning the ropes, getting her schedule to a point where she generally managed an hour off in the early afternoon. She spent it swimming, snorkeling or relaxing in the sun on the tiny forward deck, for, whatever was known about the ill effects of the sun, it had a way of melting all your cares away. She was careful with sun cream, but still she was turning a soft beige, and by the end of her first week was looking a good deal healthier than when she had arrived.

The yachting community was a world of its own, and the people who had been in it for years, such as Jill and Ronald, knew each other well.

One night when the charter guests were at a jump-up in Bequia, Ronald stayed on *Brigadoon* while the crew of a neighbouring yacht picked up Vere and Jill to take them into port for a drink with a couple of other crews.

It was a large yacht with two stewardesses. One of them smiled at Vere, and said, "Hello," in a very friendly voice. Later she sat beside Vere in the bar and said, "Nice to see you again."

She had a Canadian accent, and Vere was caught off guard. Did the girl look familiar? She wrinkled her brow. "Where do I know you from?" she asked, thinking it might perhaps be high school or a class at college.

The girl said, "We worked on *Conquistador* together for a couple of months a few years ago." Suddenly she flushed bright red, and her mouth fell open. "No, but...it can't be! What's your name?" she stammered in confusion.

This had the effect of stopping all conversation around the table. Vere said, "I've only been doing this job a short time. I know I look like someone who died when a yacht went down."

"Oh, *Incitatus*," said someone. "Last year. Horrible story." Suddenly the conversation was focused on the *Incitatus* tragedy. "They had to leave the stewardess, didn't they, because she was so hysterical they couldn't get her off." It was clear they were familiar with the public details, but this didn't stop a general discussion of them.

"They were in the Bermuda triangle, weren't they?"

"Now, who started that stupid story? They were a few hundred miles off Antigua."

"And five crew died."

"No, four."

"It was the bloody captain's fault! They tried to put the fire out and he waited too long before radioing for help."

"Should he have radioed immediately?" asked Vere.

Shrugs all round. "Who knows? Sometimes you can get a fire under control. Nothing to say there was real negligence."

"Nothing to say there wasn't. It went down pretty damn fast after they did call. By the time the rescue planes were out they couldn't see a sign of the yacht. It was twelve hours before they found the dinghy, and in the meantime, all the wounded had died. The fire must have been out of control for a long time before they radioed."

"Fires get out of hand very quickly. Anyway, it exploded, didn't it?"

"There wasn't enough of an enquiry, if you ask me. Palms got greased somewhere. With five people dead, there should have been a lot more questions asked."

"And what about the EPIRB? Why wasn't that working?"

"What's an EPIRB?" Vere asked.

"Thing that sends out a radio beacon for rescue craft," the same person explained. "He said the battery was dead. That in itself is suspicious, isn't it?"

"Is it?"

"The captain's still working, anyway. We met him in Venezuela a couple of months ago. What yacht does he have now, Barry?"

"I thought the captain was wounded in the explosion and died later. The owner was the only survivor, wasn't he?"

"There was no captain. He'd been fired. The owner was running it himself. It was probably sheer incompetence, the whole thing."

It was the first Vere had heard of any fired captain. But the conversation had too much speed for her to get any question in.

"Who *was* the owner, anyway? Canadian, wasn't he?"

"Harding. Yeah, he's big in whiskey or something."

"Harwood," Vere interposed. "William G. Harwood."

"Yeah, that's right. Arrogant bastard. Let's hope he learned his lesson," said someone in bitter sarcasm. "He shouldn't be allowed to sail a bathtub."

"Oh, come on! It wasn't his fault, was it? Most of them died when the engine room blew up, didn't they? Except for the girl."

"When you're captain you don't wait till your engine room explodes before calling for rescue. And you don't go off and leave someone to go down with a burning ship because she's too hysterical to rescue."

"What would you have done?" asked Vere.

"If necessary, I'd have punched her head and carried her into the dinghy. I certainly wouldn't have left her."

"Maybe there wasn't time. Maybe he had to choose the lesser of two evils. Obviously, he wasn't very experienced," a woman protested. "That doesn't make him a villain."

"It makes the whole thing bloody suspicious, is what it makes it."

Vere's heart was pounding in her head. "What do you think really happened?" she asked, trying to look no more than casually interested, and resolutely keeping her eyes away from Jill in case someone should intercept the look.

The speaker, who was a captain himself, stretched and yawned. "There's no way of knowing exactly what happened now, when there's only one survivor. Maybe the wounded panicked and jumped in the dinghy and pulled away before they noticed the stewardess wasn't aboard. Maybe the owner was so concerned about saving his own skin he deliberately abandoned four people in order to give himself a better chance of survival. They somehow lost the big tender during the explosion, and all they had was the lifeboat and a small emergency dinghy. Maybe he thought they wouldn't all survive. I've always thought all those deaths and burials at sea were a curious feature. Why take the bodies aboard in the first place if you're just going to dump them?''

"There was a storm, wasn't there? They were going to be swamped."

"Maybe," said the cynical captain.

Her thoughts made Vere feel faint, and without warning her stomach heaved. Carefully she set her glass down. "Are you all right?" asked the stewardess who had known Cilla.

"Yes," Vere said, leaning back in her chair so that she wouldn't fall sideways if she fainted. "I'm getting a bit of delayed seasickness, I think."

Jill came to her rescue. "Oh, that happens to new sailors all the time! You're fine until you get solid land beneath you!"

"I'm all right now," said Vere. She couldn't let this get away from her. How right she had been to come here to learn the truth! She turned to the captain. "Do you really think anyone would be so cold-blooded as to... abandon four people at sea?"

People around the table smiled cynically and shrugged. "People die at sea all the time," said someone. "It's very difficult to prove something like that even when you know for sure it's what happened."

"Myself," said someone else, "I've always wondered if *Incitatus* was running drugs or something, and it went wrong. You know, most of the crew had been taken on at La Guaira. The captain and the regular crew were all fired just before the trip."

"What does that mean?" Vere asked.

"It means he'd deliberately filled the boat with undesirables for some reason. I think they said it was because he'd sold the yacht to someone in Majorca, and it was a one-way trip, but it didn't sound right to me.''

"I never knew that!''

"No, well, they all conveniently died, didn't they? And their papers—or lack of them—went down with the ship. It's one of the reasons there should have been more of an inquest, but it's also likely nothing would have turned up. The owner didn't remember a single last name, except for the stewardess. And she was a person who *would* be missed, so he had to.''

"What about all the people who were fired?''

"Well, you don't find them talking about it much, because they naturally feel lucky and don't want to say so. Bit naf to feel divinely chosen because someone else died in your place.''

"Harry Bridges disappeared from sight for a while after that. He really seemed to take it to heart. I think he thought if he'd still been captain four people would still be alive.''

"Well, he's running his own yacht now. We saw him in Venezuela a few weeks ago," said the woman who had spoken before.

"What's the name of it?'' Jill asked.

"Now, what was the name of his yacht? It used to be owned by the guy who bought *Villeneuve* from Bill Edwards. Nice little thing—charters for four.''

"Oh, *Billy Budd!*''

"That's right! He bought *Billy Budd.*''

"Really! We passed *Billy Budd* a week or two back, near Grenada. I had no idea Bridges had her.''

"It really is weird how much you look like her," said the girl who had once worked with Cilla. "Did you ever meet her?''

A direct lie was too much for Vere. She smiled and said, "I only arrived here last week.''

"That's amazing. What's your name?''

Vere told her.

"Now, what was *her* name? Kelly? Cindy?"

Vere almost told her.

"Cilla Fairweather," said a male voice firmly, and Vere looked across at the man who'd been introduced as the engineer of the yacht *Big Business*. Another one, her radar told her. "You must get mistaken for her a lot."

"Strange men have a way of looking at me as though they know me," Vere said, hoping to keep the conversation going. "I get the feeling my look-alike left a few broken hearts in her wake."

"If she did, I'm sure you could put them back together again," said the engineer. He wasn't at all handsome, but he looked strong and as though he had a high libido. And he was looking at Vere as though he were working out in his head how to please her physically. Vere blinked fascinatedly at him, for the first time really understanding something about the kind of life Cilla had been part of. Where a man could look at you with the promise in his eyes of no more than being able to give you a good time sexually, and in some expectation of being taken up on the offer. Had he looked at Cilla like that, and had she smiled back with a promise of her own? She wondered how well he had known Cilla, and whether he could tell her anything that might be important.

"Did you—" she began, but she was interrupted by a voice just behind her.

"I don't think it's very likely," said Cass Conway slowly. He laid a hand on her shoulder, and although the touch was light, she could feel the strength in his fingers. "I think any broken hearts are going to have to take care of themselves."

Chapter 5

Vere blushed, and everybody was smiling. Cass reached out and pulled a chair from the table behind. "May I join you?" he asked. Within minutes, sitting beside Vere, he became a comfortable part of the group.

"*Vagabond?*" the captain was saying. "That's the burgundy sloop? Yeah, I've seen you around. Good yacht, that. You're by yourself, are you? How's it handle?"

It turned out that the captain had a small sailing yacht of his own in England, which he sailed whenever he was on holiday. The two men compared the relative merits of their boats, and the general conversation broke up into smaller groups. On Vere's other side, the stewardess who had known Cilla asked softly, "Is he your boyfriend?"

Vere was on the point of denying it, when she happened to glance across the table and catch the eye of the engineer. He was looking at her with frank admiration. She felt a sudden certainty that she was not equipped to handle the easy sexual attitudes that were so obviously a part of this life. And in the aftermath of the hurt she had suffered from

Rory, it might be all too easy to get hurt again. The engineer's admiration was balm to a wounded femininity, but Vere knew that for her, the promise of sexual pleasure alone would not be enough. She was too vulnerable, especially now. She would be touched, she would end up wanting more than that.

She had discussed the subject with Cilla often, and she knew that there had been some fundamental difference between the two cousins' sexuality. To Cilla, sex was a marvelous physical phenomenon and men were, first and foremost, creatures of her pleasure. But it was not that way for Vere.

If people got the idea she was already attached to someone, it might offer some protection from looks such as the one the engineer had in his eyes. So in answer to the girl's question, she said, "Sort of, yeah," very quietly.

But it was not quietly enough. The sudden stillness from her other side told her that Cass had heard the question and had listened for the answer. She tried not to look at him, but when he picked up her wrist in one strong hand and lifted it to his mouth, her eyes were dragged in his direction, completely against her will.

He kissed the back of her hand, and then the palm, and then, her hand tucked firmly in his, he drew it to rest on his leg. When his eyes met hers they were smiling; she could not help smiling back. Next time she looked at the engineer he made a face and shrugged philosophically, and Vere was sure she had as much protective cover as possible, barring a religious veil.

It wasn't till twenty minutes later, when Cass stood up, and drawing her to her feet, said, "Let's go for a stroll," that it suddenly occurred to Vere that she had left Cass himself out of her reckoning. While Cass was protecting her from other men, who would protect her from Cass?

*   *   *

There wasn't very far to stroll in Bequia. The main street of Port Elizabeth ran in a curve around the bay, and then petered out at the southern end. Here there were hotels, restaurants, shops and the bar where they had been drinking. They walked without speaking for a few minutes, taking off their shoes to walk on the beach and then putting them back on when they reached the path again. Bending over to pull on her sandals in the darkness, Vere began, "I . . . think I should explain. . . ."

"Please don't," said Cass. "Somehow I don't think I'll like the explanation much."

When she straightened up, he drew her arm through his, but almost immediately he had to loosen her again when the path narrowed. The sound of steel-band music was getting closer, its compelling rhythm so perfectly right for the warmth of the night, the black sky and the mingled scents of exotic flowers and baking bread that came to them on the caressing air.

"But I want you to understand," she said.

"Ah," he said in disappointed tones, and she knew he was laughing at her a little.

"You see, that man was looking at me, and I thought—I don't have the—whatever Cilla had that makes it all so casual. And I don't know if I even know how to resist it. So I thought that if I said that you . . . that you . . ."

"That I was your jealous lover," he supplied firmly.

"Yes, well . . . I thought maybe I wouldn't have so much trouble." In the glow of lights from a hotel, she grinned. "You look kind of . . . well, as though you could scare people off."

"Right," said Cass. "Well, let's go make it look good. Would you like to dance?"

They weren't far from the Frangipani Hotel, where the jump-up was taking place around a tiny outdoor square. It was crammed with tourists, but no one was dancing, although the music certainly invited and there was an open space that was clearly meant for a dance floor. Vere drew back. "Is it all right? No one's dancing," she protested.

For answer he simply slipped an arm around her waist, drew her out into the middle of the space, and began to move to the music. He was wearing a loose short-sleeved shirt and brightly coloured baggy cotton shorts, with his bare feet thrust into topsiders. His chin was shadowed, as if he hadn't shaved for a day, and he had the kind of deep Caribbean tan which is unavoidable on a sailing yacht. Black hair curled over his well-shaped calves. It was clear the music affected him on a physical level, and he began to dance.

He was a very sexy dancer, and he looked the complete vagabond. Vere was wearing a simple cotton dress with spaghetti straps, a tight bodice and a very full skirt, which she had bought this morning in one of the shops. It was covered in huge flowers the same blue as her eyes, and her hair hung loose down her back. The music and the heat and the few drinks she had just had made her feel abandoned, and she, too, gave herself up to the beat.

She twirled and spun, for the pleasure of feeling her skirt and her hair catch the wind, and she rotated her shoulders and hips, miming sexual enticement; and when Cass caught her to him and danced a few steps with his body pressed against her, she laughed.

His presence intoxicated her, like the music, making her feel beautiful and wild, free. She turned in his arms, and her back against him, moved her shoulders against his chest and away again in time to the music. In response he put both hands on her waist in a firm and oddly erotic grip, making her move as he directed—side to side, and forward and back. He never pressed her too far back, he didn't pull her hard against his body in any overtly sexual demand. But the mere strength of his hands in their expert manipulation of

her body was more erotic than a hundred crude hip [
could have been.

Emboldened by their presence, other people began to join
them on the dusty square, and then, feeling less exposed,
Vere got a little drunker on the music, a little wilder. When
Cass took her in his arms for a slower, pulsingly erotic
number she glued herself to him, following his moves almost before he made them. It was like forgetting who you
were, becoming an instrument of the music, of the night, of
the heat, of the dance. She was one with the dance; she was
the dance.

A prolonged skirmish on the drums indicated the end of
the set then, and Cass bent, lifted Vera's chin and kissed her,
and it was all perfection. There were beads of sweat on her
forehead and upper lip, and a little rivulet ran down her
back. His hands slipped erotically up her damp arm to her
shoulder and throat as he kissed her very, very thoroughly.
Vere felt completely and sensually alive in a way she hadn't
felt since childhood days at the lake, and she slipped an arm
up around his neck and pulled his head closer, feeling his
heat and the curling hair and his glistening, sweat-slippery
skin.

The drum was silent at last, and the other couples began
to move off the floor, some of them toward the bar.

"Do you want a drink?" Cass asked softly, his arms still
around her, hers around his neck, their faces close.

"Yes, please."

"Rum punch? Banana daiquiri?"

"Banana daiquiri."

He led her to a seat just being vacated at the edge of the
little square. "The bar'll be crowded," he said.

"All right," said Vere, sinking into the chair. "I'll be
here."

But she was right beside the short flight of stone steps that
led down to the water, and she was hot and her feet were
covered in the dust of the unpaved dance floor. After a

minute or two Vere slipped her sandals off, picked them up, and went down the steps and into the water. She set her sandals down on the last step, picked up her full skirt, and began to wade a little. The ocean was cool but not cold, and Vere sang the words to one of the popular dance numbers the band had played as she waded out.

"Vere! Vere!" called a voice, and she turned to see Jill standing on the top step.

"Oh, hi!" Vere exclaimed. She had forgotten all about Jill's existence, all about *Brigadoon*. She moved back to the steps as Jill descended them.

"Look, are you coming back to the yacht with us tonight?" Jill asked.

Vere blinked. "I guess so. I mean, yes, of course. Why?"

"Well, I caught the last of your dance with Cass. You're sure you wouldn't rather stay with him tonight?"

Vere shivered as the cool breeze dried the perspiration on her body. "Of course not," she said. "We've...I..." She didn't know what to say. She felt as though the world she had been inhabiting with Cass had been invaded, and the two realities did not meet at any point.

"Well, if you're coming with us, can you come now? We're all going."

Vere glanced over toward the bar. "Oh, I'll have to...maybe Cass could drop me at the yacht later? Would that be all right?"

"It would be all right, but it won't happen." Jill smiled. "As long as you're on board by seven in the morning, I won't ask any questions. Have a good time."

She turned, but Vere caught her arm. "What do you mean? I'll see you in half an hour."

Jill smiled again. "Honey, forgive me, but there is no way that man is going to bring you back to *Brigadoon* before the sun comes up. I saw you dancing, remember. Good night."

Vere was suddenly cold. Jill was absolutely right. "No," she said quietly. "No, I want to go with you. Can you wait while I find him to say good-night?"

Jill frowned. "You're sure that's what you want? He's a pretty sexy guy."

"Yes, he is, and I..." She faded off. She meant, she probably would have drifted straight into his bed, if Jill hadn't happened along. But she was glad of the interruption. It didn't make much sense to use Cass as her protection against casual affairs with other men, and then fall straight into bed with Cass. "I'll go find him and say good-night."

But when she went to the bar she could not find Cass. It was jammed, but she walked from one end to the other, and she knew she would have seen him, had he been there. She went to the men's washroom and stood outside while she counted four men going in and six coming out, and then returned to the bar.

At last she returned to Jill. "All set?" asked Jill.

For a moment she nearly told Jill, and asked if there were somewhere she might leave a message. But if Cass had wanted her to find him, she would have. He must have had his own reasons for abandoning her, and whatever they were, she guessed he wouldn't be checking for messages.

When the dinghy dropped Jill and Vere off at *Brigadoon*, Ronald greeted her with, "Your boyfriend called."

Vere's heart leapt guiltily. Had it really been necessary to bolt like this? "Was he—what did he say?"

"He wanted to make sure you got back safely. I said if you weren't on the dinghy I'd send out a search party. And he apologized for leaving you for so long. He asked me to tell you he got tied up, and when he got back, people told him you'd left with a woman. He said he was very sorry, and I believed him. Oh, and he won't be around for a week or so."

So he thought she'd left because she got bored waiting! Well, he must be used to it—it was the kind of thing Cilla would have done. Cilla never put up with anything from a man. "They get one chance" was another rule she'd imparted to Vere. If Vere wanted to keep her distance from Cass now, she only had to pretend annoyance at being left for fifteen minutes. "With me you only get one chance," she could say.

But she didn't get a chance to say it. After Bequia, *Vagabond* disappeared. It was only when it stopped following them that Vere realized how much she had watched for it in every port. And of course "following" was not necessarily the right term. People who sailed the Windward Islands, she knew by now, often ended up in the same ports at the same intervals. But after Bequia, *Vagabond* must have taken another course.

Brigadoon sailed only as far south as Mustique. After that they made their way back up to Saint Lucia by the end of the second week and dropped their charter guests. Then they spent another wild morning in Rodney Bay cleaning and shopping in expectation of the arrival of the next group.

Vere felt like an old hand. She had pretty well overcome seasickness, although she still felt queasy in the very choppy seas they sometimes encountered sailing between the islands. She had mastered the job sufficiently that, providing the guests weren't too demanding, she could count on two and a half hours' time off every afternoon, as well as the odd evening off when the charter guests went ashore to eat and party. And she was collecting a nice wardrobe of resort clothes, including brightly patterned sarongs, dresses and T-shirts to wear when she herself went ashore in the evenings.

She had gained five pounds, and it was all muscle. Running up and down stairs, carrying heavy trays of food and drinks, thumping mattresses around and then eating like a lion cub was a lot healthier than sitting hour after hour over the design board and lifting nothing heavier than a T-square and a cup of coffee, she discovered.

In fact, she was getting to look more and more like the picture of Cilla aboard *Incitatus*.

On Saturday morning Jill and Vere were crossing from the supermarket to the dock with another huge load of groceries. To Vere's eyes the scene was now transformed by the fact that she was familiar with it. She could see the yacht *TorBay* at the marina taking on water. The owner had left yesterday and the crew was more or less free. Jill and Ronald and Vere would be invited for drinks on board this evening, but they would not be able to go because it was the first evening for their new charter group. Two heavily laden women crew from the pretty little yacht *Pumpkin Eater* passed them, waving—they were on their way to the laundry. Jill and Vere had dropped off a huge pile of sheets and towels an hour ago.

A day-cruise catamaran was sailing up the bay, crammed to the masthead with pale bodies that were already turning red and would be horribly burnt and peeling at the end of a day spent "cruising the islands." The seabed under any place where they moored—even in the most "unspoiled" little bays—would be littered with beer cans, bottles and any other trash that the "grockles"—as Jill and Ronald called them—felt the sea was big enough to handle, evidently in the belief that any "unspoiled bay" left in the world was only waiting to be spoiled by them. It had taken less than two weeks for Vere to learn to despise these unending crowds for their mob violence against the sea. Not that the yachts had green scruples, by any means. She had seen things—even on *Brigadoon*—that curdled her blood.

She was amazed at how much change two weeks could bring. The last time she had crossed this grass, the Caribbean had been a strange and mysterious world; already it

was familiar, and Rodney Bay had taken on the coloura-
tion of "home."

They pushed their supermarket buggies to the edge of the
dock, where Ronald was waiting in the dinghy, and began
to unload. "I just saw *Vagabond,*" Ronald informed them.
"She's moored over behind *Time.*"

They both glanced smilingly at Vere, and she did her best
to smile casually back. Then she shoved the two buggies together and said, "I'll take these back," and began pushing
them back across the paved area towards the grass.

She was nervous at the thought of seeing him again. She
had been so free that night on Bequia, so unlike herself. As
though she had touched a part of herself much more like
Cilla than Vere—someone carefree, irresponsible, dedicated to the moment. If Jill had not come along when she
did, Vere knew, and was honest enough to admit to herself,
she would have gone with Cass aboard *Vagabond,* without
even pausing to consider the consequences.

Was it Cass who made her like that? Was it merely the
exotically beautiful, sensually alive surroundings? Or might
it be the sense she had of Cilla's presence with her, which she
had become increasingly aware of over the past two weeks?
Perhaps Cilla had been in love with Cass but had refused to
admit it to herself. Maybe she was happy to have Vere take
her place with him.

Whatever the answer, Vere knew that she was not the
person she had been two weeks ago, and she wasn't sure just
who this new Vere was. The whole thing made her uncomfortable, and she saw Cass Conway as a major contributing
factor, at least.

She wanted to see him again, but she wished she didn't.

The new charter group arrived late that afternoon, from
England. There were only four in the group, two married
couples, but in one way they were not very different from
the previous group. They had chartered *Brigadoon* last year,

and it was important, particularly for the men, to be sure that everyone knew it, and that Jill and Ronald remembered them.

For the women, it transpired almost at once, it was terribly, terribly important to maintain the class distinction between guests and staff. And mostly that meant Vere. As captain, Ronald commanded a certain respect. As chef, Jill was seldom seen. Vere, however, was unquestionably "staff," and the holiday was costing a fortune, and everybody intended to get their money's worth.

Within an hour of their arrival, Vere was summoned to one of the staterooms. She found the two women sitting, chatting, one in a chair and one on the bed. The one on the bed, filing her nails, pointed sideways with the nail file at a pile of clothes on the floor at her feet.

"I'm afraid a bottle broke in my luggage," she said. "Could you bring it back to me as soon as possible, please? There's a silk shirt in there I'd like to wear tonight at dinner. It needs to be washed by hand, of course."

Vere blinked at the pile of laundry and then at the woman, hesitating. Jill had said nothing to her about guests' personal laundry, but she had gained the impression that it was not part of the service provided. "I'll see what I can do," she said, bending to gather it up. The woman, however, had ceased to see her once her order was given. She was already back in her conversation with her friend.

Jill was in the galley. "What's that?" she asked as Vere entered, the laundry in her arms.

"A bottle broke in her luggage," Vere said. "She wants them back tonight."

"Well, she won't get them back tonight. She'll be lucky if we can get them to the laundry before closing time. You'd better ask Ron to come down here."

When Ronald arrived Jill indicated the pile of laundry. "You'd better warn them they won't be able to leave tomorrow, because we'll have to wait till the laundry finishes that lot, and it'll be afternoon before they're done," Jill said.

By this time everyone was on the main deck, drinking and watching for the "green flash" of sunset. Ronald explained about the length of time the laundry would take. "It means staying here another night," he told them. "We can drop the laundry off, sail out for a day's snorkeling and come back here for the night. But that means cutting a day off our traveling time. If that suits you, however, it's no problem with me. It means an extra night here instead of in Mustique, basically."

"But that's outrageous!" stormed the woman whose clothing it was. "Do you mean to tell me you can't do a little bit of laundry like that on board?"

"Vere is our only stewardess, and her job is pretty heavy as it is," Ronald explained cheerfully. "I'm afraid guest laundry is not part of her duties."

"Do you know how much we are paying for this charter?" the woman screeched indignantly. "And you tell me that laundry isn't *included?* I suppose you'll tell me next that I have to pay for it to be done."

Ronald was pretty well unflappable. "I own this yacht," he said equably, "so I know exactly how much you're paying. Laundry is not included, and I think you'll find it says so on our brochure. You'll have to pay the laundry charges, yes, but they're not expensive, considering."

"I certainly don't want to spend an extra night here if it means losing a night in Mustique, Betty," said the other woman.

"Well, neither do I, of course!" Betty's outrage was nicely bitten back. She turned to where the men were sitting, quietly absenting themselves from the scene. "Hal, can't you *do* something?"

"Can't you rinse the things out yourself?" he asked weakly. "You do at home."

"Oh, really, Hal!"

Vere abruptly tired of the nonsense. "I can probably find time to do it, if you don't mind waiting till tomorrow," she said. But if she expected thanks, she was disappointed.

"Well, I'll just have to put up with it, won't I?" said Betty.

"It's the same old story," Jill said later. "You'd better make it absolutely clear, Ron. Otherwise Vere's going to be run off her feet." She grinned at Vere, raising her eyes and shaking her head. "I knew we shouldn't have accepted their charter this year. They were absolute hell last year. Be prepared to be asked to take pictures of them with the yacht in the background so they can show all their friends back home how big a boat they were on. And you really will be run off your feet, I'm afraid."

That night, when dinner was finally over and the guests were lounging in the saloon with their drinks, Ronald answered the ship's radio and called Vere. "It's Cass," he said. "He called before but you were busy."

Vere picked up the radio in a state between reluctance and anticipation. "Yes?" she said.

"What time are they going to bed?" Cass's amused voice demanded.

Involuntarily Vere glanced through to the saloon to where the four exhausted guests were still drinking. "Never, at the going rate," she said.

"Can you get away for ten minutes? I'll come over in the dinghy."

Vere swallowed, remembering the last time he had come over in the dinghy. "Why?" she said.

"Because I want to see you. Can you make it?"

She didn't know herself, didn't understand the person whose heart was beating so hard and whose stomach was melting in clear sexual anticipation. "No," she said. "I'm very tired and it's late."

"All right," he said. "I'll come over in the morning. See you about seven."

Anticipation was winning out over reluctance; she couldn't say no twice. "All right," she said. "But I won't have very long to talk."

"I know," said Cass. "I'll be good."

She could hear him smiling; his voice was full of innuendo. As she shut off the radio and set it down, Vere felt her own lips smiling. She licked them and rolled them tightly together, but the corners of her mouth still turned up.

Chapter 6

When she went up on deck in the morning, *Vagabond* was moored close to again. She saw Cass get into the dinghy as she polished the glass door to the saloon and went to lean over the rails as he pulled up alongside.

"Hi," he said, looking at her as if the sight pleased him. "Coming down?"

His hair glinted in the sun, and his eyes were smiling, and the curve and hollow of his brown throat was very potent. She smiled and tilted her head shyly. "All right," she said. "Five minutes."

"Five minutes," he agreed, and she swung her leg over and clambered down the ladder to the little platform, stepping more agilely now into the dinghy. He kept the motor running. "Kiss me," he said, and every good intention of keeping her head was shattered by the directness of the plea. Vere slid along the edge of the dinghy and turned her face up to his; his free arm reached for her, and he kissed her mouth.

He released her lips, but for a moment his arm tightened around her back. Then he let her go. He said, "You won't always see *Vagabond* for the next little while, but if you ever need me and you call for *Vagabond* on the radio, channel sixteen, you'll reach me. When I answer, go to channel seventy-three. All right?"

She said, "I'm really not in any trouble, you know. There's no danger."

"There may be things you don't know," he said impatiently. "Will you remember that number?"

"I'll remember channel seventy-three, but can't you believe that I'm really not Cilla? I'm—"

"Hasn't it occurred to you yet that I might not be the only person to mistake you for her, and that other people might be just as unwilling as I am to believe your denial?" Cass said irritably. "Now, I'm not asking you to do anything except memorize a number in case I'm right and you're wrong about what danger you might be in. Am I making myself clear?"

She felt horribly subdued suddenly. Cilla was dead, and if she did not believe the story she had been told about the means of that death, what did she believe?

"All right," she said. "Sorry."

"I want to impress on you that even if you haven't seen *Vagabond* for days, I will get your call. Do you understand that?"

"Yes."

"I'll try to be in sight, but if it happens that I can't be, don't feel deserted."

"Cass," she said, for now she saw that he was very serious and she was frightened. "What's going on? What's going to happen? Can't you tell me?"

"Nothing so far," he said. "I wish I could hope things would stay that way. You be careful," he leaned down to kiss her again, "and stay out of trouble."

Vere nodded silently, and the five minutes were up. She climbed out onto the swimming platform. "Oh, I forgot the most important thing," Cass called.

She turned, a little breathless. "What?"

"Don't fall in love with anyone else while I'm away," he said. Then he smiled at her, revved his engine, backed away from the stern, and was gone.

"What on earth was all that noise at the crack of dawn? My God, I thought we were sleeping in the middle of Piccadilly Circus!" said Betty over breakfast an hour later.

"Port's a pretty noisy place," said Ronald, who had come down to discuss the day's itinerary.

"It had nothing to do with the port, I promise you. A boat motor going, and a man and a woman talking. It sounded as though she was on the yacht." She glared at Vere, as if she thought she had recognized her voice, but couldn't be sure. "Some girl parting from her lover. I must say, it seemed a little early for it." She laughed mirthlessly. "Or late."

All Vere could do was marvel at how a tone of voice could reduce the value of human feeling to absolute zero.

Vere didn't mind so much being run off her feet. It was, after all, only her third week on the job, and she was by no means bored with it. What did bother her democratic Canadian soul was the arrogance of the whole charter group's treatment of her. The women did not even admit her into the ranks of humanity, as far as their manner seemed to indicate, and if the men did, it was clearly only under the heading of "physically attractive female."

She struggled vainly against these attitudes, and she slowly discovered the unpleasant truth that it is not easy to establish your human right to respect with those who are determined to deny it.

"I can't understand why England never had a revolution and just beheaded all these jerks," she muttered one day in the galley, as the bell in a stateroom she had just left signaled again.

"Not forgetting Charles I." Jill smiled. "Are you imagining that this bunch is from the titled classes? Never believe it. They are nowhere near being even landed gentry. The landed gentry are far more pleasant."

"Really? What are they, then?" asked Vere, who had been imagining that at the very least they were cousins of an earl.

"They are inescapably middle-class in a society where wealth—even if they had it—does not provide an entrée into the upper class," Jill said, with relish. "That's their problem. That's why they have to constantly reinforce the idea that they are superior to you. Because they are so aware it's not true."

Vere smiled. "You sound as if you feel sorry for them."

"It must be hell to be obsessed with class, don't you think? They can't really afford this trip. You watch—they'll drink like fish the whole trip, and then haggle like market traders over the bar bill when it comes time to pay. That's why you're keeping such close accounts of the drinks they have, and making them initial all the chits."

It put things in perspective, and after that it wasn't so hard for Vere to deal with the smugness she encountered. She simply muttered "compensation" to herself, and treated them all like deprived children whose antisocial behaviour was not their own fault.

One day the women and one of the men had gone snorkeling with Ronald, and one man, pleading some slight problem with his ears, stayed aboard. He was sunning himself on the aft deck, wearing a very small, tight pair of trunks, and he called Vere up to ask for a drink. When she returned with it, he had rolled over onto his front, and he held up a bottle of suntan lotion.

"Could I ask you to rub some of this onto my back?" he asked, deceptively casual, as she set down the drink.

Vere smiled. "Sorry," she said, "I don't rub lotion onto anything less than a duke." She pronounced it *dook*.

He flushed bright red and was clearly groping for a killer comeback that just wouldn't surface. "Good God," he said dismissively after a fatal few seconds' delay. "I don't suppose this boat has ever come within hailing distance of a duke!"

"Nope," Vere agreed cheerfully. "We're not good enough for the likes of them, are we?" And while he was still thinking that one over, she disappeared.

After that, he was, if possible, even more arrogant than before. But Vere just looked at him, and somehow he began to falter.

She marveled at how fragile that seemingly overpowering sense of self-worth was. "With anybody from this side of the Atlantic, you wouldn't get through that kind of arrogance with a pickax!" she observed to Jill.

"I know," said Jill. "They're a race unto themselves, the English middle class."

It was a long, tedious haul down to Mustique, made even worse by the fact that she never saw *Vagabond* once.

Mustique is an anomaly among the islands—on the approach, with its prettily painted cottages hugging one side of Grand Bay, and its neat, tidy roads and smoothly grassed hills, it is the image of the perfect Caribbean island. But a closer look reveals that it is more like an elaborate movie set than a real island. There is no local population, no real village. The pink-and-purple painted clapboard houses are exclusive and expensive boutiques; the entire island is owned by the world's moneyed and titled. Vere had gone ashore on *Brigadoon*'s previous visit and found it clean and beautifully designed, but curiously without a soul.

But of course the charter guests loved it, because the rich and famous owned houses or visited here, and you might run into anyone at all in Basil's Bar. With this group it had been established at the beginning of the trip that the party would eat ashore on the first night, and perhaps on the second as well.

So Vere was looking forward to an evening off. She was going to do her nails, iron some clothes, give her hair a conditioning treatment and generally pamper herself.

For Jill it meant both afternoon and evening free, and the two women spent the afternoon lounging on the forward deck, away from the guests, who seldom used it. Jill, as usual on first arrival in any port, was using binoculars to check out which boats were in port.

"Oh, there's *Business as Usual*," she said. *Business as Usual*'s captain was a friend and would probably call over for a drink when *Brigadoon*'s guests went ashore. "It used to be owned by the man who runs *Big Business* now," Jill told her. Vere was getting used to this fascination with the pedigree of various ships; it was part of the life and formed a large part of the conversation amongst the yachting community. "Ronald says they ought to have called it *Monkey Business*."

"Maybe next time," said Vere with an appreciative grin.

"Oh, look! There's . . . who is that? I know—" the binoculars pressed to her eyes, Jill fiddled with the focus. "That ketch is in the way, dammit. There it is." She paused a moment, staring, and then lowered the glasses and looked at Vere.

"What is it?" Vere demanded uneasily, turning to stare in the direction Jill had been looking. "Is it *Vagabond?*"

"No," said Jill. "I'm not sure I should tell you. You see that small green-trimmed yacht over there?" Vere followed the direction of her finger. Jill held out the glasses. "That's *Billy Budd*."

Vere snatched the binoculars, jumped up and went to the rail, leaning over in the direction of the green-trimmed yacht as if a few feet could make a difference. "Is it? How do you know?" she asked, for there were several boats in between, and she couldn't see the name.

"Well, I know the shape, though the trim used to be black. But if you wait a bit, that white ketch will move around on the swell and then you'll get the name."

At that moment the bow-anchored sailboat shifted on a roll and the stern of the motor yacht became visible. *Billy Budd,* it said, in large green letters. Vere stared for a long moment, her heart beating. Then she lowered the binoculars and turned to Jill.

"You think he'll go ashore tonight?" she asked softly.

Jill shrugged. "Almost everybody does, in Mustique. Basil's Bar is kind of de rigueur."

Vere smiled, but not with amusement. "Well, there goes the manicure," she said lightly.

"Oh, Vere," Jill said unhappily. "Are you sure it's the right thing to do? You may just stir things up for nothing. What can he tell you? He wasn't there."

Vere ignored that, turning to gaze at the yacht's deck through the binoculars. She had learned by now that Jill and Ronald had known about the suspicious circumstances of the *Incitatus* disaster before Vere arrived, but hadn't told Alexa. They were sure there was no way to get to the truth, so why cause Cilla's parents more heartache than they already had? "What does he look like, the ex-captain of *Incitatus?*" she said.

"I've never met him. Ronald might know."

"His name is Harry Bridges, is that right?" There was nobody at all on the deck, no sign of life. Vere kept watching.

Jill nodded.

"Right." Vere lowered the glasses. "You don't mind if I spend the evening at Basil's?"

"I'll mind a lot less if you wear a scarf around your hair and some sunglasses," said Jill worriedly.

"Oh, no," said Vere. "I'm going to look as much like Cilla as I can. I'd like to get him talking. He might know something."

"Like what? He wasn't there!"

"Like why Cilla wasn't fired when the others were, maybe. I won't know until I try."

"Well, we're going with you," said Jill. "The yacht can look after itself for one night."

She spent a lot of time getting dressed, working to achieve the slight flamboyance that had been Cilla's trademark. She used midnight-blue liner on her eyelids, one of Cilla's tricks that made her eyes seem a more intense blue. She wore the dangliest earrings she had, and improved them by pillaging Ronald's fishing-tackle box and adding two blue fishing flies. She put on the flower-patterned blue dress she had bought in Bequia, and a small silver chain necklace, and combed her hair straight back from her face, to hang down her back in an ordered tangle. And she wore no shoes.

"The 'Barefoot Contessa,' I see," said Ronald, when she came up on deck. The guests had been safely delivered to Basil's ten minutes earlier, and now it was their turn. "I booked us a table. It's not very busy tonight."

"Good," said Vere, accepting the glass of wine he had poured and settling down to watch the sunset and wait for Jill. "Jill says you might know what Harry Bridges looks like."

The sound of a small outboard had been getting steadily closer for a couple of minutes, and now it was close enough to catch Ronald's attention. "I think we might be getting company," he observed, setting down his own drink and standing up to move to the stern. "Hello!" he called.

"Hello," said a familiar voice. "Is Vere aboard?"

Vere leapt up and ran to stand beside Ronald, her heart beating far too fast. Cass sat in the dinghy, smiling up at her in a way that melted her, his head haloed against the fire of the setting sun.

"Hi," he said. "I just got in. If you're free tonight, how about dinner aboard *Vagabond*?"

Oh, the siren call of temptation. Vere took a deep breath. "I'm sorry," she said. "We've got a table booked at Basil's."

A look crossed his face, visible even against the sun, or perhaps he radiated his moods. "Is it important?" he said. "Are you meeting someone, or is it just a meal out?"

"Just a meal out," Vere lied.

"Are you going to be here tomorrow night?"

"Yes. Can we put it off till then? I might be—"

He interrupted. "If you'll eat aboard with me tonight, I'll take you to Basil's tomorrow. Then you'll get both."

She smiled ruefully, knowing that she would rather have gone with him. She was not in a public mood, in spite of the way she was dressed. She could think of nothing she'd like better than to sit on pretty little *Vagabond*'s deck and eat nectar and ambrosia with Cass Conway. But *Billy Budd* might not be here tomorrow.

"I'm all dressed up now," she said, looking for excuses. "Why don't we do it the other way around? You come with us tonight, and then tomorrow—"

He turned and shaded his eyes from the sun. "You see that little boat out there?" he said, pointing to a small, open boat of the kind generally owned by local traders. It must have come from a neighbouring island. "That's a lobster fisherman. I just bought two lobsters from him. If we don't eat them tonight..."

Ronald, still leaning over the rail, began, "You can—" but didn't finish what he was going to say. He pushed away from the rail and went to pick up his drink.

"I want to go to Basil's," said Vere. "I'm really sorry." She was starting to feel just a little like a recalcitrant child, a not unfamiliar feeling. It was how Rory had got his own way: by putting her in the wrong.

"Couldn't we—"

"Please don't try to manipulate me," she said firmly. "My plans were made before you came on the scene, and I intend to keep to them. If you would like to join us, you are very welcome. I'm sorry about your lobsters, but you didn't ask me before you bought them."

She had never been quite so assertive in her life. Vere stopped to draw breath, wondering where the little speech had come from.

Cass smiled, but his eyes were grim. She thought, *Watch out for him. He doesn't like being crossed.*

"All right," he said. "I'd like that. I'll go and get cleaned up and meet you at Basil's." The little motor burst into life, and he turned and roared into the sun, where *Vagabond* was moored, almost invisible against its bright rays.

Basil's Bar was built of bamboo and thatch. There was a roofed section full of tables in little niches, leading to a long, wide balcony open to the air and set over the water on stilts. It was a staggeringly beautiful location, and when they got to their table on the balcony, the sky was still coloured with bright pinks and greens in the aftermath of sunset. A few stars appeared, a tropical breeze was blowing, the water shushed and splashed around the stilts and over the rocks underneath them, there was quiet music, and the smell of garlic and frangipani hovered on the air.

"Isn't this lovely?" breathed Vere as a wave rushed in beneath them. "Pure magic."

Cass came in a few minutes after their own arrival; he must have rushed. His hair was still damp from his shower, and he looked masculine and attractive and not at all manipulative. "I guess you'd rather be against the railings," he told Vere, as a waiter brought up a fourth chair. "Nice to look out over the water."

He shifted her chair as she stood, and sank down beside her. Over drinks he asked them about their itinerary over the past few days, and then they moved on to a discussion of Mustique and the best places for snorkeling.

"Have you got lobster tonight?" Jill asked, when the waiter came to take their food order.

"Oh, yes, we have very nice lobster, very fresh tonight," he said.

"Oooh, I'll have lobster!" said Vere. "Grilled, please."

Cass glanced at her, but said nothing.

"I might not get tomorrow off," Vere explained, when they had all ordered and the waiter had gone. "A lobster in the hand is worth two on the boat—so to speak."

"All right." He grinned. "I'll throw them back in, with your compliments."

"Good God, don't do that!" exclaimed Jill with a laugh. "At least, not without tethering them to the rail."

"Can you do that?" asked Vere.

"What—tie up a lobster? Why not? It's like tying up a cow, only it's underwater."

"So it'll still be perfectly fresh tomorrow," said Vere. But she had not imagined the implication, earlier, that the lobsters wouldn't be fresh beyond tonight.

"Can you eat lobster twice in two days?" asked Cass, with a smile. "If you do happen to get the night off?"

Vere opened her eyes wide. "You're talking to the girl here who has eaten nothing but cheese sandwiches and hamburgers for most of the past two years!" She laughed, tapping her chest. "The answer to your question is, yes, I can eat lobster every day for a month. For a year." She paused, considering. "Maybe, on alternate days, filet mignon."

The others laughed with her. They laughed a lot through the meal, the four of them seeming to get along easily, with no strain. They drank a delicious, strong wine, and it went to Vere's head like . . . wine. It was a marvelous evening, the company the best, and Cass was making her feel witty, beautiful and charming. If she had sat down and tried, she could not have remembered when she had last enjoyed herself so thoroughly.

Almost, she forgot her reason for being there. Almost, but never quite. Three times in the two hours they sat over the meal she got up and made her way to the toilet, and each time she walked out the short way and back the long way, so that she passed by every occupied table.

The restaurant was not very crowded, and she glanced at each face. Probably people thought she was celebrity hunting, hoping for the sight of Princess Margaret or David Bowie, but that was all right with Vere. She was glad to have a motive ready-made to cover her actions. She was willing to look a lot worse than a celebrity hunter to find out the truth about Cilla. She tried to catch the eye of any man whose build fit the rough description Ronald had given her: burly build, sandy colouring, late middle age.

They all had grilled bananas for dessert, deliciously sweet, soaked in butter, brown sugar and liqueur and then grilled under open flame; and Vere was counting on the coffee to sober her up a little and bring her back to earth.

"I take it all back," she said airily. "This really is a fantastic place."

"What's to take back?" asked Ronald. "You said that when we arrived."

"Yes, but—" she held up a finger for emphasis. Rather drunken emphasis, if the truth were known, but no one seemed to mind. "When we came to Mustique last time, I thought it was all a bit twee, you know? Too much like a movie set and not enough like real life. But a movie set can be very pleasant, from time to time, can't it? That's what I take back."

The table beside them was being cleared by the waiters; it was getting late. At the other end of the balcony, their own charter guests were making signs of leaving, and Jill glanced over her shoulder at them and then at Vere. Ronald would have to take them back to *Brigadoon,* and Vere would have to go, too.

"I think I just heard the first stroke of midnight," Vere said. She had turned down all the beds before leaving, put chocolate roses on all the pillows, filled the bedside jugs with water, tidied the bathrooms—but still, before they settled for the night, at least one of the guests would find some reason to summon her services. She was sorry, because she was really enjoying herself, and being with the charter guests would destroy her mood. And she wished she had seen Harry Bridges.

Jill said, "I've had most of the day off. I'll handle them tonight, if you want to stay on for a bit."

Vere caught Cass's look and discovered that the eyes were a powerful erogenous zone. It seemed to her that her lips became just a little swollen. She moistened them by rubbing the inside of each against the other, and the cool breeze on her wet mouth was even more erotic.

"Thank you," she said.

Jill looked at her significantly, surreptitiously tapped her watch and mouthed silently *Seven.* It meant, "But please be back no later than seven in the morning," and Vere nodded almost invisibly. The men missed the exchange entirely.

It was only a minute or two after that the charter guests got up and approached their table. "You've been enjoying yourselves," said Betty, in a belittling tone calculated to destroy the mood.

"Too much to notice whether you did," Vere agreed cheerfully. "I'm sure you found the food delicious, anyway," she added, as if to comfort a child.

Betty retaliated simply by acting as if Vere were not there, turning to join the conversation her husband was having with Ronald about whether they wanted to walk a little on the island or go back immediately to the boat.

After a few minutes Vere and Cass were left alone. By now there were only two other groups on the balcony. There was a small table vacant in the shadows of the far corner, looking out over the water on two sides, and by mutual agreement they moved to it. Cass bent to blow out the candle, and the stars took over.

"Would you like a liqueur?" Their chairs were so close now their arms were touching, and his voice was soft and caressing.

"All right," she said, although the scent of him was about as much sensual arousal as she could handle just now.

The waiter was leading a small group of latecomers to a table nearby, and Cass caught his eye and lifted a couple of fingers. "Be right with you, sir," said the waiter; and one or two of the group glanced in their direction.

With a murmured "Back in a minute," Cass stood up and took a couple of steps toward them.

"Hello," called one of the new arrivals, a large, burly man with meaty hands. "So you did make it."

Cass stopped. "Oh, hello," he said. He and the man shook hands. "I don't think so, thanks, we'll be leaving soon," Cass said, when the other man muttered something about joining them for a drink.

The waiter was beside him, lighting the candle, and in the sudden glow from the little glass globe Vere saw that the man's complexion was reddish, his hair sandy. "I don't know," one of the other guests was saying to the waiter. "You'll have to ask our captain. Harry?"

It all seemed to happen in the same second, including the sudden explosion of discovery in Vere's head. Then it was more by instinct than reasoned decision that she acted. She stood up suddenly, and moved forward behind Cass into the faint light falling from within the restaurant.

The sandy-haired man glanced from Cass smilingly to her, broke off what he was saying and stared at her. His mouth opened almost grotesquely, and he made a choking noise.

Her heart began to drum in her face, her temples—everywhere. "Hello," she said, in the best approximation of Cilla's manner she could muster. "Surprised to see me?"

It was a good thing there was nothing on the table behind but a lighted candle, because Harry knocked it over as he went down, in a dead faint where he stood, flat on his back.

Chapter 7

"What's going on?"

"Oh, my God, has he had a heart attack?"

"What happened? Harry! Oh, Lord!"

Between one second and the next, the place was in an uproar. The noise of the chairs and table being violently overturned, as well as the heavy thud of Harry's body on the balcony floor, resounded through the restaurant; that and the screams that followed captured everybody's attention.

"Well, there goes our cruise," said a calmer, more cynical voice on the edge of the little group. He was standing near Vere, but speaking to no one in particular. "Looks like he's out for the count."

Curiously, no one seemed to have noticed the part Vere's appearance had played in the collapse of their captain. They had all been chatting. They had noticed him speaking to Cass, and Vere had come up to join them, but Harry Bridges had been standing with his back to them, and so his terrible shock had not registered with anyone but Vere.

And Cass. "An old friend of yours?" he asked her softly, under cover of the general melee.

"Not mine," Vere said, banking on the hope that he had not actually heard what she said.

"Let's get out of here," said Cass shortly, taking her elbow.

But Vere had no intention of leaving. If she had wanted to speak to Harry Bridges before, now she was absolutely determined to do so. He knew something, that much was clear. There could be no reason for his fainting otherwise. "Let's wait around a bit," she said. When his grip tightened as though he would force the issue, she shrugged him off. "I'd like to be sure he's all right."

Cass frowned impatiently. "We can't be any help, and we'll be in the way."

"I took a first-aid course in high school," she said. "I might be able to help." And so saying, she pushed through the little group, now milling helplessly around their fallen comrade, and displaced the two women bending solicitously but uselessly over him. "It's best if you stand back," she said. She turned to the waiter. "Bring me a glass of water and a napkin, please."

At the sound of the voice of authority, the little group began to shift, making room for Vere to kneel by the man. Someone stepped on her dress as they surged back in, and Vere looked up to catch Cass's eye. "Can you make them move well away, please?"

Cass made short work of getting them out of the way, driving them like sheep to another table and making them all sit down. Vere, left alone with the captain, moistened the napkin with water and pressed it to his lips. She was sure he had merely fainted, not had a heart attack, but if he had hit his head badly, she had little real idea what to do for him.

He opened his eyes and stared up at her. What little light there was from the inner restaurant fell full on her face now. "I'm sorry," he babbled. "I'm sorry."

She began to think *she* might have a heart attack from sheer stress. "What have you got to apologize for?" Vere asked. He said nothing, merely breathed heavily for a second.

She had only a moment before someone would come bending over her. "Tell me what you know, Harry," she whispered urgently. She could hardly hear her own voice over her thudding heart.

"I didn't know it was going to happen that way, believe me, Cilla. I didn't know anyone was going to die. He never told me." He sobbed a breath. "I thought you were dead— you were as good as dead. I wouldn't have left you like that, but I thought you were already dead!"

"How do you know that man?" Vere asked Cass a few minutes later, as they made their way along the beach to where his dinghy lay moored. A doctor had been raised from among the guests of the island's hotel, and between her arrival and the captain's insistence that he had suffered no damage, there had been no more need for Vere's first aid.

"The way I know most of the people I know down here. I bumped into him in a bar and got talking," Cass replied. "Why?"

"He knew your friend. Cilla. He thought I was her, come back from the grave. That's why he fainted."

"Is that what it was? A faint?" Cass bent to untie the dinghy's painter from the mooring cleat.

"You didn't know him through her, I suppose?"

There was a pause as he struggled with the knot. He stood up and pulled the dinghy close to the dock. "Through whom?" he asked.

Suddenly her defenses stopped working. Her mind began to think the word that she could not bear to think. As if from a distance she could feel herself tremble. "My...

your friend, Cilla," she said. God, she'd nearly said, *my cousin.* She was losing her grip. "That man talked as if he'd...was she *murdered?*" she demanded hoarsely.

"Get into the dinghy and let's get out of here," Cass said, in answer to that.

"I want to go to *Brigadoon*," she said, not moving. She looked full into his face, letting him read whatever he saw in her gaze.

"Then I'll take you to bloody *Brigadoon!*" he exploded, as though he'd suddenly lost all control. "Get in the damn dinghy!"

It was only a minute or two before they were heading toward *Brigadoon* at what sounded like full throttle. She sat silent, not looking at him, aware that he was watching her. Staring at nothing, she saw Harry Bridges' face before her, gasping out his horrified apology. Abruptly her trembling gave way to real tremors, and then, without warning, to great spasmodic, uncontrollable jerks that tore through her body, so that she had to crouch in the bottom of the dinghy to save herself from falling overboard, while she gasped and retched air. Something terrible had happened, much more terrible than she had imagined, sitting by the table of the cottage at the lake. Oh, if only she had stayed there! If only she had never heard what she had heard tonight!

Cass let go the throttle to reach for her, but she shrugged him violently off, and he wordlessly returned to the task of driving. By the time he had brought the dinghy up to the stern, she was being shaken by loud, wretched sobs.

Jill was tidying the aft deck, and she rushed to the stern and bent over it. "What's the matter?" she cried in amazement. "What's wrong?"

Vere meanwhile shrank away from Cass's helping hand as if he had offered to punch her, and scrambled unaided onto the swimming platform, her bare feet giving her purchase. Still blindly sobbing, she pulled her full skirt up over her arm, groped for the chrome ladder and went wildly up.

Over her head, Jill's eyes, cold and stern, met Cass's. "What happened?" she asked evenly.

"I did not attack her, whatever it may look like," Cass responded with barely reined-in anger. "I don't know what the trouble is. She met someone who apparently knew her. Captain of the *Billy Budd,* named Harry Bridges. He collapsed in a faint, and she's the way you see her."

He waited only to see Vere safely over the railing and into Jill's arms before taking off again.

In the direction of Basil's Bar.

"What is it?" Jill demanded. "What happened? Did you talk to him? Vere, what *happened?* Stop crying and tell me what's the matter!"

Her sobs subsided at last, and Vere wiped her cheeks and breathed deeply to calm the aftermath. "I met him. *Incitatus*'s captain. There is definitely something much worse about Cilla's death than we were told." She was racked by a long, shuddering breath. "She was probably murdered. They lied. He was there, on board. That man helped someone do it."

"Dear God," breathed Jill. "How did you find this out? What did he say?"

"He thought I was Cilla—well, I made sure he would. It was as if he was looking at a ghost. He said he was sorry, that he hadn't known anyone was going to die. And that he only abandoned her when he knew it was hopeless, something like that. I can hardly remember the details."

Jill was deeply shocked. "What did Cass do? Why were you screaming at him?"

"I didn't—did I? When?"

"You were sobbing and howling, and when he tried to help you aboard, you screamed, 'Don't touch me!' You don't remember that?"

"No," said Vere. "Well, I didn't want him to touch me, but I don't remember saying so. He knew Harry Bridges. They were greeting each other like old buddies in there."

Jill sucked in a long, horrified breath. "Vere, are you saying—you think *Cass* might have—had something to do with it?"

Her cheeks were suddenly hot with tears again, and she shook her head as if all the weight of the world were on her shoulders. "I don't know," she whispered. "I don't know anything at all, do I?"

"I shall go back home an utter wreck," said Betty in the morning. "I got no sleep at all last night! Surely there's a better time to have hysterics than midnight."

She did not direct this at Vere, but to the world in general, so Vere felt no obligation to reply. She had not slept, either. She had cried most of the night, for Cilla. And now she was too busy with her own thoughts to have much time for anyone else's.

The truth was, she had never seriously considered what it meant to say that Cilla had not died in the way they were told. She had never thought how few reasons there are to cover up a person's manner of dying. Or perhaps, she reflected, she had not understood the huge gap between thinking that murder was possible, and facing up to the fact of it. Now, at last, she understood her uncle's reluctance to make waves, to search out the truth. To *know* that Cilla had been murdered—or even deliberately abandoned to death when she might have been saved, would be monstrous. It would change all their lives, and particularly her aunt's. It would have been far better to have accepted the story they were told.

The only thing that would make the truth remotely acceptable would be to find out who was responsible, and bring him to justice. Vere sighed heavily at the thought. It was so much more than she had imagined taking on, when

she had left home so determinedly. She had imagined un-
covering negligence, she had imagined proving cowardice...but she had not imagined single-handedly investigating
a murder that had taken place more than a year ago.

Yet if she went back without having found the whole
story, Alexa would carry a far heavier burden than she did
now. If she did not find it all out—the story of Cilla's
death—and name names, she would have to lie, pretend she
had found out nothing. That would mean carrying the burden of what she knew alone, for the rest of her life.

"I'm terribly sorry," said Betty. "Might I have decaf-
feinated coffee this morning? I'm hoping to catch up on a
little sleep later. I should have said before you poured it,
shouldn't I?"

That morning Ronald took both couples ashore for a tour
of the island and lunch at the Cotton House, leaving Jill and
Vere more or less free for the day. Vere rushed through her
cleaning, which she could always do much faster when no
one was around, to the accompaniment of some loud music, then went down to the galley, where Jill was making a
pastry for dinner.

"Why are you so sure it was murder?" asked Jill, when
they were discussing the scene again, looking for clues in
what the captain had said.

"Because he felt so guilty. I could practically touch it. His
first impulse was to exonerate himself. As though Cilla knew
he'd done something terrible."

"People feel guilty for all kinds of things," Jill pointed
out. "Betrayal, for one, and cowardice. It may have been
manslaughter, or terrible negligence."

"But he said, 'I didn't know anyone was going to die. He
never told me.' Anyway, why did they lie about who was
skippering the yacht when the disaster happened?"

"I agree that that means there was something—some kind
of conspiracy that he took part in. But it doesn't mean Cil-

la's death was premeditated. It might have happened when something went wrong in the plans. If the captain hadn't been expecting anyone to die, he might feel very guilty for having contributed to a death and then having to lie afterward to cover up the original conspiracy."

"Do you think I should go to the police?"

Jill shrugged. "They've already investigated it, haven't they? What have you got to offer them that's new that would make them think they should look at it again? A man fainting when he sees you could be put down to lots of different reasons. He's only got to deny he was there. There'll be no independent proof. That's why things at sea are so difficult to prove—there's never a casual bystander, an unexpected witness to shake an alibi."

"I don't see how I'm going to be able to unravel this thing on my own," said Vere.

Jill looked at her oddly. "Are you still planning to do it?"

"I think so. If I can."

Jill's eyebrows went up and then down again in a kind of facial shrug. "Four people died when *Incitatus* went down. If there's a possibility that Cilla was murdered, there's a possibility that all of them were."

The thought had been creeping up on her. "I know," Vere said unhappily.

"I would imagine," said Jill gently, "that a fifth mightn't trouble the conscience very much."

"*Brigadoon, Brigadoon, Brigadoon—Vagabond, Vagabond,*" the radio blared suddenly. The ship had a radio in the galley and the wheelhouse, and when Ronald was not on board it came through here.

Vere jumped and whirled, staring at it. "Oh, my God!" she said.

"*Brigadoon, Brigadoon, Brigadoon—Vagabond, Vagabond,* come in," said Cass's voice again.

Jill shook the flour off her hands and went to pick up the radio, depressing the switch. "*Vagabond, Vagabond,* this is *Brigadoon,* over."

"Hi, Jill. Go seventy-one."

"Roger, seventy-one." She punched up the new channel number. "*Vagabond,* this is *Brigadoon.* Over."

"Can I speak to Vere?"

"One second." Jill looked at Vere. "Can he?"

She felt sweat break out on her forehead, but after a moment she took the handset and pressed the button. "Hi, Cass, this is Vere. Over."

"Look, I think we need to talk. I saw your guests go ashore and I'd like to cook you lunch aboard. Are you free? Over."

Her mind seemed to stop functioning at this direct assault. "Uh . . . what time?"

Jill prompted, "Say 'over.' He doesn't know you've stopped transmitting."

"Oh, right!" Vere pressed the transmitting button again, feeling completely unhinged. "What time, Cass? Over."

"Pick you up in half an hour, all right? Over."

Vere stared at Jill. "What am I going to say?"

She was white, shaking; Jill was shocked to see this reaction. "Tell him you'll find out and let him know in five minutes."

Obediently Vere pushed the button. "I'll find out and let you know in five minutes, Cass. Over."

"Roger. *Vagabond* out."

"*Brigadoon* out."

She hung up the handset and then looked at Jill. "I don't know what to do," she said. She could feel her heart beating hard under the stress.

"What exactly happened with him last night?"

"It was the way he knew the ex-captain of *Incitatus.* Harry Bridges invited us to join them."

Jill shook her head. "Vere, everybody knows everybody down here. It doesn't mean *anything*."

"I know. But I had the feeling it did. You know, Cass happened to call the waiter as he was showing these people to a table not far from us, and the people glanced over at us—you know how you do. We were sitting in near darkness, and this man recognized him, you know? Cass jumped up suddenly and went over to them—and I know it was because he wanted to stop the man coming over to us."

Jill kneaded her pastry thoughtfully. "You're sure of that?"

Vere nodded. "And while they talked, Cass moved so that Harry Bridges's angle of vision when he looked at him didn't include me. Then when I came over, he was really angry. He saw Bridges's expression and turned and looked at me as though he wanted to kill me."

"What does that add up to?" Jill asked. "That Cass is involved somehow?"

"Don't you think so?"

"But Cass still suspects you *are* Cilla, doesn't he? Or at least he wants to believe it."

"So?"

"So this—you think Bridges is guilty of involvement in Cilla's death. But Cass has always believed she was alive, hasn't he? *He* didn't faint when he saw you."

Vere blinked. "That's right." She thought a moment, then reached for the radio handset.

Jill said, "That's not to say I think you should go to lunch with him."

"*Vagabond, Vagabond, Vagabond—Brigadoon, Brigadoon,* come in," said Vere. She shook her head, smiling. "I'm being stupid," she said. "If it were anyone but Cass, I'd have leapt at the chance to have lunch with someone who knows the captain of *Incitatus*. That's what I'm here for, isn't it? I only feel threatened because I find Cass physically attractive and I'm afraid I'll get hurt if he has ulterior motives. The trick is just not to get involved with him."

"*Brigadoon, Vagabond* here. Over."

"I'll be ready in half an hour," said Vere. "Over."

"Roger. Over and out," said Cass.

Jill frowned worriedly at this abruptness. "Are you sure you should go?"

Vere laughed, more from nerves than from real light-heartedness. "They can't murder me right here in Grand Bay, Mustique, can they?"

"That smells delicious," said Vere appreciatively. "What is it?"

"Shrimp frying in garlic butter," said Cass. "Are you hungry?"

Her stomach was certainly hollow, but she doubted if food was the cure. "Moderately," she said lamely, feeling mentally sluggish. "Just us for lunch?"

He glanced at her, then decided not to challenge that. "Yes," he said. "There's no one else aboard."

He made no attempt to get her below, but sat her down on deck where a little table was already laid with dishes and a bottle of white wine. He uncorked it and poured them both a glass, toasted her, then put down the glass and went below. "Back in a sec," he said.

The galley was just to port of the companionway, and she could watch him moving around as she drank. After a moment he handed up a basket of bread for her to set on the table. As she reached for it, their hands touched, and she felt a little shock of physical recognition. Cass looked at her for a moment longer than necessary, with dark, unsmiling eyes.

Vere set down the bread, picked up the bottle of Evian and watered her wine.

He fed her garlic shrimp and caesar salad with bread and cheese, and made no attempt to ply her with more wine than she wanted. They had agreed not to have their talk during the meal, and talked instead about the underwater world: the beauty of the coral reefs, the variety of the fish, and where the best snorkeling was in the Windward Islands. And if he seemed to take it for granted that he would be showing her some of the best places, it was so subtly done that she could find no way to correct this misapprehension.

"Would you like to take a look at the boat while I clear this?" Cass asked, when they had finished. "Then we can talk."

Vere naturally wanted to look around, and she followed him eagerly down the companionway. Since she wanted to use the toilet as well, she did that first.

There were two doors out of the bathroom, and by the time she had washed her hands she had forgotten which one she had come in by. She opened one of them at random and found herself looking into the main cabin.

In the confined space of a sailing boat, the cabin was naturally dominated by the double bed, and looked cosy and inviting. It was clear that this was Cass's bedroom, and in spite of herself, Vere stood at the threshold, gazing around.

There was a framed photograph on the built-in chest beside the bed. From the other entrance door to the cabin the photo itself would not be visible, but from this angle, coming in from the bathroom, she got a glimpse of the face of a woman.

Suddenly catching her breath, Vere left the door and advanced to the bed and, as if hypnotized, knelt on it, leaned over, and stared at the pictured face. Then, her mouth open and her breathing audible, she slowly reached out and picked up the frame.

How long she knelt there, frozen into immobility, staring at the photograph, she could not have said. Time seemed to have no relevance, as if she had left the dimension in which it had sway.

She remembered the day it had been taken; a day of perfect Canadian summer by the lake, three and a half years ago, after her university finals. The cousins had taken a week at the cottage by themselves to talk and catch up after a long time of not seeing each other. Cilla would fly out to Antibes in the Med the following week to join a yacht, and Vere would get down to the business of starting a business.

One afternoon they had gone out for a walk around the lake, and at the last minute Cilla had picked up the camera. She had snapped Vere leaning against a tree in full sunshine, squinting a little as she looked out over the water.

"There you are, gazing into the future, all serious and determined," Cilla said later, when the photos were developed. "That's my Verily." She had asked Vere to get a blowup made and send it on to her in the South of France.

At the bottom, Vere had written, "Lots of love, Cilla" and signed it with the little squiggle that had always been their secret code.

She had never seen it again, until today.

How did it come to be in Cass Conway's possession?

Chapter 8

She sat on the bed, the photo in her hand, staring at nothing. She scarcely noticed the door opening behind her.

"Everything all right?" Cass asked.

She awoke from her trance then, turning slightly to face him. She frowned thoughtfully as she stared at him, trying to see what this could possibly mean. "What is it?" he said, seeing that there really was something wrong. "Ci... Vere, what's wrong?"

"Where did you get this?" she asked levelly.

He took a breath, and said carefully, "Where did I get what?"

"This photo of me. How did you get it?"

"Is that a photo of you?" His voice was even, and he looked at her with an expression she couldn't read.

"Of course it's a photo of me!" she snorted, her nameless fears finding an outlet in anger. "You've only got to look at it!"

"You're sure of that? You've seen it before?"

Afterward she wasn't sure what kept her from detailing the day and time it was taken. Perhaps the fact that Cilla had taken it, perhaps simple forewarning of some kind. She said harshly, "I think I recognize my own face! How did you get this picture?"

For an answer Cass crossed to the bed and took the frame from her hands. He set it facedown on the bed and slipped the cardboard backing from the frame, then lifted the photo out.

He turned it facedown in front of her. On the back, she could see, there was a stamped caption of the sort used by newspapers and press agencies. Cass's long, strong finger pointed it out. "Perhaps you'd like to read that," he said.

"A photo of Cilla Fairweather," the caption read, "the stewardess who lost her life in the *Incitatus* disaster in November last year. A suitcase containing the photo was washed ashore this week on Glass Beach. There was nothing else in the suitcase and no identification, but police believe it came from the wreck." Underneath this caption was the stamp of the Eastern Caribbean Newsphoto Agency.

She didn't think her heart had ever beat so hard and so fast in her life. Vere gazed openmouthed at the caption, then turned the photo over and stared at her own face. She understood exactly what must have happened. "Lots of love, Cilla" read the inscription, and for those who didn't understand the little squiggle below, that "Cilla" must have looked like the signature. "Lots of love *from* Cilla," instead of "Lots of love *to* Cilla."

Vere tried to calm her heart with a long, slow breath. Just in time she remembered that this was supposed to be the first time she had seen Cilla's face. "That's amazing," she said at last. "Is that really her? Of course, I should have noticed the inscription, but all I saw was the face. She looks just like me. We could be twins."

"It's not you after all, is that it?" Cass asked dryly.

She trusted herself to meet his eyes now. "What would a photo of me be doing in a suitcase washed up on a beach?"

Cass did not reply as he took the photo from her, replaced it in its frame and set it again on the bedside table. Then he sat on the bed opposite her and looked at her as if choosing his words. "Look," he said at last. "I'm trying to help you. I'm on your side. Why won't you trust me? Why not tell me the truth?"

But trust him was exactly what she couldn't do, not when he was friends with Harry Bridges, not when she didn't know what there had been between Cilla and him. "What truth?" she demanded. "That I am Cilla Fairweather? I'm not. I really am not. My name is Vere Brown and I..."

"And that's not your photograph?" he asked softly.

There was no way out except a lie. "That is not my photograph," she agreed flatly.

He dropped his eyes from hers then, and looked down at his hand where it lay on the patterned coverlet. "Vere," he said. "I know you're lying. I know as surely as you're sitting here now that that is a picture of you." He looked at her again, and she saw with frightened surprise that he was telling the truth. Somehow he knew it was her. She felt goose bumps crawl up her back. She swallowed.

"I know you think you have to lie to me," he said, before she could speak. "I know you must have your reasons. But believe me, whatever they are, you're mistaken. You have nothing to fear from me." He reached out and caught her hand in his, lifting it and pressing his mouth to the palm. "I love you. Please tell me the truth."

"I am not Cilla Fairweather," Vere said woodenly, closing her eyes briefly against the physical jolt of his touch.

His dark eyes got darker; they seemed to want to burn a pathway through to her soul. "Then how is it you recognized the captain of *Incitatus* last night?" he demanded roughly. "How is it you said, 'Surprised to see me?'"

Her eyes slithered guiltily away from his, and it took a force of will to meet his gaze again. "I don't know what you're talking about," she said; it would be ridiculous to start inventing some previous meeting, or some confusion of Harry Bridges with another man. Perhaps a moment too late, she added, "Who's the captain of *Incitatus*?"

He shook her wrist impatiently. "Vere—I heard you myself."

She looked at him with a blank stare, behind which her brain was working frantically. Of course she had had too much to drink, that was why she had so stupidly decided to say what she had to Harry Bridges. She need not have said a word.

"If you're talking about that man who fainted last night, he mistook me for your friend Cilla. It had nothing to do with anything I said to him." Cass merely looked at her. "How long have you known him?" she asked.

"I met him in Grenada a few weeks ago. We were taking on fuel at the same time and went for a drink together."

She decided to risk believing that. "Did you know before you met that he used to be the captain of the boat your friend Cilla was working on?"

His eyes fell, but she wasn't expert enough on body language to know if that necessarily preceded a lie. "I had reason to suspect that that was the case," he said after a moment.

"Did you talk to him about the accident?" she asked. She realized with a little shock that her presence was going to confuse the issue. If Cass had been asking Harry Bridges whether it was possible that Cilla had survived the disaster.... Her brain gave up trying to work through the ramifications.

"No," he said.

This was starting to sound like a police interrogation, but she didn't care about that. As long as he was willing to answer questions, she would ask them.

"Last night, I got the feeling you were trying to prevent Harry Bridges from meeting me."

"Did you?"

"Were you?"

"I thought it would be better if he didn't see you, yes."

"Why?"

He looked grim. "Because there were three possibilities... A—you are Cilla Fairweather and you escaped a disaster in which everyone thinks you perished; b—you are Vere Brown, and you happen to look enough like Cilla to make people think you are her; c—you are Cilla, and certain people know that you are alive." He paused, marshaling his thoughts. "In either of the first two cases, I felt that a confrontation would be unwise, and possibly even dangerous. It would be better for you if the captain—and through him, perhaps, other people—didn't find out about your existence until we have some idea what their reaction is likely to be."

She said, "Do you think there was something strange about your friend's death?"

He looked at her, very straight. "That's as much as I'm going to say at the moment."

"That man was apologizing last night as if—I really got the creepiest feeling that he'd watched her being killed by someone and hadn't done anything to stop it. Seeing me, he thought she'd managed to survive." She licked her lips. "If Cilla died in the *Incitatus* disaster, it can only mean he was there, too. But then, how did he escape? He wasn't on the dinghy when the rescue boat picked them up. It means..." she broke off. The alternative was even worse to contemplate: that Cilla hadn't met her death aboard *Incitatus* at all.

He was watching her steadily. "What did he say, exactly?" Vere told him, as near as she could remember. "And you think he participated in murder?"

She said cautiously, "Jill says four people died in that disaster, including your friend. We think that there must have been something else going on, and the captain was part of it. But he didn't expect it to involve people dying.''

"What do you think was going on?"

"I don't know. The most obvious is drug smuggling, isn't it? But I don't see . . ." she broke off, thinking. "Is it possible there was some kind of battle between rival drug runners and *Incitatus* was deliberately burned?" She shuddered. "What a *horrible* thought!"

Cass said, "I wish you'd tell me everything. What can I do to convince you that I love you and that you are safe with me?"

She said, "It's not me you love. It's Cilla Fairweather. How can I trust you when you can't . . ." she had been going to say *"Can't even tell the difference between us?"* but she didn't get that far. Cass's hand, clasping hers, slipped up the inside of her bare arm and then, gripping her upper arm firmly, gently dragged her down till she was lying flat on the bed, looking up at him.

He bent down over her and gazed into her eyes at point-blank range, and the intensity of that look thrilled her to the bone. She could think of nothing to say, and lay staring up into his black gaze as if the rest of her life were written there.

"It is you that I love," he said huskily. And then he kissed her, softly, carefully, still savoring the newness of it, and the blood roared in her ears like the sea.

He lifted his mouth to smile at her, slipping his arm tightly around her waist; with his other hand he caught hers again and brought it to his mouth and, closing his eyes, brushed his lips across the palm, forward and back, before pressing his mouth firmly in the centre, his breath damp and erotic against her sensitive skin.

She was not used to dark eyes; she found his look disturbingly passionate as his long black lashes swept up and he gazed past all her barriers straight into her being. She felt her heart jump in response, as though her body understood the promises she saw there, even if her intelligence did not.

Her flesh shivered into awareness, and she lifted a hand and stroked the curling hair above his ear, threading her fingers through its thickness.

He kissed her throat, holding her hand prisoner over her head, wrapping her even more tightly with his arm around her waist, half lifting her helpless body to meet his lips. Her breasts arched up, and her head fell back, offering the curve of her brown throat. When he ran his lips and tongue slowly along its length, she felt her abdomen tighten in a building sexual excitement, and her hand in his hair closed into a fist and she pulled gently against his scalp.

This time his mouth smothered hers with a passionate and demanding kiss, filled with unmistakable urgency. He squeezed her wrist so tightly she thought he would crush it, then let it go to slide his strong hand under her head, cupping it and lifting her mouth more firmly against his.

When he freed her lips this time, she was gasping with a deep sexual arousal, and every touch of his body on hers was the centre of a shivering erotic pleasure; ripples of sensual response spread out over her body to meet and set up new vibrations, building to a deep and powerful spiral of need.

"Cass!" she whispered helplessly, her arms around his strong back now, pulling him down close against her. Inflamed by the expression of her desire, he wrapped her tightly in both arms, crushing her to him, and buried his face against her neck.

"Cilla," he breathed the name passionately, not knowing what he said. "I've waited so long for you."

Chapter 9

She would not have believed that all the flame of the world could go out like that, between one second and the next, leaving nothing but cold ashes in her mouth. Safely back aboard *Brigadoon* twenty minutes later, Vere felt so let down, physically and emotionally, she could have wept.

She told herself there was no reason for it. She had known from the beginning that it was Cilla he loved—it was *Cass*, not she, who was confused.

Yet when she thought of his passion, his dark eyes gazing so unsmilingly into hers, when she remembered his voice saying, "It is you that I love," it was hard not to feel a sense of loss. That was the kind of love women dreamed of, longed for from a man, and it was hers...if she would only pretend to be someone she was not.

She knew, too, that, thinking this, she was fooling herself almost as much as Cass was fooling himself. If he had really loved Cilla as much as he said, wouldn't he *know* that Vere was not Cilla? Why didn't his inner being recognize that she was not the woman he had known? And if, as seemed more likely, he did know she was not Cilla, what were his motives for pretending otherwise?

Whatever his reasons, she'd be keeping him at arm's length in the future. She'd been bruised enough by Rory falling in love with Marta. She didn't need a man who was already in love with another woman.

"*Billy Budd*'s guests have gone to Basil's for lunch," Jill told her, when she got to the galley. "With the captain."

"Omigod, really?" said Vere, all other thoughts being driven from her head immediately. "When did they go? Are they still there?"

"They went in about half an hour ago. They're sitting on the balcony, if you want to look."

Vere snatched up the binoculars and rushed up on deck. She was trembling too much to focus properly, but there was no question that it was him . . . there, suddenly he was in focus, laughing at something he was saying to the woman on his left. She watched riveted for a couple of minutes, until it occurred to her that she was wasting time.

"I've got to get over there! Can we get the speedboat down?" *Brigadoon* had both a dinghy for running errands and a small speedboat for taking guests water skiing. "Oh, God, Jill, do I even know how to drive the thing?"

Jill, lining her pastry shells with slices of ham, eyed her skeptically. "Are you sure you want to meet this man again, in cold blood?"

"Yes. Oh, yes. How else am I going to find out what really happened?"

"You think he's just going to confess to you?"

"I think he might let something drop. I know—I'll just swim in! It's not far." She rushed out, and then guiltily went back. "I won't be long. We're not expecting that bunch to come back again for a while, are we?"

"Ronald promised to keep them ashore as long as humanly possible. Vere . . ."

"Yes?"

"Please be careful. You don't know what you may be getting into."

"I'll know better after I talk to him. I'll be careful," she added reassuringly.

It took no time at all to change into a swimsuit and then fold a towel and a cotton dress into a waterproof bag. There was a short strip of white beach below the balcony of Basil's; she slipped gently off the swimming shelf and struck out for that.

It took only a few minutes to get there, and by then she had decided on her course of action. She came up out of the water, her blond hair streaming down her back, pushing her way slowly through the thigh-high waves, as if oblivious of everything except the physical pleasure of sun and sea. She pulled out her towel, dropped her bag on the beach, and dried her body and her hair slowly, before slipping the little dress over her head. She knew that they could not help watching this display from the balcony, but she did not look that way as she put the towel back in the bag and climbed barefoot up the beach to the bar's entrance.

She made her way out to the balcony and took a seat at a table for two by the railing, from where she had a direct line of sight to Harry Bridges. She ordered a drink, shook her wet hair down her back in a gesture that was so much one of Cilla's it nearly broke her heart to do it, and settled down to wait.

Of course, if he hadn't come, she would have gone to him, but he came. He smiled as he approached. "I think I owe you my thanks for a little first aid last night," he said. "May I buy you a drink?"

"Thank you," she said, inclining her head, and he sat down opposite her.

He was looking for a way to open negotiations, but she took charge. "Do you know me?" she asked.

He couldn't have been more shocked if she'd pulled a gun on him. *"What?"*

"Last night you—you called me by some name, as if you knew me. Do you?"

A curiously devious look came into his eyes. "Why are you asking? It's a very strange question, isn't it?"

Vere smiled pathetically. "Not when you know the reason for it. I've got amnesia. I thought perhaps you..."

"Got amnesia!" he interrupted in amazement.

What she had decided on the swim ashore was that, if even for one split second he had imagined Cilla might have survived... she could make him believe it was a real possibility.

"Do you know me?" she asked again, smiling.

"I... no, I doubt it. For a minute, in the dark, I thought you were someone I knew, but you certainly can't be her. It was a trick of the candlelight."

"Oh." Vere smiled sadly. Her drink arrived, and he ordered one of his own as she picked it up and drank.

"How do you come to have amnesia?" he asked, after a moment of staring out to sea. She could see the effort he was making to sound casual, merely curious.

"Well, that's what no one knows. I was brought into— well, more abandoned at—a hospital in Miami, Florida. No one knows how I got there, and I don't know where I came from. I was naked except for a brand-new sheet that might have been bought anywhere. I was in a coma, and when I woke up..." she shrugged. "That's all I know."

She could see he didn't know whether to believe her or not.

He said questioningly, "Last night, you said something, I forget what. But I thought you were someone I knew."

"You were staring at me, so surprised, and I thought— well, that I'd found some clue at last. Are you sure I can't be... ?"

He shook his head, scratching his ear. It was clear he had no idea how to attack this.

"Is the woman you know dead?"

"What makes you say that?"

"You were apologizing, as if she'd died, and you'd done nothing to help."

"No, no," he said hastily. "So, you were just left at a hospital?" She could see that he wanted to tell her as little as possible, while getting as much information as he could from her. She let him manipulate her a little. She hardly knew herself where she was going with this.

"Yes." She nodded calmly and sipped her drink. "Of course, the police were called. At first they thought I was faking it. They thought I was an illegal immigrant, but my accent made that seem unlikely. And I knew all about the geography and politics of the States. Then one day I saw a television program about sailing, and it seemed to be a life I understood. So they thought maybe I'd been hurt while on a drugs ship—you know—that I was helping to smuggle drugs, or something." She watched covertly as she said the word, but he didn't twitch. "So then they really got mean with their questions."

She had a vague recollection of an interrogation scene of a fake amnesia victim from some television drama, and was throwing it in for colour. In fact, she must be lifting the entire story wholesale from somewhere, it seemed to come from distant memory, and she could only hope he had not seen the program.

"What are you doing here, then?" he asked, very friendly.

"Oh—well, I had to do something, didn't I? I mean, it's over a year now, and the doctors say that probably I'll have to live without my memory for the rest of my life. And I saw a lot of big yachts moored and...I thought maybe they were right. Maybe I had been involved in something at sea. I certainly knew my way around yachts."

She paused. "Are you *sure*," she asked sadly, "that I can't possibly be your... friend?"

He took a deep breath and glanced involuntarily out to where *Billy Budd* lay at anchor. She wondered who he might be wishing he could consult. "I don't think so," he said apologetically.

"What was your friend's name?"

He made up his mind. "Cilla Fairbrother," he said, watching her closely.

"Oh, Cilla—that's right. You said that last night. Cilla Fairbrother." She repeated the deliberate mistake, tasting the name. "What happened to her?"

"She was lost on a yacht at sea."

Vere gasped. "Really? When?"

"Just over a year ago."

"And she just—fell overboard? Is that how it happened?"

"There was a fire at sea. You can't be her. She was caught on a burning deck, and panicked. She wouldn't get aboard the lifeboat."

"You were there?"

He blinked. "No," he said, as if suddenly remembering what his alibi was. "No, they... told me afterward."

"But last night you apologized for not doing anything."

He looked at her with the look she was waiting for, a look that said he thought—in the face of whatever he had seen— she might really be Cilla.

"I should have been there," he said, clearly pleased with his acting ability. "I was the captain, but I wasn't on that trip. They wouldn't have died if I'd been there."

"Oh, that's terrible! But it sounds so strange. I don't think I'm at all afraid of fire. I rescued somebody from a fire once, and I was the only one who didn't panic."

He didn't like that, she could tell. But it was a bad slip. Before he could dwell on it, she wrinkled her forehead and said, "Was she your girlfriend?"

He stared at her, fascinated. It was as if he were afraid that seeing him might cause the doors of her memory to open then and there, and accuse him. And if she had known the facts, she might have pretended that.

"Why?" he asked.

She blinked in pretended confusion, and then laughed. "I don't know! Isn't that funny? I just—it just came into my head to ask."

"She wasn't my girlfriend. She was a stewardess and I was skipper."

Vere allowed her eyes to grow huge. "Really?" she said, drawing it out incredulously. "Snakes alive!"

He jumped. It was Cilla's idiosyncratic expression, derived from a childhood misapprehension of her grandmother's "Sakes alive!" and kept on as she grew up because, as Cilla said, at least it made sense. Vere had never heard anyone else use it. Clearly neither had Harry Bridges.

"What do you mean?"

"But that's exactly what I'm doing now! I'm a stewardess on a charter yacht!" She set down her glass and got serious. "Look, can't you tell me more about what happened when your ship caught fire? What if it's me? What if I'm her? I might remember, if you told me. Are you sure, absolutely sure, that she couldn't have survived?"

"I'm sure," he said. "She died. The ship blew up while she stood on deck. That's what they said."

"Who was there? Who can I ask about it?"

"Nobody. They were all killed except one. It wouldn't be you, believe me."

"But just for a moment you thought it was me. You must have thought it possible, just for a moment."

But Harry Bridges could take no more. "It's impossible," he stated brutally. "It was a trick of the light."

She gazed at him as he stood up. "I'm sorry," he said. "But it wouldn't be right to let you get your hopes up. You don't even look that much like her."

Vere put her hand on his arm as he dropped money onto the table to pay for their drinks. "Harry," she said. "Last night you said you were sorry. What were you apologizing for?"

"For nothing. I told you. None of it was my fault."

"You said, 'I didn't know anyone was going to die. They didn't tell me.' Did somebody try to kill me, Harry?"

He wrenched his arm from her grasp and strode away without another word.

Chapter 10

The following day *Brigadoon* set off on its return journey
north. The trip back up to Saint Lucia was just as unpleasant as the trip down, but at least they knew they would be
dropping their passengers at the end of it. Primarily it was
Vere who suffered, but Jill came in for her share: at almost
every meal now, the guests were demanding individual
menus. "I *simply* can't eat chicken in olive oil! Might I have
some sliced ham or roast lamb, please?"

But at last they were free of their passengers—not without some disagreement over the time they were expected to
vacate their cabins. "But our plane doesn't leave for *hours*
yet! What *do* you mean?"

Ronald said tiredly, "The charter agreement very clearly
states that the staterooms and cabins must be cleared by ten
o'clock. You're welcome to sit on the deck and have a drink
after that, but Vere's got to be able to clean the cabins for
the next charter."

Of course an argument ensued, and of course that argument extended to the drinks bill, and even Vere could see

where it was all heading—toward a righteous failure to tip anybody. At the end of it, Ronald—always even-tempered— got angry and informed the guests that their business would not be welcome next year. They left then, with as much pomp and circumstance as the Changing of the Guard.

A few minutes later, Vere flopped onto a deckchair on the upper deck. "I can't believe Cilla did this for fun!" she exclaimed. "I've never met such horrible snobs in my life!"

Ronald was at the flying bridge on the upper deck, manoeuvring the yacht away from the dock where they had taken on diesel, and out into the bay to find an anchorage. For a few minutes Jill and Vere lounged beside him in the warm sunshine, laughing with the release of tension after the unpleasant little scene, while Jill poured out coffee. Soon they would start the madness of getting the yacht ready for the new group.

"Never mind," Jill said. "The next bunch are Americans, and will be so democratic they'll want to help you with the ironing."

"Really?" Vere laughed, tilting her head back to catch the sudden sprinkle of rain on her face. "Have you had them before?"

"Not this particular group, but Americans always want to help you with the ironing. And they want you to call them by their first names, and be friends."

"Well, they'll get no argument from me!"

"Ahh," said Jill, in a tone of interested discovery. "Who's that?"

Coming into Rodney Bay was a large, impressive cream-coloured megayacht. "Haven't seen that before," Jill said. "Vere, can you reach the glasses?"

Vere handed her the binoculars, glancing briefly at the mammoth yacht in the distance. She hadn't yet become infected with the yachting compulsion to know all the boats, who owned them and how they came and went.

"That's got to be fifty metres," Ronald said. "Can you see the name?"

"*Phoenix,*" Jill read out obediently. "From Curaçao."

"Never heard of it," said Ronald. "Must be a new one."

"I wonder who owns it," said Jill. "It looks pretty luxurious. They've got the aft deck covered in."

"Well, that'll be American or Canadian owners, then," Ronald said. Jill nodded, not taking the glasses from her eyes.

"What do you mean?" asked Vere. "How can you tell?"

Jill said, "Europeans like an open aft deck. They want to go to places like Monaco and be seen to be there. North Americans like air-conditioning."

"There seems to be a certain tendency toward cultural stereotyping in the yachting community," Vere observed dryly.

"The world is full of cultural stereotypes," Jill responded without apology. "People act like the people they feel are most like themselves, and the people most like them are usually their own nationality. It's just not popular to say so at the moment."

Vere leaned up on the railing and looked at the megayacht, now sailing slowly and impressively toward them off the starboard bow. The yachts would pass each other on opposite sides of the bay. "How much will you bet that it's not owned by a North American?"

"You'll lose," said Ronald cheerfully.

"I—" Vere stopped, frowning in concentration as she looked at *Phoenix*. "That's weird," she said softly.

"What's the matter?"

She lifted her shoulders and shook herself. Her body was suddenly covered with goose bumps. "Nothing," she said. "That boat . . . somebody just walked over my grave."

She felt the strangest sense of apprehension, almost of destiny, as she looked at the creamy sides of the yacht. She thought, with complete certainty, someone on that ship knows what happened to Cilla, and then shook herself and wondered where the thought had come from.

She turned from the railing then, and looked at Jill and Ronald with a little frown of perplexity. "Is there any way to find out about a particular yacht?" she asked.

Jill shrugged. "Gossip in the bars is the fastest way, out here. Why?"

Vere turned back and looked at the megayacht. One crewmember was visible on the upper deck, in white-and-navy. Almost absently Vere reached for the binoculars dangling from Jill's hand and set them to her eyes.

As though drawn by her scrutiny, the crewmember turned suddenly and leaned on the railing, gazing out at the bay. Her flesh began to crawl with anticipation even before she got the focus clear. When his face was finally before her, she didn't even gasp. Her mouth opened as she stared, making sure.

But there was no doubting it. The face before her was the face of that clean-cut farm boy she had last seen on the plane that brought them both to Saint Lucia.

Phoenix was new, out of an English shipyard, and had just come up from Honduras, where it had been fitted out. It was for charter, and was looking for crew. It would remain in Rodney Bay till it was completely staffed and equipped, and then it would be joined by its first charter guests.

By tradition the charter guests of *Brigadoon* spent the first evening aboard, and that meant so did the crew. But at about ten-thirty Ronald had found the space to go ashore, and had spent half an hour drinking with *Phoenix*'s engineer. Late that night, when the new guests were in bed, he and Jill and Vere sat in the galley, talking over what little he had found out.

"Looking for crew," Vere repeated thoughtfully. Jill looked at her apprehensively.

"You're not thinking of trying to get a job aboard her, are you?" she protested.

"Can you do without me? Could you find someone else?" Vere asked.

"There'll be no problem finding another stewardess," said Jill. "But I don't feel right about you going aboard that yacht."

"Why not?" asked Ronald in surprise.

Jill shrugged. "I've just got a feeling. That man was very interested in finding out where Vere would be at the airport, but then I notice he never tried to look her up."

"Maybe he didn't have time. Maybe he lost interest."

Vere and Jill exchanged glances. There was no point trying to explain to a mere male. They both had a feeling about the yacht, and it couldn't be explained in masculine, rational terms.

But whereas Jill was convinced that the yacht would be dangerous to Vere, Vere's feeling told her that she should try to get aboard.

It was in the nature of things that Jill had to give in. The next morning, before they sailed, Vere went ashore, where *Phoenix* was at the dock, and spoke to the captain.

He looked at her without any start of recognition, took the résumé and the glowing reference Jill had typed the previous night and glanced over them. "Why are you leaving *Brigadoon?*" he asked, but without much curiosity. It was not unusual in the yachting fraternity to make such changes.

"I'd like to work on something bigger," said Vere.

The captain read the reference again. "Extremely good worker, efficient…" He looked at Vere. She looked healthy and intelligent, and more important, she was very attractive. Everybody preferred a sexy stewardess, including himself. "All right," he said. He told her the salary offered, and she accepted it. It was higher than she was getting from Jill and Ronald, but she wasn't thinking about salary. She'd have taken anything. "All right," he said again. "When do you want to start?"

Vere wasn't surprised. She had known almost from the first moment of seeing the yacht that she would get to know it very well. "I'll be back in two weeks, maybe one if they find a replacement sooner."

The captain shook his head, scratching his scalp as he squinted up into the sun. "Two weeks is fine. We'll be here till then anyway, and one stewardess is enough when we have no guests aboard. No point in your coming before Christmas. All right, see you in two weeks."

He put out his hand. "Vere, is it?"

"That's right."

"My name's Hugo." He was English, like many of the captains she had met. "You'll meet the rest when you get back, I guess."

Ronald meanwhile faxed a message to Martinique. A stewardess they knew on a yacht moored there was bored and was looking to change jobs.

"In fact, if at the last moment you hadn't turned up last month, we would have flown her down then," Jill said.

There was no necessity to fly her down to Saint Lucia now, however, since the new charter group wanted to sail north to the French island of Martinique and then to Dominica. They could pick the new stewardess up en route.

Jill was worried and apprehensive now, but Vere was calm. She had the deep inner sensation that the course she had chosen was the right one; not necessarily the easiest, but the best. It wasn't that she didn't expect to meet trouble. She expected to be able to handle what trouble she met.

"Golly," said a young female voice. "Do you really have to do all that ironing? Would you like some help?"

It was a good thing Jill wasn't in the galley. Vere laughed a little, but kindly, and smiled at the girl. "That's very kind of you, but you don't want to spend your holiday helping me iron. You go up on deck and enjoy yourself."

She looked about fifteen, awkward but pretty. She had come aboard with her parents and two brothers. She pushed a load of clean linen out of her way and sat up on the table opposite the ironing board. "Yeah, but it's so boring. Mom says I'm not allowed to lie in the sun and get a tan because of skin cancer. Do you think I'll get skin cancer? You have a tan. And you look gorgeous."

Vere ironed a napkin. "The sun's very hot down here, you know."

"I'm used to it. Minneapolis gets very hot summers."

Vere smiled. "I think the sun here is much stronger than in Minneapolis, even in the summer. It's a lot hotter than we get in Toronto."

The girl rolled her eyes. "Toronto is *miles* from Minneapolis! It's in Canada! They live in igloos!"

"Mmm," said Vere, folding the napkin she was ironing. "Take a look at a map one day," she suggested with a grin.

"Why?" said the girl, whose name was Paula.

"It's a question of where the igloo latitude lies." And in spite of Paula's curiosity, she would say no more.

She was forced to give way on the ironing, however, and for the next half hour Paula sorted and folded and ironed along with her. As a result the ironing took longer than usual, but as Vere said to Jill later, it made a nice change.

"Paula, there you are!" said her mother, coming into the galley at the end of the half hour. "We're just passing Saint Anne now. We're going ashore as soon as we've cleared customs, and Ronald is going to take us up to the shrine. Come out and have a look."

Vere had not been on a French island before, and she turned off the iron and went out on deck with Paula for her first sight of the island where Napoleon's Josephine had been born.

Saint Anne was a pretty town, the buildings white and clean against a background of green hills, the shrine, high up, dominating the town. The island was unlike any of the English islands she had seen—it was clean and apparently affluent and romance and mystery seemed to be in the very air.

They motored slowly up the bay towards Marin, the port of entry at the top, and found a convenient anchorage not far out. The sun was fabulously bright in a sky with only a few clouds, and a cooling breeze blew steadily from the land. It was a perfect day, a perfect place: a tiny French tropical town.

Vere stayed on the deck longer than usual, looking around, drinking in the promise of atmosphere ashore. That was how she eventually noticed the burgundy hull neatly moored between two other sailboats, close in to shore.

They met Cass in the afternoon at Saint Anne, when everybody except Jill came ashore to walk up to the shrine with Ronald. Cass called to them as they tied up the dinghy, and started walking beside Vere. Within a few minutes he had detached her from the group and at his suggestion they turned off the route to a pretty little café with outdoor tables that smelled of Gauloise cigarettes and good coffee.

She knew she was being weak. But the day was beautiful, and so was the island, and so was Cass, and it would have seemed like ingratitude to the Divine to have turned up her nose at so much sheer physical beauty.

He steered her to a white table under a tree and pulled out a chair for her before sinking into one beside her. They both breathed in satisfaction at the same time, and relaxed to look at the scene around them. When the waiter appeared they had still not spoken.

They ordered espresso and water, and when it came, Cass put his elbows on the table and leaned over his cup, absently dropping in sugar cubes and stirring it with the tiny spoon. At last he dropped his arms, picked up the cup, drank, set it down, and then leaned back in his chair.

"Where are you heading this time?" he asked.

"Up to Dominica and back, I think. What about you?" He looked at her. "Up to Dominica and back."

Her pulse started to thud in her temples. "What does that mean?" she asked levelly.

"I told you what it meant a few weeks ago." He looked full at her, and the message in his eyes was amazingly potent.

"You haven't been following us up till now," she protested in surprise.

"Haven't I?"

"Have you?"

He absently added another lump of sugar to his coffee and stirred it again. He seemed to make up his mind not to answer the question, picked up his cup, eyed her over the rim and asked softly, "Have you felt abandoned because I was out of sight? I told you I would be. But you've always been within reach of help if you needed it."

The suggestion that she had missed him in any way was not a welcome one, probably because it was too close to the truth. Vere stiffened. "How could I have felt abandoned because a total stranger isn't—"

Smiling, he interrupted. "I'm not a total stranger."

"No?" She was feeling hostile without quite knowing why. It seemed that whenever Cass got inside her defences, it made her angry. She wondered if that was her instinct telling her not to trust him.

"No. I'm the man you're going to marry."

Her hand shook, and she set the cup down. As if it were the most important thing in the world, she concentrated on pulling a tissue out of her shorts pocket and wiping the spilled coffee from her hand. Then she scrunched up the tissue and jammed it underneath the side of the saucer.

He watched her in silence. Then, as though he had a right, he reached up and grasped the brim of the baseball cap she was wearing, and gently tugged it off. Her hair fell out of it, down around her shoulders, and he set the cap on the table and put his hand on her head, stroking her hair from crown to tips. "You'll wear flowers in your hair," he said. He caught a lock between finger and thumb and simply held it, stroking the curling end around his strong forefinger and watching her with a quizzical half smile on his lips.

She shivered at the touch, and burned at the look in his eyes. She knew she was within an inch of being swept away by sheer physical attraction. Unable to tear her eyes from the look in his, by pure determination she raised her hand and removed the lock of her hair from his grasp. She said, in the tones of one using a mantra of self-defence, "You love Cilla—"

She stopped abruptly, as a thought fell neatly into her head—ready-made, as though it had been formed and packaged in her unconscious without the news getting out until it was complete. Coming without forewarning, it had all the impact of a central truth. The thought was this: if he had been looking at *her* picture for the past year, it was no wonder he had her so thoroughly confused in his mind with Cilla and didn't see the difference. Perhaps a year of staring at her photo had indeed shifted the target of his love. Maybe, in some curious way, it really was now Vere that he loved and not Cilla.

With this thought, the last of her defences against him was fatally undermined. What could she now say to keep him at bay—and, more important, to keep her own deep attraction to him under control? She looked at him in something like terror. If he wanted her now, he would have her. She had lost her shield.

She picked up her cap from the table in front of her and concentrated desperately as her finger traced the yacht's name printed across the peak. "I'm leaving *Brigadoon* next

week," she said. Her arms felt leaden and lethargic as she
wrapped her hair into a knot, piled it on her head and
shoved it under the cap.

"Where are you going?"

This was her chance to escape him. All she had to do was
refuse to say, or lie. She could say she was flying back to
Toronto, and with a little luck she would never see him
again.

"To a megayacht called *Phoenix*," said Vere; and realized with a sudden insight that wild animals that are captured and tamed have only themselves to blame. For a brief
moment she had a glimpse of the inevitable and laughed,
partly at her own human foolishness, partly in the delight of
anticipation.

"I don't think I know it."

"No, it's new. Just up from Honduras."

His eyes narrowed momentarily at a thought. "When do
you join it?"

She told him about the arrangements she had made with
the captain, and about picking up her replacement in Fort
de France. "There'll be two of us on the way back," she
said.

"Right," he said, as if he were thinking of something else.
"It's a megayacht?" She nodded. "How big is it?"

"Ronald said at least fifty metres. But I don't know for
sure. Why?"

"How many crew?"

Vere shrugged. She hadn't asked. "There are two stewardesses at least, that's all I know. They've got one aboard
already."

He thought for a moment. "It may be harder for you to
get access to the radio. We'll have to work something out."

"Mom'll kill you if she finds out." The voice, coming
from the other side of the tree, penetrated her consciousness, and Vere blinked as if coming out of a trance. Involuntarily she glanced through the branches to the table on the

other side, where the two teenage boys from the yacht were sitting, their backs to the tree. They clearly had not seen her. They were good-looking boys, the younger fourteen, the elder seventeen. The elder, Eric, had a pack of Gauloises on the table in front of him and a cigarette between his lips.

"Mom won't know, unless you tell her," he said now. He adjusted his sunglasses on his nose. "French cigarettes make a man sexy," he said.

Vere caught Cass's eye and began to giggle. "If only it were that easy," said Cass. Their soft shared laughter blended like music on the pleasant breeze, and for a moment they were in perfect harmony, and it seemed a promise of things to come.

"Butt the smoke, Eric," his younger brother told him sarcastically. "You haven't got a hope."

But Vere scarcely heard. The look in Cass's eyes was for drowning in, and she thought, If I could be sure of trusting you...

"Why don't you just tell me?" he suggested, in a low voice.

Her nerves tightened. "Tell you what?" She leaned forward to take a last sip of her coffee, trying to find normality in this sea of feeling.

"There's something you could tell me, but you don't. Why not?"

She laughed lightly. "There are lots of things I could tell you, starting from birth. What in particular do you want to know?"

She knew as soon as she'd said it that it had been a dangerous thing to say. Having got the opening, Cass was going to use it. He drank some of his coffee, set down the cup, and absently stirred the dregs. He watched the spoon's movement intently as he spoke. "I want to know why you're here. I want to know why you first say that picture I've got is of you, and then that it isn't. I want to know why to me you say you're someone else entirely, and to...others, you pretend to have amnesia. I want to know why you're afraid to get involved with me when we both know we're sitting on a volcano."

He stopped speaking suddenly, as if what he said had aroused his own sensual awareness, and turned to look at her. The deep, involuntary passion in those dark eyes stirred her without him having to put a hand on her. She stared at him, feeling a kind of vertigo assail her stomach, then deliberately blinked and turned away. She knew she was lost, knew her only hope of safety was to keep him from knowing.

But she had looked away that split second too late. She felt the stillness as Cass absorbed it in some purely physical, nonrational way. "Vere?" he said softly.

She dropped her eyes from the mountain and turned her head away. Her body, understanding her surrender, was suddenly a clamour of desire from blood and bone and cell. Waves of physical attraction and longing vibrated between them, so that it seemed to her, in the shadow of the tree, that they sat in full sun.

"Oh, here you all are! What a fabulous view! You really missed a terrific walk! What have you been doing, Eric and Michael?"

"Nothing much."

The waves of heat subsided a little as Ronald pulled out a chair at the table where Vere and Cass sat, and asked, "Anything to drink for you two?" He signaled the waiter.

"I'll have a *pastis,*" said Cass, and she could hear the effort it took him to control his voice. Vere didn't even try, just shook her head.

"What have you been doing?" asked Ronald, when he had ordered.

"Well," said Cass, "we've been thinking that if you won't need Vere after you pick up your new stewardess in Fort de

France, I might take her for a holiday in *Vagabond* for a few days over Christmas before she joins *Phoenix*."

Ronald stretched and leaned back in his chair. "Sure," he said. "You can have her at the end of the week."

Chapter 11

A week later aboard *Brigadoon* Vere packed her belongings in a queasy state between nervous fear and anticipation. She was nearly twenty-six years old, but she had never in her life gone off like this to an assignation with a man, knowing that by nightfall she would be making love.

The last thing she packed was the photo of Cilla aboard *Incitatus*. "I'm taking a leaf out of your book, Cilla!" she said aloud, with a certain amount of bravado. "I sure hope somebody knows what I'm doing!" Then she tucked it carefully into a zip pocket of her case.

Cass picked her up in the dinghy late one afternoon in Fort de France. She had said her goodbyes to the charter guests earlier, before they went ashore. Now there were only Jill and the new stewardess to wave her off.

"Keep in touch," said Jill, hugging her warmly. "Probably we'll see you quite a bit, but if we don't, you know we always pick up mail in Saint Lucia. And there's always the radio."

"Yes" was about all Vere could say. She was too aware of Cass in the dinghy, his dark eyes and his waiting arms.

They sailed down the coast to a pretty little emerald-green bay where the lush hills came down to the water's edge, so that it had no village or settlement except for a rather dilapidated old farmhouse or fisherman's cottage on a small rise. Cass anchored just before sunset, at a good distance from the two other yachts moored there. She watched him make everything fast for the night, and then he jumped down into the cockpit and said, "Right. What would you like to drink?"

What she needed most was a sedative. Her heart was going far too fast, and her imagination was simply unstoppable. But she said weakly, "Wine, please," and turned to watch the sunset as he went lightly down the companionway.

He returned with a glass of white wine for her and a beer for himself, and sat beside her on the cockpit seat. He propped one foot up on the seat then, and drew her gently back against his chest. They sat mostly in silence for ten minutes, drinking and watching the sun set, crying out in triumph together as they saw the "green flash." Cass held her with one arm across her chest, his hand curving over her shoulder. They drifted easily into conversation as the darkness became complete, and when the stars were bright, and she was just beginning to wonder whether they would have a cooked dinner, Cass lazily consulted his watch and said, "I guess we'd better go."

Vere sat up in some surprise. "Where are we going?"

One long, strong arm pointed into shore, to the little farmhouse she had seen earlier. A single bright light glowed from the porch. "We're going in there, to eat. Aren't you hungry? I am."

It only took her five minutes to change from shorts into a flowered dress and a pair of sandals, brush her hair neat and apply a little mascara and insect repellent, and she was ready. Cass steered the dinghy into a tiny bay that was all but invisible in the greenery until you were on top of it, and moored at a sagging wooden dock. The only light came from the bulb on the porch, and she was grateful for Cass's arm as they made their way along the rickety dock.

Inside a squeaky screen door was a large room that had once been the kitchen of the house, and still was. The difference now was that one half of the room was given over to half a dozen small tables and chairs. Once, presumably, it had held one large table with chairs for a dozen or more. There were two groups of four and a couple sitting at different tables.

A black woman in flowered cotton and a large apron greeted Cass from where she stood by a stove and called out something incomprehensible to a pretty young woman with creamy caramel skin and the looks of a fashion model, who was about seven months pregnant.

The latter showed Cass and Vere to a table by the far wall, went to a large Welsh dresser at the back of the room and brought out napkins, plates and cutlery. She set the table in front of them in a matter-of-fact way, and then fetched salt and pepper and a couple of little bowls of lethal-looking sauces. "Le menu est à," she said, bringing a blackboard and leaning it against a neighbouring table.

Vere's French vocabulary wasn't up to the variety of dishes offered, and Cass translated for her. When they had decided on fresh broiled lobster, the chef called from across the room to ask what they wanted. Cass called out their order, and the young woman was dispatched with a bucket down to the shore.

Vere watched her as she disappeared out of the glare of the porch light and down towards the water. "Where is she going?" she asked Cass in laughing bewilderment.

"Down to the lobster-holding pens, I guess," he said. "It does say fresh."

She smiled in bemusement at the room around her. There was aging but very clean black-and-white linoleum on the floor, and the tables were covered with mismatched oil-cloths whose patterns had faded from long use. Walls and ceiling were clean and painted within the past two years, but the wooden dresser that held the dishes was so old it was hard to see quite how it remained standing. Each table had a candlewick floating in a bowl of oil, with a tiny pastel-coloured shade reducing the glare and casting a soft glow among the shadows.

In the other half of the room the chef stood surrounded by an old-fashioned black cast-iron stove, a charcoal grill, a sink, a butcher's block and at least two dozen ancient and deadly looking knives, some of which had been sharpened so often their blades were no wider than a finger, and one of which she was wielding now with ferocious skill on some onions. When she worked at the butcher's block she faced the room, and she was chatting volubly with a French couple sitting nearby. The glare of her working light was cut off from the tables by a panel of wood running the width of the room above the butcher's block.

The atmosphere was an indescribable mix of home, soup kitchen, bistro and...a centuries-old Caribbean kitchen; and those who had lived and worked here seemed barely the flicker of an eye away.

The screen door whined open and banged as the pregnant waitress came in with her bucket, heavy now and covered with a round wooden lid. She carried it into the kitchen and set it down, exchanged a few words with the cook, and then came over to them again.

"Vous voulez du vin?" she asked. When Cass intimated that they did, he was invited to the kitchen to look in a refrigerator that held the wine. He poked around happily inside for a few minutes and came back to the table with a bottle of white and a corkscrew. When he had poured the wine, Vere felt its smoky flavour on her tongue with sybaritic pleasure.

"Mmm!" she said. "That's delicious! It tastes like... smoked silk."

He smiled at her, his eyebrows flicking upward. "A natural connoisseur, I see," he said admiringly.

"What is it?"

"Pouilly fumé," he said. It was a name she had never heard, but then, it was probably expensive, and in the last three years there had been little eating out of any kind and none at all with good wines.

"Well, it's got my vote," said Vere, taking a sizable swallow to prove it.

Whether it was the wine, the atmosphere, the company, or the fabulously delicious food, Vere knew this was a night she would always remember. Everything was perfect, including the crazy, inconsequential conversation, their laughter, and Cass's black eyes, watching her with admiration, anticipation, promise and desire.

She had never laughed so much, or talked so much, since her childhood. She had never felt so free, or so witty, or so beautiful. She had never drunk so much wine, or cared so little for the fact. She had never felt so strongly that the future would take care of itself if she allowed the present just to be.

She had never fallen in love before, not like this, drowning in a pair of eyes, and as hungry for a man's hands and mouth and body as she was for the tender white flesh on her plate.

She had never been so much like Cilla.

He laid her on the bed in her pretty flowered dress and slipped her sandals from her feet. Lazily, she bent a knee, and the full skirt of her dress slithered down her thigh, and he bent and lightly kissed the little patch of white cotton that this movement exposed. The sensation was so directly erotic

that she grunted, and half lifted a hand in surprised pro-
test. He caught her hand and kissed that, then bent to her
knee and kissed the tender inside flesh there. His mouth
slowly, slowly trailed down her inner thigh, not with dry,
light pecks, but with his lips opening and closing on her
flesh, so that her skin felt the heat and wetness of his mouth,
the inside of his lips.

He did not stop where her thigh met her body, and this
time she gasped, for the kisses on her thigh had been a sensual caress, but this was an erotic assault upon a system already alight with desire, so that between one second and the
next flames leapt up to scorch her.

"What are you doing?" she asked faintly, and Cass lazily lifted his head and looked at her.

"Don't you know?" he asked with a caressing smile.

"No—I—"

He blinked at her, as if he were a large cat. "Ah," he said
with interest, and nodded and bent his head again. He
started on the other knee this time, but his mouth led him
inevitably to the same goal. This time she had anticipation
adding to her other pleasures, and when his mouth arrived
she trembled and moaned.

He smiled as if he were pleased to find her so apt a pupil,
and then his hands cupped her hips and his fingers found the
edge of her briefs, and he slowly dragged them down over
her hips and thighs, kissing the flesh thus left bare, and then
down her long legs and off.

He pushed the skirt of her dress up higher, looked first at
her face, then at her naked body; and a look of passionate
need crossed his face, and he closed his eyes and breathed
for control. This time his mouth went straight to her centre, and he did not raise it again.

She had really had no idea there was so much pleasure in
the world, let alone in her one body alone. She had read,
and even heard, that a man might be so dedicated to giving
a woman pleasure, but she had not really believed it. She hit

the first peak with a tremendous feeling of release as well as pleasure, for her body had struggled to achieve it, and she heaved a deep sigh of gratitude. But the second needed no struggle and came within a few seconds, without warning, and surprising her into a series of broken cries. Then the third and the fourth, and then she lost count and simply lay gasping and shuddering under the onslaught of such a mass of pleasure it defied everything she had previously known on the subject.

By the time her lover raised his head she felt weak, as though every muscle in her system had achieved a state of complete relaxation. Her body was glowing with sweat, tendrils of hair stuck to her forehead and cheeks, and as Cass stood up she raised an arm that limply fell back onto the bed. She could scarcely even open her eyes.

He was undressing beside the bed, stripping down to nothing, and she saw his aroused body with a kind of detached hunger, as if it was what she wanted, but she could do nothing about it. Distantly she imagined that it would be wasted on her.

When his hands were on her, pulling her over and lifting her hips, her back and her arms in order to drag her dress off her, she found in surprise that his touch still had the power to arouse her; and when he kissed the brown breasts thus exposed, she shook her head in bewilderment. It was as though the state of utter exhaustion she was in had merely lowered the threshold at which pleasure could enter her body. The sensations she felt now were deeper, richer, fuller, and profoundly arousing in a way she had simply never dreamed of. Lazily, curiously, she opened her legs as he rose above her, and anything but lazily Cass thrust into her.

"Oh, my God!" she cried involuntarily, for it was as if that one thrust reached the end of every nerve and the heart of every cell of her entire being. Her sensual amazement was very great now; she had entered a new world only to become completely lost. She wandered like an innocent abroad, crying out at each new discovery; and her surprise and delight were music to him.

He moved in time to that music, providing the thudding bass while she cried and sang and soared in strange, wonderful harmonies and tremolos above, and then, as the climax approached, their lines moved closer to each other, and the bass rhythm became more dominant, more insistent. She lost her sense of time and place, and her orientation in space, and her certainty of being a separate being. She was merely a note within the great music of the spheres, and the music crashed and sounded around them, and they were part of it. Suddenly his rhythm broke and she felt the liquid heat of his pleasure, and her own pleasure burst out and soared to one high, keening note of pure sound, the central note of vibration of the universe, which, astoundingly, came from her own throat. It lasted for one infinite, unknowable moment of perfection, and then, running down through the levels of divinity, arrived at the earth again and died in a sigh.

In the morning she was awakened by rain falling in through the hatch onto her face. Vere stirred sleepily and licked her dampened lips: after last night, even this physical stimulus was a pleasure. She knelt up and poked her head out into the rain to look around.

The bay was perfectly peaceful. Two other boats had come to moor in the night, but they were far enough away to maintain the sense of isolation in paradise. Under the lowering cloud, the green of the water had deepened and was glowing with its rich inner life and the promise of its great fertility. Around the bay the thick, palm-covered hills climbed up to their background of grey cloud. For a moment she had a vision of being in them, naked in the rain dripping from their branches.

What had a minute ago been a sprinkling of drops on the surface of the water was increasing in strength, and as she watched, the hills became obscured by the fall of water and her head was soaked. Rain ran in heavy rivulets along the gunnels of the boat and around the hatch opening.

It was also coming inside. Vere cut short her sense of communion and oneness with Mother Nature, and drawing her head inside, pulled down the hatch. Cass was lying awake, one arm under his head, watching her with a half smile on his face.

"I'm soaked," she said, leaning down over him to dribble water on his bare chest.

He ran his hand appreciatively over her wet shoulder and down her back, both of them enjoying the slippery touch of the water between his skin and hers. "I thought you might crawl out and dance in the rain."

"I nearly did," Vere admitted. "It's lovely, isn't it?"

"You're lovely," he said. Water was dripping down over her breasts and beading from a nipple. He raised his head and lightly took the nipple in his mouth, drinking the rain from her. She felt a sense of atavistic shock deep in her stomach, as though they had just repeated a part of some ancient rite of worship of the all-giving Mother. Wordlessly she offered him the other breast, and he drank the water of life from that, too. Then he followed the trail up between her breasts, to her throat, over her chin and at last, lying back and drawing her down on top of him, to her mouth.

Her cells were all still swollen with the pleasure of the night, and between his hands and the tickle of rain on her skin and face, she was quickly aroused. So was he, and he impatiently threw off the sheet that covered his hips and drew her leg over him so that she knelt on either side of his body. She felt the pressure of his arousal, and his hand guiding the way, and then, his two hands firm on her hips, he pulled her down against the thrust and pressed his way home.

She felt urgent and languid at the same time, her body full and lazy, the tendrils of pleasure slumbering along her back and limbs as if by a kind of osmosis, of transmission through the liquid that swelled her being. There was a deep, heavy sensuality in her flesh that seemed slow moving, so that she reached the peak with surprise, not having known she had got above the foothills. Her pleasure was deep, solid, satisfying—without the high, singing response of the night before, without the knife edge of balance between pleasure and pain.

When she fell forward, her hair falling around Cass's head, supported on her arms as she shook and pressed against him in her pleasure, he gave himself up to it, and gripping hard to still the movement of her hips and force her down to enclose and envelop him fully, his body bucked and jerked with his release and he grunted with satisfaction at each upward thrust.

She pulled her hair to one side off his face then, and at his hands' urging lay on his chest and relaxed against him.

When they awoke for the second time, the clouds had gone and the sun was streaming in through the closed hatch, making the cabin hot. Vere lifted herself and their bodies separated, and she fell down beside him on the bed.

After a moment Cass knelt up, opened the hatch and looked out at the day. A welcome breeze sailed in to cool their bodies and the cabin. "We're almost alone," he said. "Everyone's gone except the cat down at the end. Want to go for a swim?"

It was an unaccustomed luxury to have slept so late, and to wake without the responsibility of other people's needs on her. And it felt fabulously luxurious to be able to go swimming in the heat of the morning rather than taking her usual quick dip at a quarter to seven.

Under the bright sun the water had changed colour again and was now a nearly unbelievable emerald green, deep and clear and utterly enticing. The white catamaran was a fair distance away, and they swam naked, the water soft and ca-

ressing and as fine as the silk that passed through a needle
in the old fairy tale. After a while they put on snorkels and
masks, watched a few fish and lazily chased the school of
the little silver fish that could always be found in the shadow
of a boat. There were hundreds of them, but she saw with
ever-present amazement that they moved as one organism,
turning and twisting in perfect unison as they evaded the
shape of the large fish they thought threatened them.

"Why can't humans be like that?" Vere asked, when they
had surfaced and climbed out onto the swimming platform
to shower the salt off with fresh water.

"I've always imagined that that was what was signified by
The Fall," Cass said.

"What?"

"The discovery of human consciousness, and the awareness of individuality. I imagine that before that stage in human evolution we did operate much as the fish do—as one
great organism."

"Oh," said Vere, as she took this in. "But that's—kind
of depressing in its implications, don't you think? Does that
necessarily mean that evolution presupposes separation?"
She passed the nozzle to him and climbed up onto the deck.

Cass held the nozzle to his head and rubbed the water into
his scalp thoughtfully. "Well, one stage of it, it seems. But
perhaps we are meant to discover individuality and carry it
back into union. Then union has a higher value, since it's
engaged in consciously."

Vere, drying herself on the deck above him, blinked and
frowned. "Does it? How do you know all this?"

"I don't know it. I'm merely extrapolating from what the
various sources on the subject say."

This was even more perplexing. "What sources? I've
never heard of anything like that."

He laughed in real amusement, his eyes twinkling up at
her. "They're usually called sacred scripture. I'm talking

about the Bible and various other religious books and traditions.''

She stared at him for a long moment in deep perplexity. "You are?" she said at last.

"Don't you ever read religious texts?" he countered.

She shrugged. "My parents and my aunt and uncle sort of didn't worry about things like that. They said people could lead a moral life without recourse to religion."

"Well, so they can. But there's more to religion than leading a moral life, isn't there?"

"I ... guess so," said Vere. After a moment she asked, "Like what?"

He leapt up the chrome steps to the aft deck, grabbed his towel and began vigorously rubbing himself dry. "Like learning to be like the fish again, and operating as one organism under divine will."

He was so unembarrassed by this speech! As if it were all self-evident and logical, as if he were telling her he hoped to make an engine work!

"So then, what religion are you?" she asked faintly, half dreading the answer. She wrapped the towel around herself and stood watching as he did the same, his wet black hair tousled and glinting in the sun, his body sleek and firmly muscled, the bright red material around his hips a perfect complement to his vibrant colouring.

He smiled, a long, slow smile that saw and understood what she was thinking. "All of them, Vere," he said gently. "Since they all say the same thing, what is there to choose?"

This was enough spiritual confusion for Vere for one morning. "I'm starving!" she said. "What's for breakfast?"

"Whatever you like," said Cass, not evincing any reluctance to let the subject drop. And the thought occurred to her, unbidden, that somehow that was more than just a statement about breakfast. With Cass, she could have whatever she liked. She could have it all.

* * *

They sailed on. The next morning they found another bay, more populous, that held a small fishing village just beginning to give itself over to tourism. There they wandered ashore, climbing the hills for a fabulous view of several perfect bays, circles of white sand between magical blue waters and thick green forest. They sailed to those bays, too, and to busier ports. They walked and talked and held hands and kissed, and returned to the boat to make love in the afternoons, in the evenings, in the mornings, whenever it suited their fancy.

He watched her like a flower unfolding, and she knew he was right in that—this was her real sexual awakening. She had never understood before what a source of pleasure her body could be, or what a delight another's body could offer her. He made her free, by the simple means of being entirely unashamed himself. He encouraged her in wildness, in subtlety, in secret and open. He made her dictate to him exactly what he should do to please her, and then he did it. The freedom this gave her at first frightened, and then overwhelmed her. She became demanding, and by his attitude and actions, he said that that was right. He, too, was demanding, showing her sometimes by word, and sometimes by direct physical commands, what he wanted of her. The discovery of how much her body could offer him in the way of pleasure was as sexually thrilling to her as the equal and complementary discovery of how much his could offer her.

Sometimes they lay on the bed for hours, exploring each other. She had never experienced such a dedication to pleasure. On one such afternoon, she told him so, and asked why it was.

He had a lock of her hair between his fingers and lying on one elbow beside her was trailing it over her back to send sharp little shivers of delight over her skin. "Ah," he said easily, "there are three kinds of men in the world: those who have no idea that it is their duty and responsibility as a man to give a woman sexual pleasure; those who, knowingly or unknowingly, resent the obligation; and those to whom it is the greatest delight. I am lucky enough to be among the third group.''

"Really?" Vere was fascinated by this view. Rory had certainly belonged to the second group. She rolled over and faced him. "How does it happen? I mean, is it—inborn? Or developed?"

"It must be training." He trailed the hair he still held across her breast and tickled the nipple. "Men get sexually selfish because they start out badly, with young girls who don't know enough to be demanding. Later, when they meet a woman who knows what she wants, they resent her demands. If men get their first taste of sexual excitement inextricably bound up with a woman's pleasure, instead of entirely their own, it lays down a track in the brain that they will ever afterward be delighted to follow. But that seldom happens in our culture, sadly for us all."

She blinked. Sometimes it was as though he inhabited some other world entirely from the one she thought she was in. "And how did it happen for you? Did you—was your first lover an older woman or something?"

"No, I got my sexual training, indirectly, from my father. He gave me a set of books to read when I was thirteen. I was eighteen when I got through them, and I started in again at the beginning."

"What was it—*The Collected Works of D. H. Lawrence*, or something?"

Cass grinned. "No, much better. It was Richard Burton's translation of *The Thousand and One Nights*."

"I didn't know that was sexy!"

"Well, it is. Very sexy. And most of the women in it are wildly sexual and demanding, and most of the men ascribe to the ancient warrior code. And that is that a man must be a stalwart warrior, must give the hospitality of his house to strangers and must keep his woman sexually satisfied."

"That's an ancient warrior code?" Vere said in tones of disbelief.

"Oh, yes. It still survives in the mountains of Central Asia and amongst some desert Arabs, I believe. Treatises were written on the means and methods by which men could satisfy women."

She raised her eyebrows. "And have you read those?"

He grinned. "I have." He dropped her hair then, and ran his hand along the length of her body from shoulder to hip, where he closed it with a firmness that thrilled her. He bent and kissed her. "Now," he said. "Have you ever heard the story of Bahloul, the fool at the court of King Mahmoum?"

Chapter 12

They sailed into Rodney Bay on Friday afternoon. Vere was due to report aboard *Phoenix* on Saturday, at no particular time. They had decided to eat their last evening meal aboard *Vagabond*. Vere planned to make spaghetti, garlic bread and a salad, and they went together to the supermarket for supplies.

It was only when they had returned to the boat that they realized they had abandoned two bottles of wine somewhere ashore. Cass was about to get into the dinghy when a radio call came through for him from a friend who had seen *Vagabond* arrive.

"Go seventy-one," said Cass.

"Hi there! Long time no see!" said the male voice, when they had changed channels. "What are you doing? Over."

Cass, standing at the navigation station, smiled across the width of the boat to where Vere was at work in the galley. "Enjoying myself," he said succinctly. "What about you? Over."

"Just hanging about." The accent was Australian. "Why
don't you come over for a beer? Over."

Cass raised his eyebrows at Vere. "Want to go? They're
nice people."

But the real world would arrive sooner than she wanted,
anyway. She didn't want to invite it in. Vere shook her head.
"I'd rather cook," she said. "Can you go by yourself?"

So Cass went off to find the lost wine, or buy some more,
and then to visit for a half hour on his friend's sailboat. She
wasn't sorry to be left alone. She liked cooking, she knew
she made good spaghetti and she enjoyed the thought that
she was cooking for Cass. She hummed to herself as she
chopped the onions and garlic and fried the meat and
roughly measured out the salt and pepper in her palm and
tossed it in.

Cass was going to suggest something, she knew. It had
been a fabulous few days, but it was more than just an in-
terval for both of them. Something had happened between
them, and she knew they couldn't possibly throw it away.
What he would suggest she didn't know... that they should
sail away for a while? That they should get engaged? That...
Vere shook her head and executed a little dance step in the
confines of the galley. Whatever it was, she knew in advance she would like it. She would dress in her prettiest
dress, comb her hair down, make the simple meal as perfect as it could be and be ready to listen.

She would be ready to talk, too. It was time she trusted
him with the truth. She would tell him tonight, and then she
would know whether it was her he loved, or Cilla. And if it
was her, she would ask him to help her find out the truth.
Vere sighed. It would be a relief to have him know. She
hated living a lie.

The meat, onions, garlic and a little green pepper, nicely
browned, all went into the saucepan along with the tinned
tomatoes and tomato paste, and that was it except for a little wine and the spices.

Where on earth were the spices? The salt and pepper, of course, were right there, but where was the basil and the cayenne and the mixed herbs he had assured her he had in stock? Vere slid aside the plastic doors of the little cupboards above the work space and carefully sorted through the jars of jam and mustard . . . she bent down to the cupboard that she knew held only pots . . . no spices, no herbs.

Suddenly, she turned her head. Of course. The tiny cupboard behind the companionway. She had seen him take spices from there. Vere put her finger awkwardly into the little hole in the door and pulled back the catch that kept the cupboard closed at sea. She opened the wrong side, where there was only a cardboard box with files in it, closed it and opened the other side.

There they were, all the spices and herbs she could want, inserted in little holes in a double shelf designed to keep things steady at sea. She poked through them, looking for the familiar and the unfamiliar. Perhaps she would add something new if it smelled right.

The door to the other side hadn't caught properly, and she left both open as she pulled out various spices, turning to add them to the bubbling sauce behind her. Oregano, lots of basil, garlic powder for good measure, cayenne, paprika . . . she wasn't sure how it was that her eye caught what it caught. Each time she turned around, her eye glided past the other side of the cupboard, without looking at the contents, but somehow the name filtered through.

She had added a little more cayenne, for good measure, and had turned to replace it on the shelf, when she paused, almost involuntarily, and looked for the first time directly at the cardboard box in the other half of the little cupboard.

It was a narrow box that had once held a dozen jars of dill pickle, doing service as a small filing cabinet. It was upright, and the top had been cut off. It had file folders standing in it. They were labeled across the top in thick felt marker.

The first one was labeled, "*Incitatus.*"

She was sitting at the navigation table when he returned, the box on the wooden divider wall facing her, several files on the table open. There were files on people she hadn't heard of, and on some she had. There was a file on Harry Bridges. And one on Cilla Fairweather.

It was scarcely half an hour since he had left, only ten minutes since she had found the files, and he came aboard in silence. He hadn't gone to his friend's boat. It was as though he already knew.

Certainly he showed no surprise as he came down the companionway and found her turned in the chair, staring coldly up at him.

"Ah," he said softly, pausing briefly on the middle step and then continuing down. He carefully set two bottles of red wine on the counter edging the galley and then turned to meet her gaze again. "What have you found?"

He knew what she had found, she read it in every line of his body, in the tone of his voice. "Who are you?" she demanded coldly.

"I might ask you the same thing," he pointed out, lifting his eyebrows.

She gestured contemptuously to the material lying in front of her. "You've got something to do with *Incitatus,*" she accused him.

"I have. Have you?"

"You're only with me because you think I'm Cilla Fairweather."

"And are you?"

She snorted. "It's not very nice, is it?"

"No. It is decidedly ugly." He came across to her then, and began shutting the open folders and slipping them back into the cardboard box. "And you are a little too nosy." He was angry, but no angrier than she.

"That's a file on Harry Bridges," she pointed out, as he folded it up and replaced it.

"Is it?"

"It says I told him I was Cilla Fairweather and had amnesia."

"Does it?"

"Why have you got that in there?"

"Why were you talking to Harry Bridges?" he countered softly, as though he really wanted to know.

"I talked to Harry Bridges because he spoke to me," Vere said through her teeth. Her heart was beating faster now, too fast, threatening to choke her. How right her instincts had been when they warned her not to trust a man who was the confidante of the captain of *Incitatus!* Oh, if only she had listened! "Why did *you* talk to Harry Bridges?"

"I watched you come on deck and train your binoculars on Harry Bridges. I watched you swim ashore to Basil's. I watched the sensual display on the beach that had their eyes out on stalks. And I watched you sit where you could watch Harry Bridges. Don't tell me that all happened by chance."

"I'm not telling you anything," she said levelly. She shivered in the tropical heat. "Are you watching me? Do you watch every move I make?"

"Yes."

There was no response to that. She could hardly allow herself to take it in, because of what it meant to the last few magical *lying* days. "Tell me why you asked Harry Bridges what I'd said to him, and why Harry Bridges told you."

"I asked him because I was interested. He told me because he was drunk. And because it scared him to hell to think that you were alive and suffering from amnesia."

"Good," she said.

"You are not suffering from amnesia," Cass said flatly, in a tone that allowed no contradiction.

"No."

"Why in the hell did you tell him you were?"

She looked him full in the face to gauge his reaction. "Because what he said, when he thought I was your friend Cilla, made me think he'd conspired in something very ugly, and I thought he deserved to live in fear of exposure for a bit."

His eyes got darker. "You thought—for God's sake! Tell a man who thinks he killed you that you're not dead after all, but know what he did? Are you crazy?"

"Does he?" she asked.

The question threw Cass. "Does he what?"

Very softly she said, "Does Harry Bridges think he killed Cilla Fairweather?"

"He did not confide in me so far. Even drunk, he was smart enough to keep that to himself."

She was still leaning on the last folder—the one labeled Cilla Fairweather. There wasn't much in the file: an old résumé that took her up to the last yacht she'd worked on before *Incitatus*, a couple of letters of recommendation from various captains, newspaper clippings of the disaster that featured her name and death, another copy of the photo that she had found framed beside his bed. Cass had arrived before she had had time to go through it minutely.

"Tell me," she said conversationally, folding this file together and looking at the name, feeling as cold as she hoped she'd ever feel, all her life long, "Were you ever Cilla Fairweather's lover before that day you saw me on the dock out there?" She jerked with her head in the direction of shore.

He looked at her calmly. "Don't you know the answer to that?"

"Yes," she said, because now, she did. "You never knew her intimately at all. You were never her lover. Isn't that so?"

His eyes were black, watching her.

"And you never loved her. What you told me that day was a lie."

His eyes dropped momentarily, and then he looked at her again, and that, oddly, hurt more than anything that had gone before. "What exactly did you hope to gain?" she asked, biting her lip for control.

He looked straight at her. "You," he said.

She threw Cilla's file at him. It struck his chest and fell to the deck, the papers spewing out at his feet. "You make me sick," she said.

It was as if he tried one last time. "Why don't you tell me the truth?" he asked urgently, as if he really meant it.

In his eyes she saw the ashes of those days they had spent together, in a fool's paradise made just for her. "The truth is," she said, staring at him and biting the words out, "you make me sick enough to vomit."

After that there was nothing but the awful anticlimax of going into the stateroom and packing her things while he waited for her. She called *Phoenix* and asked if she could come aboard a day early. Then they got into the dinghy together, and he took her to the megayacht where she climbed aboard, wordlessly took her bags from him and turned away without saying goodbye.

The yacht still didn't have a full complement of staff. She was shown to a cabin with two bunks, but the other was still uninhabited. As soon as they left her alone, she cried.

"Well, hello," said a hard, masculine voice, pleasantly enough. "What brings you here?"

Vere, standing at *Phoenix*'s stern next morning looking out over the bay, turned her head to look into the face of the man she had sat beside on the plane, and gasped in astonishment. She had forgotten! In all the excitement and turmoil of the past few days it had slipped her memory that he would be aboard!

"Hello!" she exclaimed, smiling and holding out her hand. Perhaps, on reflection, it was just as well she had forgotten. At least her surprise looked spontaneous, and something told her he was a man who would easily be made suspicious. "What are *you* doing here?" She eyed his yacht uniform. "Are you working aboard?"

He took her hand and smiled the curiously unexpressive smile that reached no depth. "That's right. I guess it's time we introduced ourselves. My name's Greg."

"I'm Vere." She was wearing the yacht uniform, too, a fact he ostentatiously noted.

"You must be the new stewardess."

"And you must be the new bodyguard."

But if she had hoped to embarrass him, she failed.

"And security," he said, nodding. "My boss has chartered *Phoenix* for the season. He'll be joining us in a day or two. I've come ahead to make sure everything is . . . settled. You changed your job quickly," he observed. "Bad luck with your last employers?"

The tone of friendly interest nevertheless had an edge. Perhaps he suffered from a professional need to be suspicious of everyone, but Vere didn't like it.

"It's a bigger yacht and the crew quarters are a lot more pleasant than on *Brigadoon*. And the money's better." She was about to go on with her excuses when she realized that to give too many would look suspicious. People babbled to cover up guilt, and this man made her nervous. "Actually, I had quite a good relationship with the owners of *Brigadoon*. I've been having a pretty good time, considering."

"The work's pretty hard, I guess."

"Slave labour," Vere agreed. She decided to move the battle across the field before he could ask anything more. "So, what are you doing? Do you have to check the yacht for bugs?"

He grinned. "Par for the course," he said.

"And maybe plant a few," Vere offered without thinking.

He didn't like that, though she knew it only in the way his eyelids dropped over his eyes and he examined his hand on the chrome railing. "Now, why should I be doing that?" Greg asked calmly.

She smiled and shrugged, as if what she had said was of no significance. "I don't know, isn't that what people do these days? Is your boss planning on running important meetings aboard? Doesn't he want to have everybody on tape?"

"I haven't heard anything about that," he said. He lifted his head and gazed at her levelly, and Vere shivered involuntarily.

"Where's the new stewardess? Vere! There you are!" said a female voice behind them. They turned. "Hi," said the tiny, curly-headed brunette named Alice, who was the other stewardess. They had met last night. "Do you wanna come with me and I'll show you around and we can discuss time-tables?"

Vere wasn't reluctant to leave Greg. She followed Alice into the saloon without looking back. But she didn't forget the conversation, nor the fact that Greg was certainly lining the yacht with bugs.

Phoenix was in another class entirely from *Brigadoon*. Vere had never seen such luxury ashore, let alone afloat. Two huge saloons, a glassed-in aft deck that was so full of plants it was practically a conservatory, staggeringly ornate furnishings, a master stateroom with a Jacuzzi, another Jacuzzi on the lower aft deck, huge mirrored walls in two of the guest staterooms... and gold-plated fittings.

Vere stopped and eyed the Jacuzzi. "That's for real?" she asked gently. "We are looking at gold-plated taps in the bathrooms here?"

Alice burst out laughing. "You should be a comedian," she said. "You make it sound so ridiculous."

"It is ridiculous." She paused. "Isn't it?"

Alice laughed again, and shrugged. "Well, some people say gold plating is very practical. It lasts longer, and it stays polished and all that. I don't know."

"This thing must cost a bomb to charter," said Vere. "Who's this guy who's taking it for the season? Is it some-one rich and famous?"

"I guess he's rich enough," said Alice. "As for fa-mous—his name's Bill…oh, heck, I know it! He's in beer."

"Canadian?"

"Oh, yeah—what's his name?"

"Bassett?" Vere suggested.

"No, he's not that big—Woodman?" Just then a little clock beside the bed chimed the half hour. "Whoops! It's time for the crew breakfast," she said. "I'll show you the galley and stuff, and we can set the table."

She followed Alice to a fabulously appointed galley amidships on the main deck, just behind the wheelhouse and the captain's cabin. There was a huge walk-in freezer, cooking surfaces that looked as though they belonged in a Cordon Bleu restaurant, and a large and comfortable table with bench seating that constituted the crew's mess.

"Breakfast is nearly ready," the chef told them, and the two girls hurried to lay the table with place mats and china as the rest of the crew began to filter in and take their seats.

Full complement, Vere discovered, as she was introduced around and they all chatted together, was nine crew—two or three stewardesses looked after not just the charter guests, but also the captain, engineers and deckhands needed to run such a large yacht.

And, of course, the bodyguard.

"I understand your boss is in beer," said Vere to Greg, who was sitting beside her. The breakfast table was noisy and friendly, but conversation had moved to the history and movements of some boat Vere had never heard of. She had still not learned to share the general fascination of yachting people for the background of every boat afloat.

"Josiah Bach was his great granddaddy," the farm boy agreed.

Vere raised her eyebrows with interest. "Oh, Bach Beer? Is it still a family concern?" she said. "I didn't know there was so much money in a small beer company."

"So much money as what?"

She waved a hand to indicate the yacht. "Well, you said he'd chartered this for the season." As she spoke, the name suddenly triggered a deafening clangour in Vere's head. Her whole body went horribly hot, and she felt the flush creep up her face. Her heart pounding, she reached for the orange juice and with trembling hand poured herself some. She kept her face averted. She could look at no one.

Liz, the chef, who was sitting beside Greg, noticed nothing. "Bill Harwood's got a lot more money than that," she was saying. "He used to own a megayacht as big as this one, but it sank last year, remember? And I guess he will again, when the insurance pays up. The *Incitatus* disaster."

"Really?" demanded Alice, fixing Greg with a look as the whole table now moved into the conversation. "Did your boss own *Incitatus?*"

"I guess he did," said Greg.

William G. Harwood had been the registered owner of *Incitatus*. Vere pressed her hands to her cheeks in a vain effort to cool them, and squeezed her eyes shut against the nausea that gripped her.

She had walked straight into the viper's nest. God in Heaven, what should she do?

"Didn't you know?" asked Greg, beside her, and she thought, in terror, he's known about me all along. Bill Harwood has known I was here ever since his bodyguard sat beside me on the plane. No wonder I got the job.

Chapter 13

The days went by, but Bill Harwood did not join the yacht. The crew ate and slept and talked and waited. Every night they went ashore for sundowners, or to other yachts, or had the crews of other yachts aboard. Both the captain and Greg, the bodyguard, began to act as if Vere should be flattered by their sexual interest in her. In Hugo, it might mark real interest. She knew Greg was pretending, and it terrified her. Everybody was bored, except Vere, who was in a constant state of nerves, waiting for the man who never came, wondering whether to stay or go.

One day they were all at lunch when Gordon, the engineer, arrived from the engine room late and covered with oil. He stood at the sink in the galley and scrubbed his hands vigorously with detergent. "Nothing wrong with the oil," he told the skipper. "False alarm. Must be the oil-pressure sensor itself."

"Right," said Hugo. "I'd better send a fax to the yard and get a replacement part sent out. You get onto the repair this afternoon. Let's try and have the repair done as soon as possible. We don't know when our man is arriving."

Vere smiled in perplexity. "How can Gordon start fixing it before the new part arrives?"

"We carry replacement parts on board," Gordon explained briefly, his real attention on Greg. "Any idea when Harwood'll be arriving?"

Greg just shrugged.

After lunch that day Hugo went ashore for the ship's mail, collected from the marine office. There was a letter for Vere from Alexa, and another from Jill, telling her that *Brigadoon* was taking a one-week charter to Martinique and would be in Saint Lucia again the following Saturday.

Vere almost laughed aloud in relief. She had not expected them to return for two weeks, by which time *Phoenix* might be long gone. Today was Monday, and it was possible that Bill Harwood would not arrive until the weekend. If she could talk to Jill and Ronald, maybe she could come to a decision about how dangerous what she was doing was.

On Tuesday Vere went ashore with Hugo to stock up on groceries. On the way back they passed *Vagabond,* and Cass was on deck. They were sitting side by side in the front seat of the large tender, and Hugo had his hand on her near shoulder in a casual touch that was nothing she could object to, but which she irritably understood meant he was staking out future territory. Vere steadfastly refused to look at Cass as they went by, but she could feel his eyes on her. Suddenly the hand on her shoulder was intolerable.

"I'm hot," she said unapologetically, shrugging it off. Hugo, as if in absentminded good nature, transferred the possessive palm to her bare knee.

This was a move she could counteract directly. Vere firmly picked his hand up by the wrist, moved it over his own thigh and dropped it. "Hands off, Hugo," she said. He looked over, opening his mouth as if to object, but the unapologetic self-possession which he met in her glance silenced him. They traveled the rest of the way without speaking.

She wished she could have trusted Cass.

Lunch was waiting for them when they got back, and Vere, as usual, got sandwiched in beside Greg at the table. She was abruptly aware that if she were not afraid of him, she would never have let him get away with this. It was only because she knew that his interest was not what it pretended to be that she was putting up with it. "No, you sit inside," she said, standing up before he had quite settled himself. "It's easier if I'm on the outside."

He obliged, but immediately began to use a low voice meant to separate the two of them in a private conversation. "Nice time ashore?"

She looked at him. "Yeah, I got some really stupendous bottles of ketchup, Greg."

"That's nice," he replied without offence, from which Vere deduced that irony would be lost on the bodyguard.

At that moment the fax machine in the wheelhouse began to make noises, and Hugo got up to investigate.

"I sent the wrong bloody number to the builders," he said, coming back into the mess waving the fax. "That's the number I've got in the log. You'd better get it off the engine for me, and I'll send again," he said to the engineer.

Gordon nodded, chewing. "Weird," he said.

Vere would scarcely have noticed the exchange, except for trying to avoid conversation with Greg; but she noticed what came later. She was loading the dishwasher in the galley when Gordon came up from below to speak to Hugo, who was pottering in the wheelhouse.

"What?" she heard Hugo explode. "Damn it, what kind of game are they playing?"

He immediately sat down to fire off another fax message. As he sent it he looked at his watch. "Hell, they'll be closed by now in Portsmouth! A day lost!"

"Why does he have to send all the way to England?" Vere asked Liz curiously.

"I guess because that's the yard where it was built," Liz said. "It's not like a car, where you can just pick up a spare part anywhere. Every ship is different, so everything has to be ordered according to the ship's number. I mean, they're all custom designed, these megayachts."

"Phoenix, Phoenix, Phoenix—Vagabond, Vagabond."

Vere jumped when she heard the familiar voice and turned to watch as Hugo pushed the last button to send the fax and simultaneously reached for the radio mike. *"Vagabond, Vagabond, Vagabond, this is Phoenix—go ahead."*

"Phoenix, go sixty-eight. Over."

"Roger, going sixty-eight." Unmoving behind him, Vere watched as Hugo punched up the number.

"Phoenix, Phoenix, Phoenix, this is Vagabond. Do you read?"

"Roger, *Vagabond*. What can I do for you? Over."

"Could I speak to Vere Brown? Over."

"Roger, *Vagabond*, here she is." She didn't have time even to open her mouth to say no before the mike was in her hand.

"This is Vere. Over," she said nervously.

"Hi, Vere," he said. "Are you free for a drink aboard this afternoon, over?"

She glanced involuntarily up at Hugo. "Sure," he said. "Make the most of your time before the punters get aboard."

Her heart racing, Vere pressed the button. "Sorry, Cass, no can do. Thanks, anyway. Over," she said.

"Another time," he said. "Over and out. *Vagabond* going sixteen."

Vere handed the mike to Hugo for the final repeat of the liturgy. There was sweat on her forehead, and she knew it was because in spite of everything she had wanted to go. It wasn't just because he called to her physically, though she would have liked to tell herself that. It was because she desperately wanted to trust someone. She wanted to trust Cass.

"Still not forgiving him, eh?" Liz called from the galley. "He's an awfully good-looking guy."

At breakfast on Wednesday, another fax came through. Ralph, one of the deckhands, sitting next to the door, got up to tear it off and handed it to the captain. Vere, counting the days till *Brigadoon*'s arrival, felt her heart thud with the fear that this was a message announcing Harwood's arrival. But Hugo swore colourfully while he read it and then frowned across the table at Gordon.

"They still say there's no such number," he said.

"No such number as what?" Liz enquired.

"This ship we are on doesn't exist," said Hugo flatly. He looked at the fax message again. "We're the *Flying Bloody Dutchman*, aren't we?"

He nodded at Greg, who was stoically eating his eggs and bacon, and taking no apparent interest in the conversation. "Your boss, if he ever arrives, is going to be stuck in Rodney Bay till we get this sorted," he said.

"What are you going to do?" asked Vere, as he quickly finished his meal.

"I'll fax George." George Pagliatis, another wealthy Canadian whose name everybody knew, was *Phoenix*'s owner, but the crew had scant hope of seeing him aboard. *Phoenix* was a business proposition for him, not a pleasure yacht.

Hugo shrugged as if it didn't mean very much, but Vere happened to be looking right at him as he spoke, and she saw a curious expression in his eyes, wary and puzzled, and even a little suspicious.

Whatever he said, Vere knew the incident worried him.

That night they all went ashore for a pub crawl, except for the one deckhand whose sad turn it was to remain aboard as watch. At the first bar, Vere enjoyed herself, forgetting her problems under the influence of alcohol and steel-band music. At the second bar, Hugo and Greg, both getting a little drunk, began making their intentions even clearer than they already were. Her pleasant haze was destroyed then, because she knew that Greg wasn't drunk at all. In the third bar, they ran into Cass, sitting alone at a table by the window. He looked up at Vere with a smile that melted her, and then glanced at the captain walking beside her. Hugo immediately lifted his arm from Vere's shoulder, and somehow the party ended up dragging another table over and sitting with Cass.

He made no effort to separate her from the group, but simply joined in their fun, with the social ease she had noticed in him before. The conversation was casual and witty, and nothing of any substance got said, but at the end of an hour it was clear that both Greg and Hugo had been warned off. If she hadn't been so relieved, she might have been more annoyed than she was. But she knew that after such a public showdown, even Greg would have to back off.

Only when they decided it was time to go home did Cass make any effort to get her on her own, and then everybody conspired with him so that it was impossible for Vere to avoid it.

They all imagined, no doubt, that as they stood on the dock in the cloudy moonlight he was making amends. She knew by now that they had all watched fascinated when she arrived a day early at *Phoenix,* not speaking to Cass. But Vere and Cass both knew there were no amends he could make. They stood in silence for a long minute, while Vere wished she didn't wish he would kiss her. She felt angry and betrayed, but still standing beside him was enough to puff the embers of her being into flame. That made her angry with herself. "Good night, Cass," she said, just at the moment when his arm went round her waist.

"It's a big yacht, you might not have access to the radio," he said. "If you need help, come on deck anywhere and wave something—a scarf, a hat, a cushion—if there's anything at all in your hand, I'll know. All right?''

She did not answer.

"I'm sorry you can't trust me," he said then. "I wish you could." And then he pulled her swiftly against himself and kissed her mouth in the moonlight, and her blood was so hot she thought she must burn him. She was scarcely conscious of putting an arm up to his shoulder, but he felt it, and his grip on her tightened nearly unbearably and his kiss became deeply passionate.

When he lifted his lips she had forgotten most of her firm intentions. He pulled her face close in against his neck and bent to press his lips against the place left bare by her shirt, that sensitive spot where shoulder met neck.

"Come back with me," he said, the urgency in his low, deep voice melting her where she stood.

She wanted to. If she listened to her body, she wanted to go anywhere with him, forever.... Vere drew away from him a little and looked up into his shadowed face, hesitating. She was close to forgetting everything she knew in the overwhelmingly primitive urge to mate with this particular member of the masculine half of the species. In spite of the cool breeze, she felt perspiration bead her upper lip.

"Why won't you trust me?" he said then, as if the words were torn from him. "Trust me, come with me, and tell me the truth!"

Well, of course, that was what he wanted, wasn't it? she told herself roughly. Some kind of confession that she was Cilla, for whatever his own purposes were. He was as bad as Greg. He wasn't in love with anyone—certainly not her, and not even Cilla, though unlike Greg he was very good at counterfeit passion.

"Leave me alone, Cass," she said. They were calling jocularly from the tender to know whether she was joining them or not. "I'm coming!" she called, pulling herself out of his tightening hold and running lightly along the dock, away from her own desire, to where there was nothing she wanted except safety in numbers.

Ever since she had learned that Bill Harwood was going to be aboard the yacht she had been dreaming of Cilla, and that night was no exception. A few months ago the dreams had been simple images of Cilla, saying, "It's not right." Now they were different. Now she had long, urgent conversations with Cilla. The problem was, she could not remember them when she awoke. Was Cilla trying to warn her away from *Phoenix?* Was she urging her to stay? It was like trying to see through fog, like listening down a bad line.

The foggy feeling sometimes stayed with her during her waking hours, and after a few days she felt Cilla's presence on the yacht almost constantly. Not since the time of Cilla's death had Vere felt the kind of pain that comes from unconsciously expecting to see a loved one around a corner or through a door and then remembering that the loved one is dead.

She slept in the lower bunk of a comfortable cabin. If and when another stewardess was hired, she would share the cabin, but for the moment she was alone at night. Once, as she lay reading a book in the soft light of her bedside lamp, she laughed aloud at something she was reading, and began, "Did you know—"

She stopped there, with a little gasp of horror. The person she had been speaking to, as though she lay in the upper bunk, was Cilla. Vere dropped her book and breathed deeply, trying to still her beating heart. Was she going mad? Dream messages from the beyond were one thing. That she could accept. But the breakdown of the barriers between reality and unreality in the human mind was...

Vere sat up and looked around the room. Of course, it felt like their bedroom in the cottage up at the lake. When they were young they had had bunk beds, and there was that same cosy, secure, shut-in-against-the-storm feeling that their little room had always had. And the nearness to water. Drowsy and concentrating on her book, her rational mind had lowered its defenses and memory had slipped in. That was all.

Yet as she turned out the light and slipped into sleep, she knew that it was a lie. She had felt Cilla's presence in a way she hadn't experienced since the terrible moment when she had heard her say goodbye.

But she didn't know what it meant.

On Friday morning the new oil-pressure sensor was delivered by courier.

"Well, that's fast enough, anyway," Hugo observed. "George can obviously get ass moving at that yard when it's necessary, even if I can't." He held up a fax from the owner instructing his captain to order all parts through him in the future until the problem with the yard was straightened out.

It was sorted out just in time. An hour later Greg got a phone call to inform the yacht that Bill Harwood and party would be arriving on Saturday. "How many in the party?" Liz and Alice asked simultaneously.

"Five, he said," Greg told them. "There's the boss and his girlfriend, another couple and my partner."

Alice looked at the bodyguard. "Is your partner going to be a guest or—"

Technically, Greg wasn't really crew; he was a member of the charter party. But he had made it very clear from the beginning that he didn't expect to be treated as a guest. He looked after his own cabin and made his own bed like the crew members, leaving Alice and Vere with no duties in his cabin except regular vacuuming along with the rest of the yacht. He was always present when they did so. Vere was certain it was to prevent anyone searching the cabin. But she couldn't imagine what it was he was hiding.

"Noah will share my cabin. We'll look after ourselves," said Greg. For some reason he looked at her as he said it.

* * *

Phoenix was sparkling when Hugo and Ralph left in the tender after lunch on Saturday to pick up the charter guests. Hugo had changed his casual uniform polo shirt for more formal whites and a shirt with epaulets. He and Ralph would drive all the way to the south of the island to meet the guests at the airport; it was a ninety-minute trip over very bad roads.

The staterooms had all been polished as if for royalty, including the gold taps; the lounge looked like the picture of a thirties luxury liner; there was a snack of champagne and cold lobster waiting in the fridge, and the crew were all freshly laundered and pressed an hour before the earliest time they could expect the arrival.

Vere played nervously with the table fittings in the main saloon, already perfectly laid, and now there was nothing to do but wait. And worry. Having got her training on a smaller yacht, she was a little surprised at the formality— and dismayed. She had been hoping that she would be able to keep out of sight for a while when Bill Harwood came aboard, putting off the moment of coming face-to-face with him. But a megayacht meant megamoney, and such people were different from the charterers of small yachts. Bill Harwood and his guests apparently would expect to meet the entire crew when they came aboard.

Torn with indecision, not able to meet Jill and Ronald before Harwood's arrival, she had let apathy take its course, and had remained because that was the choice that required no decision.

A dozen different ways of delaying the moment of recognition had run through Vere's mind, from dying her hair to faking illness today, but she had rejected all of them.

Although she was convinced *he* would recognize *her*, she wasn't certain of recognizing Harwood. She had only seen a photo in the newspaper over a year ago. Greg had said, when she asked him, that he was a big man but had no beer belly, and had given her the kind of look that simply stopped her asking more.

She felt nervous and stupid, as though hypnotized by a snake at long distance. She was afraid. And yet, in some part of herself, she had to know.

She heard the sound of a dinghy motor killing its speed at just the distance that meant it was headed for *Phoenix*. She ran out to the deck and looked over, her heart in her throat, though she knew it couldn't possibly be the *Phoenix* tender yet.

It was Cass. He saw her instantly, looking up as if her gaze had drawn him. "Hi," he said, without preamble. "Can I talk to you for a few minutes? It's urgent."

Already afraid, she shivered. "What about?"

He didn't smile. "It's also private."

Liz was on the upper deck, relaxing after her labours with the lobster. She leaned over. "How long do you want her for, Cass?"

"Half an hour."

"All right, you can go, Vere, but be sure you're back here in time. And don't get your uniform all messed up." Liz had taken a liking to Cass; she was happy to promote his cause with Vere. If she'd been a few years younger, she might have fallen for him herself, but she could give him ten years and Gordon suited her.

Vere stood hesitating. Had Harwood already found out about her? Was this some way of getting rid of her before he arrived, so that suspicion wouldn't fall on him? She gazed at Cass, trying to find a way to say no without sounding as terrified as she felt. But he lifted a hand and beckoned imperatively, and resistance died in her. He had an animal hold over her that she could not resist.

So she climbed down and clambered into the dinghy. "Don't let her sit on any oil!" Liz called down with a grin.

Cass shouted something back, nodded and waved, and in two minutes they were at *Vagabond*.

"What do you want?" Vere asked as she climbed aboard the pretty maroon sailboat.

Cass followed her aboard and tied up the dinghy in silence. She stood facing him on the aft deck, her hands in her shorts pockets. "I said, what do you want?"

"Will you sit down?" he asked, a little roughly, as though her attitude had reminded him of his own uncertain temper. He stood with his shirt blowing open over his bare chest, the sun behind him blinding her as she looked at him, holding the rigging with one arm and looking every inch a civilised pirate.

Vere stood her ground. She wasn't risking sitting down, or relaxing in any way, or letting him get near her. Her control around him was precarious, at best, and she had not forgotten that a couple of nights ago, knowing what she knew, she had weakly let him kiss her. Whatever he wanted, he would know how to use any advantage she allowed him.

"What do you want, Cass?" she repeated steadily. The boat rocked as the wake of a passing motorboat hit it, and she grabbed for the boom to steady herself.

He said abruptly, as if giving up any hope of approaching the subject obliquely, "Do you know who is going to arrive aboard *Phoenix* this afternoon?"

"Yes," she returned flatly.

"And does the name Bill Harwood mean anything to you?"

"You tell me," she invited softly.

"Bill Harwood was the owner of *Incitatus*. If you're Cilla Fairweather, maybe you know what you're doing, but I doubt it. If you're Vere Brown, do you have any idea what kind of danger you might be walking into?"

Not for anything would she admit fear to him. "What kind of danger?"

He shook his head irritably. "Don't go back there," he said. "I don't know what game you think you're playing, but allow me to tell you it is potentially fatal."

"What's your interest, Cass?" she asked softly.

"My interest right now is your safety."

She was shaking her head before he had finished. "No, it isn't," she said. "You've had another interest right from the start. I'm incidental." She laughed mirthlessly. "What happened, did Bill Harwood double-cross you?" As soon as she said it, she believed it. That would account for his behaviour, at any rate—tailing her, thinking she was Cilla, clearly in the belief that she would lead him to Bill Harwood. And so she had.

She leaned closer. "I am not Cilla Fairweather," she said, spacing each word as if for someone simpleminded. "And whatever scam you and Bill Harwood were running, I know nothing about it. All right? Now, Bill Harwood will know that, even if you don't, so I won't be in any danger from him." It was as if she were convincing herself, and maybe she was. Certainly seeing Cass's concern, her own had lessened, so much easier is it to dismiss your fears if they are expressed by someone else. "If he's the one who killed her, he won't be very likely to think she's returned from the dead."

"Your presence will make him feel threatened. He's not the man to reason with any feeling of threat."

She frowned. "What do you mean?"

"He's a man who just gets rid of a threat, isn't he?" She felt her heart choke her. "Whatever scam Bill Harwood was running isn't over yet. He won't run the risk of being wrong about you."

"So he'll just murder me? Murder isn't that easy."

"Murder is a lot easier at sea than anywhere else in the world," Cass said. Vere gasped. "Tell me the truth. I can help you."

He had lied about Cilla, and he had lied about loving her, and he had secret motives of his own. Yet in spite of all that, she wanted to trust him. Vere glanced at her watch nervously. "They'll be looking for me." What should she do?

The question was answered for her. Cass caught her arm as she turned to look over at *Phoenix,* and put his other arm roughly around her waist, pulling her to him and kissing her before she had a chance to scream. There was no one on any boat close enough to see that she struggled as he dragged her down into the cockpit, and there, out of sight of all, he lifted his mouth from hers and clapped his hand over it.

"We're going below," he said, in a voice that terrified her. "If you struggle, you may fall and hurt yourself. Don't struggle." Then he was behind her, his hand over her mouth, his arm around her waist, and he lifted her bodily through the hatch. Her feet groped for the companionway steps, her hands clutched at the hatch, but he was too strong for her. She struggled, but the fear of falling meant she gave in in the end.

He got her onto the sofa, his hand over her mouth, his arm keeping her arms pinned. "I'll take my hand away if you don't scream. The moment you try to scream I'll gag you. Understood?" said Cass.

Chapter 14

"*Vagabond, Vagabond, Vagabond—Phoenix, Phoenix*—come in."

Cass looked at her, and she stared back, her eyes black with fear. "I'm sorry," he said. "But I have to stop you going back there."

"*Vagabond, Vagabond, Vagabond—Phoenix, Phoenix*—come in, please."

Cass heaved a breath and, still holding her arm, got up and forced her to move with him to the nav station and the radio. "*Phoenix, Phoenix, Phoenix*—this is *Vagabond*, over."

"Damn it, Cass." Liz's voice came irritably, "Where is that girl? They're arriving already!"

A pair of binoculars lay on the nav desk, and without pausing for thought, Vere grabbed them up and smashed wildly at his head, landing a glancing blow. He let go the mike and her arm and reached for the binoculars, but Vere dropped them and went for the companionway, leaping up the first three steps in one, grasping the hatch to lift herself and flinging herself through into the cockpit. She heard Cass call her name once, but in another second she was at the side and over into the water. The water in the harbour wasn't the cleanest, but it was by no means disgusting, and when she surfaced she put her head down and broke into a strong racing crawl.

It wasn't a long swim, though her clothes slowed her down. She lifted her head to look back once, and saw Cass on deck, very still, watching her. She didn't look again. He would not be following her.

There was nowhere to go now, except to *Phoenix*.

A few minutes later she arrived at the stern and saw with a sinking heart that the tender was already there: Bill Harwood was aboard. She had no choice but to face him.

The sliding doors of the conservatory were open, but no one was on the aft deck as she approached. Vere manoeuvred around the tender and in its shadow found the swimming ladder down. She reached for it, hauled herself up onto the swimming platform and then, her shoes squelching, her hair plastered to her scalp and face and her wet shirt dark and clinging, up the short ladder to the Jacuzzi deck.

She hadn't looked up, for fear that her own attention would draw some in return; but as she crossed the deck she felt the sensation of being watched, and one hand on the next ladder, she paused and looked up.

Directly above her a man on the main deck was staring down at her, a cigar in his hand; and she had been wrong to imagine she had forgotten what Bill Harwood's face looked like. She would have known him anywhere, the eyes cold and even deader than they had looked on newsprint.

"Who are you?" he demanded, as another figure joined him at the stern. Hugo. Vere shrugged and climbed the ladder, and Bill Harwood watched her, through narrowed, calculating eyes, all the way up. "Who the hell are you?" he demanded again as she reached him, and Vere knew with complete certainty that she was looking at Cilla's killer, and that he would not be apologizing for it.

Turning, she clutched the railing and threw up her lunch all over the nice new cream-coloured paintwork.

"I think you'd better pack your bags," said Hugo, when she had recovered and was wiping her mouth on the warm, wet cloth Alice had brought her. "Sorry about this, Mr. Harwood."

Harwood waved his hand as if Hugo were a fly, and stared at Vere with flat inhuman eyes. "Who hired you?" he demanded softly.

She glanced at the captain apologetically. "Hugo," she said.

"Don't give me that," he said contemptuously. "I mean, who hired you to come up out of the water like that? Who told you to get a job on this ship and pretend to be that girl?"

They were all staring at him, except for Jonathan, who was already hosing down the yacht's sullied paintwork. "What she says is perfectly true, Mr. Harwood. I hired her, and I've fired her. She won't trouble you again."

"What's your name?" said Harwood. Hugo might as well not have spoken.

She had to convince him she knew nothing. "Vere Brown. I apologize for arriving the way I did. My friend's motor died and he couldn't get it going again. In the end I just decided to swim for it. I thought I'd get here before you and have time to change."

He glanced at Hugo, cutting across her explanation. "That the name you hired her under?"

Hugo was seething. "Yes, it is," he said, very clipped. But his English displeasure made no impression on Bill Harwood.

He was watching Vere again. "Right," he said flatly. "You're not fired."

* * *

Vere hurried along to the forward companionway and down to her cabin. As she dropped her soaking clothes onto the floor of the bathroom, she shivered. Why hadn't he let Hugo fire her? Was it because she didn't worry him, or because she did? She almost wished he had let her go.

Yet, much as part of her wanted to get off *Phoenix*, another part of her was deeply convinced that she could not go, in spite of the danger. Never had she been closer to knowing the truth of Cilla's death. Her instincts had led her here, and it must be for a reason.

She didn't like it, but she knew she had to do it. She had never been so scared, so sick, or so determined.

She noticed that someone was with him every minute of the day, wherever he went. He was always accompanied by one or both of the bodyguards. Noah in particular never left him. Sometimes she wondered when he slept.

Noah was from the islands. He had smooth, dark skin and a wide smile, and he spoke softly; and Vere was glad it wasn't her job to assassinate Bill Harwood, because Noah looked dangerous. He carried his gun against the small of his back, and they had seen him draw it once, with a hand that really was quicker than the eye.

It was on an evening that some young thugs had tried to come aboard *Phoenix* when she was in dock loading fuel. The incident was over before it began, but Alice had been girlishly impressed by Noah's quick draw and had tried to make him repeat it. Noah had steadfastly refused; he never drew his gun unless he intended to use it. And try as she might, Alice did not win. "It's a gun," he kept saying. "It's a gun."

So they were no amateurs, Harwood's security men. Vere added that to her mental file on Bill Harwood.

* * *

"C'mere, honey," he said to her one day, when he and Greg were sitting in the saloon together talking, and she had come in to see to their drinks.

There was a tone in his voice that sent an unpleasant shiver down her spine. She carried a tray with nuts and chips, but even though she had been on her way to the low table where they were sitting, his command made her actions seem servile.

"What'd you say your name was again?"

She told him.

"What was your mother's maiden name?" The shiver chased itself all over her back and arms, and to her scalp. She looked into those eyes and knew that she would not be able to refuse to answer. The lie came to her quickly, as if by an inspiration, and she used it.

"My mother's maiden name was Brown," she said, staring at him with her eyebrows slightly raised, as though she found him importunate. But Harwood was immune to anything indirect and to most things direct. "She didn't know who my father was." She had been born in 1968. It wasn't an unbelievable story, if what she had heard from Alexa about those times was true.

There was a notebook open on the table in front of Greg, but he wasn't writing in it. Her heart sank. How easy was it to check birth records?

"Where were you born?"

"Why are you checking up on me?" she countered. "What is it you want to know?"

"Where were you born?"

So powerful was his ego, his will, that it was all she could do not to simply obey the demand. She was actually shaking with the effort it took to resist. She stared at him in silence, trying to work out what to do, when it suddenly occurred to her that the easiest answer was silence.

Vere bent down and carefully removed the attractive little bowls of nuts and chips from her tray and set them on the table. She consolidated the leftovers of two others into one, then picked up Harwood's empty glass and went to the bar to refresh it.

"You ever hear the name Fairweather?" The voice, admitting no defeat, followed her across the ornately appointed lounge.

"Somebody mistook me for someone with a name similar to that in Bequia once," she said. "I know there's someone who looked a lot like me. Did you know her?"

He didn't answer. Suddenly Vere was tired of being afraid of the man. Carrying his whiskey and a beer for Greg, she returned to set them down.

"I've heard she worked for you, too, Mr. Harwood," she said. She tidied the coffee table, changing the ashtray unnecessarily.

"Eh?"

"Somebody told me there was a girl who looked like me who used to work on your old yacht." She looked at him. "The one that sank."

He grunted, and puffed at his cigar. Greg was watching her in fascination.

"They say you abandoned her to die." She was crouched beside him, picking up a peanut from the carpet at his feet—Bill Harwood was not a tidy eater. For a week she had been wearing Cilla's favourite perfume, a strong scent called Youth Dew. She looked up into his face. "Was that horrible, watching her die?"

He stared at her with a deep malevolence. "Get out," he said quietly, jerking his head, and her heart beat as if with the approach of physical danger.

Vere stood up. "Did she burn, or did she drown?" she asked ghoulishly. Harwood did not answer. She moved back to the bar to set down her tray and cloth. "I guess it must have given you a real scare that day when I climbed out of the sea." She laughed stupidly, a stupid woman attracted to secondhand horror. "For a minute you must have thought I was her come back to haunt you!"

"Get the hell out of here," said Harwood. But even then he didn't raise his voice.

For over a month they sailed among the islands, picking up and dropping various guests in various ports, and through familiarity her fears subsided. Bill Harwood came and went, though his girlfriend, Portia, remained aboard. Noah always left with Harwood. Greg always stayed on *Phoenix*.

Somehow the crew picked up the knowledge that *Phoenix* was for sale, and that Bill Harwood would get a commission from the owner if he managed to sell it to one of his friends. From the commission, the crew would be well rewarded for their cooperation. This seemed to explain everything, including Harwood's clearly uncharacteristic generosity, and the fact that the yacht seemed to travel entirely at the whim of whatever guests he had aboard.

But Vere kept her eyes open in case there was more to it than that. As stewardess, she was in a good position to know what came aboard, both as supplies and as personal luggage. She would have known if any bag that came aboard remained unpacked, for example; she did her best to count the bags as they arrived on the yacht, in case one disappeared before getting into the guests' cabins, and as they left. But she never saw anything that looked like evidence that the yacht was involved in drug shipments or anything else that might be illegal.

They had taken on another stewardess, and Vere no longer had her cabin to herself. Debbie was a red-haired Vancouverite, and so the yacht now had the full complement in its stewardesses, as more than one of the male guests pointed out: a brunette, a redhead and honey-haired Vere.

For the most part they were a happy crew, getting along well together with few disagreements. Vere enjoyed their company, but she was very alone. There was no one she could confide in. She did not see *Vagabond* again, and in spite of everything, the knowledge that Cass was no longer there made her lonely. And although *Brigadoon* was often nearby, only once or twice had the two yachts actually been in the same harbour together, and there had been no chance of her seeing Jill or Ronald. She had written to Jill to tell her about Harwood's presence, but she was afraid to commit too much to paper. Sometimes she suspected that Greg would not be above intercepting her mail. Jill wrote her, too, in very guarded terms.

At last, however, one morning in Mustique, Vere came out on deck before lunch to see *Brigadoon* sailing into the bay. Dropping her polishing rag, she rushed into the wheel-house, where one of the deckhands was pottering in the absence of the captain. "Can I use the radio for a minute?" she demanded.

When he nodded, she picked up the mike. *"Brigadoon, Brigadoon, Brigadoon—Phoenix, Phoenix!"* she called.

"Phoenix, this is *Brigadoon,"* said Ron's familiar voice, and when they had moved to a clear channel, "How's it going, Vere, over?"

"Great! I'm dying to see you! Will you have any free time today, over?"

"We'll work something out. When are you free, over?"

She hadn't worked that out herself. "I'll have to find out and call you back, over."

Ron chose his words carefully. "Is everything all right, over?"

"So far, so good," she said. "Over and out."

Alice and Debbie agreed to serve the evening meal without her, and Hugo let her have a couple of hours off. When Ron had dropped his new stewardess at Basil's Bar, he stopped at *Phoenix* to pick Vere up. It turned out *Briga-doon* had no charter guests this week, and they were pleasing themselves. They had followed *Phoenix* to check up on Vere.

Jill was cooking a simple meal when they arrived, but she dropped everything and wiped her hands to come and give Vere a hug. "What's been going on?" she demanded. "I've been so worried, you there with that terrible man!"

Vere and Ron settled at the table while Jill went back to her cooking, and Vere did most of the talking. She told them about Harwood's reaction to her dramatic entrance from the sea, about his questions, the way Greg watched her, how Harwood came and went, how she kept track of the luggage. They discussed everything that she had seen and heard, but after an hour they were no closer to a guess at what had really happened aboard *Incitatus* when it went down.

"And what about Cass?" Jill said.

Vere's heart thumped in spite of herself. "What about him?"

"He's very worried. We've talked to him once or twice. Have you discussed this with him?"

It made her nervous to think he was talking to her friends behind her back. "We haven't spoken since he tried to kidnap me," Vere said dryly, producing all the amazement she could want with the little bald announcement.

But when she had explained the incident, Jill merely shrugged. "I'd trust Cass, myself," she said.

"I don't," said Vere flatly.

There was an awkward pause. Jill said, "Time to eat. Will you open the wine, Ron? Vere, will you set the table? Let's talk about more pleasant things over the meal."

They ate without any more reference to *Phoenix* and its inhabitants, and Vere could see that her hopes of coming to some resolution through discussion had been in vain. There was simply nothing to say, nothing to think. That Cilla's death ought to have been treated as suspicious was now nearly certain, but she had no leads, no direction. What could she do?

Vere became steadily more depressed throughout the meal. Surely they had not covered everything! Surely if they got together again, they would think of something!

"How long are you staying here in Mustique?" she asked when they had finished dessert, because it seemed likely *Phoenix* would remain another day.

"We're leaving first thing in the morning," said Ron. "I've got to pick up a part in Bequia. Fuel pump went and I don't like travelling without a spare. It's waiting for us there."

"Oh!" Vere exclaimed. "That reminds me! Can you believe that with a brand-new boat like *Phoenix* the builder's yard has got the numbers all screwed up? Hugo couldn't order a part, because the number on the engine didn't exist at the yard! Isn't that odd?"

Ron was frowning. "That's ridiculous!"

Vere described the conversations she had overheard. "And now if he wants to order any part, he has to get in touch with the owner. He's the only one, apparently, who can get anything out of the builders."

"That's a load of bull," said Ron. "If they read the number off the engine, that's the number the builder's got. And if they made a mistake between their records and the yacht, all they have to do is change the number at the builders'. Something's wrong there."

Goose bumps began to chase themselves all over Vere's skin. She put down her spoon and gazed at Ron as he spoke. "Really?" she said softly.

"There's something damned funny going on," said Ron.

But they could none of them guess what.

Something was nagging at her as she returned to *Phoenix* and began to help Debbie and Alice with getting the staterooms ready for the night. Was there something, some clue, that she had forgotten to mention to Ron and Jill? Something that she had noticed but hadn't consciously considered? All through the ritual of turning down sheets and filling water carafes and all the other little touches that made traveling on the megayacht a "luxury experience," Vere combed her memory for the elusive clue she knew was in there.

Later, undressing in her own cabin, she pulled out the only photo she had of Cilla, aboard *Incitatus,* and stared at it, willing her cousin to tell her what she was missing. When she settled down for the night, she set the photo on the little wooden rail that ran along the bulkhead above her bunk, and lay staring at it long after Jonathan, who was using the upper bunk these days, had said good-night and put his own light out above.

"What is it?" she whispered to herself, to the picture. "What am I missing?"

She fell asleep with her light on, and awoke two hours later, remembering no dream, but knowing the truth. She came upright in the bunk, nearly bashing her head on the bed above, and snatched at the photo of Cilla. She stared at it for a long moment. "Of course!" she muttered. "Of course!"

It accounted for so many things—why Bill Harwood had "chartered" the yacht for the season; why Hugo hadn't been able to order parts with the number on the engine bulkhead; why she had felt Cilla's presence so strongly ever since coming aboard; and how it was that Harry Bridges had been at the scene without escaping in the dinghy.

She looked at the photo with an eye more expert in judging yachts than it had been a few months ago. All the differences were superficial: *Phoenix* was cream-coloured, *Incitatus* had been a more conventional white; *Phoenix*'s aft deck was closed in with glass, *Incitatus* had had an open deck. The upper deck supports were square-cut on *Incita-*

tus, curving on *Phoenix. Phoenix* had a large chrome extension like a little bridge on the bow, which altered the apparent shape of the bow. Her designer's eye must have seen the truth long ago, perhaps as early as that first, premonitory sight of *Phoenix.*

Incitatus had never caught fire, never gone down at all. She couldn't have done. As sure as Vere was sitting there, *Phoenix* and *Incitatus* were the same ship.

Chapter 15

Then what had really happened that day at sea? Vere shook herself in disbelief. It was almost too difficult to believe in such an extravagant fraud. How and why would such a disaster have been faked? What had happened to the ship after it was abandoned by Bill Harwood, and how had the crew, including Cilla, died?

Vere tried to remember what she had heard and read of the details of the *Incitatus* disaster. The yacht had been en route to Palma de Majorca, where it was due to be delivered to a buyer. There had been no guests and no captain except Bill Harwood, the owner, making his first Atlantic crossing as skipper. The yacht had been very lightly staffed by temporary crew, hired just for the one trip to deliver the yacht across the Atlantic. Only Cilla had remained from the regular crew.

Incitatus, therefore, had been running with one stewardess, also acting as cook; Harwood, acting as captain; an engineer; and two deckhands. Its full complement would have been at least five more. The engineer and the deckhands had been fighting the fire in the engine room when the explosion occurred, killing two of them instantly and wounding the third. When Bill Harwood and the wounded engineer had abandoned ship, they had managed to get the two bodies into an emergency dinghy, which they towed behind them. But Cilla had panicked and had been unapproachable, running all over the ship away from them and finally locking herself in her cabin with the fire raging only a few yards away.

Through sheer and awful necessity they had abandoned her. Later, in rough and threatening seas, they had been cut loose from the dinghy, which was never found. Later still, the engineer had died of his wounds. The rescue homing device hadn't worked, and it was twelve hours before the rescue aircraft had seen Harwood's last flare. He had buried the engineer at sea an hour before he was spotted.

That was the story. But it fell apart completely if Harry Bridges had been there. There had been a conspiracy, and he had not expected anyone to die.

Why *had* the four crew died? If the yacht hadn't sunk, there had been no fire to panic Cilla, no explosion to kill the crew. No need, presumably, to abandon ship.

Vere sat there in the small hours of the night, lighted by her tiny reading lamp, staring at the photo of her laughing, carefree cousin. "What happened, Cilla?" she whispered urgently. "What really happened?"

The next day *Brigadoon* left for Bequia without Vere having any chance to talk to Jill and Ron again. She was allowed a quick exchange with Ron over the radio, and told him that Hugo expected *Phoenix* would be following them to Bequia in a day or two. "I really hope I see you again soon," she said, trying to communicate a sense of urgency with the sentence, because there was nothing else she could say with Hugo listening and over open airwaves.

"You bet," said Ron, but she couldn't be sure he had understood the urgency.

Portia, Bill Harwood's girlfriend, was an attractive blonde in her thirties, and Vere had the impression that she had known Harwood for several years. She was friendly, looked intelligent and had a very dry sense of humour. She liked Vere's company. On the occasions when there were no other women guests aboard, as sometimes happened, Portia had got into the habit of chatting with Vere, inviting her to go snorkeling or to lie on the deck with her in the afternoons.

So it wasn't difficult to open a conversation with Portia. One day, when Vere was cleaning the master stateroom and its bathroom, Portia came in and flopped down on the bed. "God, that woman's thick!" she said. The woman in question was the girlfriend of one of Bill Harwood's many friends.

Vere laughed encouragingly. "If she doesn't stop moaning about not being able to find a decent hairdresser in the islands, I'm going to go in there one night and shave her bloody head!" Portia declared. "Look, have you finished in here?"

"Pretty much," said Vere.

"Well, go out and get us some drinks and bring them back here and put up your feet for half an hour. I've got to get away from them for a bit."

So Vere went out and loaded a tray with Portia's favourite whiskey and some white wine and a bottle of water, an ice bucket and a couple of bowls of chips and snacks. "God, do I need alcohol!" said Portia gratefully when she returned. "Put it down right here!"

She tossed some ice into the glass and poured the whiskey freely, as she offered, "Help yourself." Vere poured herself some white wine and watered it well. "Is that all you want?" asked Portia. "Rather you than me."

She quickly got onto the subject that was clearly eating at her, but which she hadn't been open about until now: the fact that she was fed up with Bill Harwood and with being his lover and with living in luxury without having any real freedom or anything constructive to do. "I don't know how I got myself into this," she said.

"How did you?" asked Vere, to whom this opening came as a gift. "I mean, how did you meet Bill?"

Portia shrugged and finished off the whiskey in her glass, sitting forward to give herself a refill. "I used to be the head of the advertising team for Bach Beer. You know, I worked for an agency, and Bach was one of my clients. Bill likes blondes—but I also think he was threatened by me—he didn't like dealing with a woman in business. So he started asking me out, and then once he'd got me into bed, he sort of had me where he wanted me. He started to nag me to quit and come and live with him, and eventually, like a fool, I did."

"How long ago was that?"

"Oh—more than three years ago now. What a waste of a career!"

"So you knew him when he owned *Incitatus*," said Vere, as casually as she could.

"Oh, yeah—in fact, I named her." Abruptly Portia laughed, as if at a private joke.

"It's an odd name, *Incitatus*. I've often wondered what it means," Vere said, although the truth was she had never thought about it.

Portia laughed again. Clearly she had been drinking before she came into the stateroom. "He wanted some significant name, something regal. So I told him he should name her after a Roman emperor's horse." She drank deeply and giggled. "He liked that idea, did our Bill. 'A Roman emperor's horse!'" she mimicked his deep voice. "But he never thought to ask me which Roman emperor it was."

"Who was it?" asked Vere.

Portia eyed her, as if trying to assess whether she would get the joke when told it. "Caligula," she said, and it took Vere only a moment to recognize the name of the megalomaniac lunatic who had murdered half of Rome, declared himself a god and made his horse a consul.

Suddenly the two women were shrieking with laughter.

"I've never told that to anyone before," Portia said at last, with belated caution, "and to my knowledge, no one has ever got the joke."

"It's not the sort of thing that leaps to the eye," Vere said. In their present mood this seemed much funnier than it was, and they laughed again.

"I wonder how the horse died," Vere said, when they had calmed down at last. The laughter seemed to bring them closer together.

"Caligula was assassinated, to everybody's relief," said Portia, wiping her eyes, and still shaken by gusts of laughter, "but I think history does not record what happened to the horse. Why do you ask?"

"I was thinking about the *Incitatus* disaster. Were you aboard when it went down?"

"No, I'd split up with Bill then. I wanted to get back into advertising."

"How did you hear about it?" She wondered if the question was too obvious.

"What? *Incitatus* going down? Oh, I don't know—it was on the news, wasn't it, when he was found?"

"And that's when you went back to him?"

Portia nodded, making a face that said she regretted it.

"So you changed your mind? You never went back to work?"

Portia shrugged. "The recession changed my mind. Advertising was a big casualty. My old firm was cutting its staff by nearly half, and lots of good firms were folding." There was a silence then, as if she were watching the past on a screen. "Bill had taken his account away from my old agency by then, and I asked him to pull some strings to get me a job with the new agency that had the account. I thought he could do it. In the eighties, Bach Beer was big. They were really expanding, going international. Bill had a lot of clout with us when he was a client. But it hadn't been a success. They'd had to pull out of the international market completely, except for the northeastern U.S. Bach sold well down there.''

She sat forward and refilled her glass again. ''Anyway, Bach Beer was no longer such a big, important account. Bill couldn't have got me a job even if he'd been willing to try, which he wasn't. When he said I should come back to him, I did.''

She yawned. ''What's your story?'' she asked Vere, lying back again and pulling the pillows comfortably up around her head.

''What do you mean?''

''Well, you haven't always been on boats. Any fool can see that you had a career once. What did you work in?''

Vere smiled. ''Design.''

''Really! Did you work in an agency, too?''

''No, I had my own company. We went belly up last year.''

Portia shook her head sympathetically. ''Maybe, when this damned recession is over—if it's ever over—you and I will get together and run our own advertising agency.''

''Maybe,'' said Vere. Then, as if at a sudden thought, ''Did you know the stewardess who died when *Incitatus* sank?''

''No, I never met her. Bill started up with her after we split, I think.''

''Was he having an . . . were they lovers?''

Portia shrugged. ''Oh, yeah. Almost certainly. She was a blonde, wasn't she? That would be why he hired her. An easy replacement for me. Why?''

"Apparently she looked a lot like me. One or two people have mistaken me for her, down here. It's kind of made me curious about her, you know?"

"Really? I didn't know that."

"Yeah, even Bill thought I was her for a minute."

Portia frowned. "Really? He never told me." She waved an arm in well-rehearsed discontent. "Well, but he wouldn't. He doesn't tell me anything."

They sat in silence for a while, the companionable silence of women contemplating the iniquities and inadequacies of men.

"Is this boat a lot like *Incitatus?*" Vere asked gently then.

Portia made a face. "It's about the same size, I guess. I liked *Incitatus* better. It was less ornate. But that's George. George wants to sell, and he thinks he'll have a better chance with the Arabs if there's a lot of gold plating and thick carpeting." She drank. "He may be right, but no takers yet."

"Do you know the owner?" Vere asked in surprise.

"Oh, yeah. He's a good friend—well, a business associate—of Bill's. That's why Bill's got the charter of *Phoenix* and why he stands to make money if he can sell it."

"Why would George design and build a ship just to sell it?"

Portia shrugged. "Money. He gets it done on the cheap in Honduras, and sells it for what it would cost to fit in the States. Anyway, he didn't build it—he just bought an old yacht and refitted it. That's a helluva lot easier."

"I thought it was brand new," Vere marveled innocently.

"No, that's what he wants everybody to think. God knows where he got it from. George is always running some scam. He and Bill are in something together right now. That's why I'm left here, entertaining all these people with more money than brains. As long as he doesn't tell me what it is, I don't care. When Bill comes crashing down, I want to be on the sidelines watching, not smashed up with him."

* * *

They met up with *Brigadoon* again in Bequia. The harbour was crowded with boats of every kind now that the Easter break was approaching. *Phoenix* anchored at a distance from the centre, barely within the confines of the bay, behind a green catamaran and a smaller motor yacht. *Brigadoon* was further in.

It wasn't easy to find a way to talk to Ron and Jill, but at last they arranged to meet her ashore for half an hour that afternoon. Vere took the photograph of *Incitatus* and met them at a bar far around the bay, with outdoor tables. They chose a table out by the water, where no one would be passing.

They hadn't much time, and she came straight to the point. Laying down the photo, she said, "I don't believe *Incitatus* sank at all. I think I'm sailing on her."

That got their attention. Ron, taking a sip of his drink, choked and coughed liquid over his bare knees. Jill's mouth opened slowly and remained that way as she stared at Vere. "What!" she breathed. "Is it possible?" She turned to Ron. "Do you think it's possible?"

Vere lifted the photo. "There's a picture of *Incitatus*, and there—" she pointed out beyond them, where it lay at anchor "—is *Phoenix*. Are there any differences that are more than superficial?"

Ron picked up the photo and frowned down at it, then out towards *Phoenix*, while Jill leaned over his arm. After a moment he dropped the photo and shook his head. "Not easy to say for sure. The deck supports are different, and the bow, and the flying bridge, but those are cosmetic changes, as you say. The aft deck is closed in, but that's nothing. And she's been repainted, of course." He paused, and looked out into the bay again.

"And you think I'm right," said Vere, excited.

Jill picked up the photo and looked at it again.

"The thing is to get proof," said Vere at last. "I'm right there aboard her. There must be something, some evidence somewhere, that will prove which ship it really is. So how can I do that?"

"Most ships the size of *Phoenix*," Ron explained, "will have a yard number assigned by the builders themselves, for the purposes of parts supply. Or at least that's true of Baker and Wild, the yard in Portsmouth that built *Incitatus*. We had a Baker and Wild before we got *Brigadoon*. They keep records of any ship they build, and those records include parts numbers. Do you follow? One yacht might have a pump that's flanged at the side and another a very similar part that's flanged on top, because of space restrictions. When I order a part from the builders, I want to know they're going to send me the right one. So I count on them knowing what part they installed in the first place. Got that?"

"Got it," said Vere.

"That's the number that was incorrect in the captain's papers and on the engine-room bulkhead. If what you suspect is true, it means those numbers were changed on the ship to prevent any casual discovery of the fraud. But until and unless they change the engine, the original yard number still has to be used to order parts."

She breathed but said nothing.

"Right. Now, in addition to that, there's what's called the Official Number. That's a number that's assigned to a ship by, in this case, since it's an English yard, the British Register of Ships. It's called the Carving Note, because in the old days of wooden ships the number had to be carved into the main transverse beam of the ship."

He paused to let that sink in. "The Official Number is used for identification purposes, and legally it's never changed under any circumstances, even though the name of the ship might be."

"All right," said Vere, nodding.

"The law still requires that the Official Number and the yacht's tonnage be permanently fastened onto or etched into a main transverse beam. It's supposed to be readily accessible.

"Now, if your theory is right, we know that they changed the yard number when they refitted *Incitatus*. The question is, what did they do about the Official Number?"

"What could they do?" asked Jill.

Ron crossed his arms and stared down at the table for a moment. "They could have simply obliterated it, but if they're now trying to sell *Phoenix*, they'll need a number of some kind, so they should have put a new number onto the beam. Or they could have left *Incitatus*'s Official Number where it is, and be counting on using a shady surveyor when the time comes to transfer ownership."

"Which would be better?"

Ron was absently tapping the table leg with his foot as he thought. "In fact, he's going to need to buy off a surveyor whichever course he chooses—whether he's using a false Official Number or *Incitatus*'s real one. If it were me, whichever course I chose, I'd do one thing: I'd make sure the number wasn't as readily accessible as the law requires it to be, and I'd rely on special pleading if I were caught, saying the interior design just worked out that way."

"What does that mean?" asked Vere, who'd suddenly got lost.

"It means the Official Number should appear on a main transverse beam in an area of the ship where it's uncovered. Like the machinery space or the generator room. I'd get the ship designed so that that part of the beam was above one of the staterooms or a corridor and therefore had to be hidden by an internal ceiling."

"So first you think I should look . . ." Vere breathed.

"No!" Jill protested. "Ron, it's too dangerous. Why don't we just call the police?"

"What can we tell them?" Vere demanded. "Harry Bridges fainted when he saw me. Bill Harwood is suspicious of me. *Phoenix* is the same length as *Incitatus*."

"And there's a problem with *Phoenix*'s yard number," Jill said firmly. "That should get them interested."

"Somebody muffed the investigation the first time round. What if that was the result of bribery?" Vere said. "We've got to have something ironclad or he's going to get away with it forever!" Now that she was so close, she felt almost panicked at the thought of Bill Harwood's escaping again.

Ron said, "Jill's right. You certainly can't take such a risk. The Carving Note might be anywhere, and *Incitatus* may well have more than one main transverse beam. If I'm right, you'd have to demolish the place to find it. It's not something you can do silently, and you wouldn't be able to put the place back together. They'd know it was an inside job."

"Unless it wasn't," said Vere.

Bequia was a favourite port with everyone. So when the guests announced their intention of eating ashore and attending the jump-up at the Frangipani with the captain and the chef that night, it was taken for granted that the crew would go ashore themselves for the evening. It meant everybody except the man whose turn it was at watch duty was free until at least midnight.

Mark, a handsome if rather unintelligent deckhand, drew the short straw, and his face fell like a child's. He was a good dancer and a good drinker, and he liked to show off, with a childish pleasure that offended no one. Jump-up was just his style.

"I'll stay aboard with you," Debbie offered. Lately, Vere had been sharing her cabin with Jonathan, the engineer's assistant, so that Debbie and Mark could share. There was no secret about it. The yachting community was full of quick, easy affairs.

"Right," said Hugo. "So that's one trip for the guests and one for the crew. Jonathan, you come in with me and the guests and you can bring the tender back for the crew. We'll each take a phone and liaise later."

It was a chance just too good to miss. It was as if, hot on the heels of her discussion with Ron and Jill, fate were offering her the perfect opportunity. As soon as she could, Vere went to the wheelhouse and asked to use the radio to call *Brigadoon*. "I've got the night off," she told Jill. "Any chance of a meal with you, over?"

There was a pause, and Vere could almost see Jill thinking over what this meant. "Sure," she said. "Want us to pick you up, over?"

"No, I'll get dropped off. See you later, over."

"Roger, *Brigadoon* out."

Vere hung up the mike, then leaned out the wheelhouse door to call to Jonathan, who was on the forward deck, "Will you drop me off at *Brigadoon* and pick me up again when you're on your way back?"

"No problem," said Jonathan.

So it was very clear to all where Vere would be spending the evening.

"Tell me what I've got to do," said Vere.

"You want the centre of the ship, say from here—" Ron had made a rough outline of a hull and was marking it with pencil "—to about here. Your main transverse beams will be in that part. The best place to start is probably in the machinery space and the engine room, places where the Carving Note ought to be and you can look for it without touching anything. Also you'll be able to establish the line of the transverse beams. If you don't find any evidence of a number or damage to the beam, then move out into the adjacent areas along the line of the beams. What's the ceiling like on the lower deck?"

"White leather panels."

"They should be easy enough to pull down."

"And exactly what am I looking for?"

"It might take several different forms. There'll be a six-figure number, and a number marking the tonnage. These could be etched on a metal plate that's welded and screwed onto the beam, or they could be bead-welded into the girder itself. The number you want is the six-figure number. Alternatively, there may be a damaged place on the girder where it's been carved off. If you see something like that, give up. There'll be only one reason for a mark like that, and even if they've put a fraudulent number someplace else, it'll be absolutely useless as proof that this is *Incitatus*."

"For God's sake, don't forget the time!" Jill warned. "If you can't find it, get out, don't keep on till you're caught."

"Right," said Vere. That was when her heart started to pound....

"Me," Cass agreed. "Surprised?"

"What are you doing here?"

"Watching you get yourself into a heap of danger for no known reason. What did you think you were doing over there?" He sounded angry, and his hands squeezed her shoulders as if he would have liked to shake her. Light from the searchlight in the dinghy flashed over his features again and cast a huge shadow on the bulkhead behind.

"None of your business," she said hardly, trying to disguise from herself the staggering knowledge that finding Cass here was a tremendous relief. Rationally, she might distrust him. Intuitively, after the first moment of shock, she had relaxed with the inner certainty that she was safe.

"You've made it my business," he said. And then he pulled her into his arms and kissed her with a rough and hungry impatience that was fired by the fear he had felt, seeing her so close to danger.

When he lifted his lips, she was conquered. Now she knew. The terrible stress and its aftermath had told her what she ought to have known from the beginning: whatever he was doing here, whatever his motives, she could trust Cass with her safety, with her life. Under his caress she heaved a sigh of homecoming.

"Right," he said, a little unsteadily. "First things first." He looked over to the porthole, where the searchlight was still flashing over the water under the cat and intermittently into the cabin. "Stay below." The tone of his voice made her shiver. She might trust Cass, but her danger was by no means over.

He left her, and a minute later she heard him on deck calling out to the men in the dinghy. What was the problem? What were they looking for?

A thief, a vandal had been aboard the yacht next door. Had he seen anything? Nothing? the porthole below had been open when they first passed, and then closed. Could someone have come aboard without his knowing?

"I closed that," said Cass. "Your engine woke me and I closed it to shut down the sound. Certainly no one came in. Did you get a look at him?"

None at all. Small footprints, lightweight; probably a kid. They thanked him and went away.

Cass came below and turned on a light. Vere was sitting on the bed in her one-piece suit, shivering a little. "They're unconvinced," he said. "We'll have to be careful getting you off." He walked to a tiny door at the end of the bed and opened it to take out a navy seaman's jersey. He shook it out and bunched it up to the neck opening. "Lift your arms," he said, and when she did so, he pulled it over her head.

Feeling oddly comforted by this enforced childish dependency, Vere slipped her arms into the sleeves and stood up, pulling the jersey down. It came well over her hips and her shivers subsided.

"Jill and Ron will have seen the fuss and will be worrying. Can we call them?"

Cass opened the door and led the way to the saloon which sat between the two hulls. At the nav table, he lifted the radio mike. *"Brigadoon, Brigadoon, Brigadoon—Vagabond, Vagabond."*

The response was immediate. *"Vagabond, this is Brigadoon, over."*

"Go seventy-three, over."

"Roger, seventy-three."

Cass punched up the number. *"Brigadoon, this is Vagabond, do you read?"*

"I read you, Vagabond." Ron's voice didn't sound nervous, but Vere knew that he was. "How's it going, Cass, over?"

"Pretty well. I've...ah, got some news for you." She could see that he was racking his brains to find a way to tell them without alerting anyone else who might be listening.

"Ask if I'm with them," she hissed, when he let up the button for a moment.

He raised his eyebrows, but pushed the button again. "Is Vere with you tonight, over?"

There was a bit of a pause, then, "Yes, she is, over."

"Tell her I've got something of hers. I'll drop it off later. She was worried about it. But it's safe and sound with me, over."

"Roger," said Ron cheerfully. It was clear he thought he'd got the message. "Right, we'll look forward to seeing you, over."

"Roger. As soon as possible. *Vagabond* out."

"Brigadoon out."

Cass looked over at Vere. "Right," he said then. "Now let's have the truth between us."

Chapter 16

"What are you doing here?" she demanded as she sat at the table in the saloon. She shivered again. "Where's *Vagabond?*"

"Not far away. I took *Cat's Whiskers* because I didn't know what you might do if you saw *Vagabond* still following you after what happened."

He poured a cup of coffee, sugared it liberally and set it on the table in front of her. After a moment he put out a plate of cookies. Vere drank gratefully. Her nerves had suffered in the past couple of hours more than she would have believed.

"Please, what's going on?" she begged. "Who are you?"

"I'm a lawyer," Cass replied. She opened her mouth in amazement, but before she could interrupt, he went on, "I'm a partner in a Toronto firm, and one of our clients is Seaworthy, the marine-insurance company that is holding the bag for a large part of the *Incitatus* claim. They didn't like the smell of it from the beginning. It's a biggish claim—

$12 million U.S. They've been holding off paying out while they investigated.

"I guess you know there wasn't a very thorough inquest here when it happened, but when there's only one witness, investigation is almost useless. At sea there aren't any chance witnesses, and any kind of crime is nearly impossible to prove. You have to hope for some kind of break, some slip. I had a sabbatical planned, anyway. I said I'd spend some time down here sniffing around to see what I could find."

"Do you mean they think it was done for insurance fraud?" Vere demanded on a long breath.

"Yes. What do you think?"

"We—I thought maybe . . . drugs or something."

"Drugs are no reason to sink a ship."

"No. Of course, you're right." She laughed as this piece of the puzzle fell into place. "Of course! It all makes perfect sense!"

"Does it? Well, Seaworthy certainly thinks so."

"But they said they were satisfied and would pay the claim," Vere protested.

"Yes, they did. Nothing at all was happening down here. It was a last-ditch attempt to see if, once the pressure was off, someone would relax and make a move." He looked at her. "Someone did."

"What?"

"You came on the scene."

She gasped. "Oh, my God! Oh, how strange! Yes, it was when we heard the news of the insurance company giving in that I knew we'd never find out unless we did it ourselves." She bit her lip and opened her eyes at him with new understanding. "And you thought I was Cilla, returned from the dead. You thought I'd been part of the scam and felt it was safe to reappear."

"That's what I thought. What's the truth?"

"The truth is, I'm Cilla's cousin." She saw it sink in, saw by his slow nod that he was accepting it at last. "My mother and aunt were identical twins, and Cilla and I were almost identical. You'd have known us apart if you ever saw us together, but for some reason it was nearly impossible for people to tell who it was when they saw only one of us." She smiled in misty memory. "We used to pull some pretty good scams of our own when we were kids."

"So you came here..." He broke off questioningly.

"Neither my aunt nor I was ever satisfied about what they said about how Cilla had died. That was the first thing. Cilla wasn't afraid of fire, she just wasn't, and she was the last person to panic in an emergency. The second thing was, my dreams." She told him briefly about them. "That was what really did it in the end. I just couldn't rest with Cilla saying things weren't right. So I decided to do just what you did— come down here and sniff around. I had the advantage of looking like Cilla. I thought it might get people talking. I was right."

"What made you take a job aboard *Phoenix?* How did you know Bill Harwood would come aboard?" Cass asked.

She looked at him, wondering how he would react. "I didn't. That was just intuition," she said. "The first time I saw *Phoenix* I just thought I should get on board if possible." She wondered now how much had been intuition, how much Cilla, and how much an unconscious recognition of the yacht by her designer's eye.

"What were you doing tonight? I saw you go aboard, and a flashlight playing around."

"Did you know it was me?"

He grinned. "I didn't know it, but I had a sinking feeling. What were you looking for?"

"I was looking for the carving note. Someone told me it might be on the central girder."

He frowned at her in sudden curiosity. "The carving note?"

"What does your insurance company think happened to *Incitatus?*" she asked.

"There aren't many choices. Arson or scuttling seemed most likely."

"You're sure it happened, though?"

He looked at her steadily. "Sure what happened?"

"You think *Incitatus* is on the bottom?"

He went very, very quiet. "What do you know, Vere?"

"You tell me why that scares you first."

There was a long pause. Cass pushed up his shirtsleeves and watched her. "Someone in the builder's yard who would like a share of any reward money reported a few weeks ago that a part may have been ordered using *Incitatus*'s yard number. Unfortunately there's no trace of it beyond that. No record was kept of where it was sent, and he stumbled on the business by accident. We haven't been sure whether to put any weight on it or not."

"Well, you should," she said.

He looked at her. "You know that, do you?"

"Especially if the part involved was an oil-pressure sensor."

He didn't move an eyelash, watching her. "What are you telling me, damn it?"

She leaned back and pulled the curtain away from the tiny windows behind her. "If you want to know what happened to *Incitatus,*" she said, with the pleasurable thrill that comes from giving exciting news, "look out there. She's been refitted and renamed. She's called *Phoenix* now."

The sudden roar of a dinghy motor and distant shouting interrupted their conversation. When they looked out, there were lights on all over the deck of *Phoenix.*

Vere gasped. She had forgotten all about the aftershock of her break-and-enter. "What if they tried to pick me up from *Brigadoon* before coming back?" she said. "I've got to get back there!"

Cass grabbed her arm as she moved for the sleeping cabin. "Where do you think you're going?"

"I'm supposed to be aboard *Brigadoon* tonight. I'll have to swim back."

"The hell you will. I'll take you in the dinghy."

"You can't! They'll see me!"

"They'll see a man and a woman heading ashore at a not unreasonable hour. If they catch sight of you in the water, what chance will you have?"

She hesitated. It made her nervous to think of getting into the dinghy in full view of the yacht.

"And with all that activity going on, you could be run over and cut to pieces if they don't see you. I'll find you some jeans to put on."

They got into the dinghy quietly but not furtively, and Cass cast off and pretended to fiddle with the gas tank and motor for a few minutes, while they floated on the swell and were carried near another moored boat. Then he started the engine and they ran quickly to *Brigadoon*.

Jill was on deck with the binoculars, anxiously watching the activity around *Phoenix*. "What on earth happened?" she demanded. "I've never had a worse two hours in my life!"

"Has anybody come to pick Vere up?" Cass asked.

"No." They both heaved a sigh of relief. "Ron is out there looking for you, just in case. We weren't sure what your message meant." She picked up a radio and called. "Come back," she said briefly. "She's here."

"I'd better hurry, in case they come for me," said Vere.

Cass didn't want her to go back aboard *Phoenix*. He thought it was dangerous and unnecessary.

"Can your friends get a search warrant and look for the carving note?" Vere asked.

Cass shrugged. "I don't know till I try."

"Well, if they can't, you're stuck, aren't you?"

"I'd rather lose the twelve million dollars than let you put yourself at greater risk. I think you've done enough."

"For you it's twelve million dollars," Vere pointed out. "For me, it's the murder of my cousin. Unless we get evidence that *Phoenix* is really *Incitatus,* he's going to go free, isn't he?"

Cass looked at her, his eyes grave. "If he killed your cousin, and possibly three others, do you think he'll have any hesitation about killing you, if he thinks it necessary to silence you?"

"There's no reason for him to think I need to be silenced. Anyway, he may not come aboard again for who knows how long."

They were all opposed to her going back aboard, but she overrode them. "I am not going to dream of Cilla for the rest of my life, knowing there was something she wanted me to do and I chickened out!" Vere said at last, and there was no way they could stop her.

The tender to *Phoenix* pulled alongside just after eleven. "I'm going in to pick up the crew now," Mark called up to them. "I'll stop for you in about five minutes. There's been a break-in on the yacht. Nothing taken." He pressed the accelerator knob forward and roared off towards the Frangipani.

Ron and Jill said good-night and left them alone on the aft deck. Cass stood up and drew Vere to her feet, then walked with her to the rail. "Don't go back," he whispered. "Trust me to find a way."

"Cass—" she began protestingly, but was silenced as he wrapped his strong arms around her and bent to her mouth with a kiss full of longing.

"I've missed you," he whispered urgently in her ear. She pressed against him, wanting him, and felt his body respond to the touch of hers. His arm around her waist grew tighter.

"Come with me now. We'll solve this thing together."

She said, "They'll be suspicious of me if I don't go back now. They'll know I was involved. This way, there's nothing to make him suspicious. If they take fingerprints, of course mine will be all over the boat anyway. I'm sure no one got enough of a look at me even to know I was a woman."

"It's dangerous. I love you. Listen to me."

She drew back. "Do you?"

"You know I do."

"No. I thought that was just faking, to get close to me."

"I have never lied to you about loving you."

"But you lied to me about loving Cilla, and you thought I was Cilla."

He didn't answer that, and immediately there was the sound of the tender returning. Cass held her and kissed her, and then let her go. "Remember, when you need me, call for *Vagabond*," he said softly, "and go immediately to seventy-three. If you can't get to the radio, come out on deck and wave."

She nodded wordlessly, because she couldn't trust herself to speak. She pulled out of his embrace and ran lightly down the ladder to the swimming platform just as the tender pulled alongside.

"Was that Cass?" asked Alice.

"Yes."

"Aha! No need to ask if you've had a good time! Where'd he spring from? I haven't seen *Vagabond* around for ages."

Her heart started beating. "I think he's been staying on a friend's boat. What happened tonight?"

"Somebody broke in! Mark thinks he's really going to catch it—he wasn't watching the monitors. But luckily Greg was aboard, so they didn't get anything."

So it was Greg who had come up from below. Vere wondered why he had come back aboard. They all gabbled excitedly until the tender pulled up behind *Phoenix*, and then everybody rushed aboard. Hugo and Gordon and the deckhands were trying to get the ceiling panels into place.

"What were they after?" somebody asked. "What was up there?"

"Maybe they weren't after anything. Maybe they were just vandals."

"Golly, it was lucky they were heard so soon."

"Did anybody see them?"

"Nobody saw anybody clearly," said Greg, in the kind of voice used to command, and they all fell silent and looked at him. "But there was only one person involved, and we think it was probably a woman."

Vere whirled to face him in surprise. "Really?" she said. She realized her mistake immediately, but had to go on. "Why?"

"Whoever came aboard was wearing those flippers," Greg said, and there was a relentless tone in his voice that simply terrified her. How could she have forgotten? "Too small for most men. It might have been a kid, but then how did a kid reach the ceiling panels?"

Suddenly she felt Cass was right. She shouldn't have come back. How could she be certain Greg hadn't seen her? Arrogance in criminals was usually their downfall, wasn't it? She should have thought longer.

Later, when she went to her cabin, she discovered that her things had been searched. Had Greg been searching her cabin when the noise she made interrupted him, or had he searched it since, believing her to be the intruder?

Vere slept fitfully, then not at all, watching dawn through her little porthole. At last she got up, slipped on her uniform, and went into the galley. She made coffee in the cafetiere and took a cup up onto the upper deck in time to watch the sunrise. She was still there twenty minutes later when Greg appeared.

"You're up early," they both said simultaneously, and then smiled at their own stupidity.

"I couldn't sleep," Vere said. She yawned. "I never seem to watch the sunrise anymore. I'm getting jaded. When I go back home, I'll think of all the fabulous sunrises I never bothered to get up for, and then I'll feel guilty."

"Sounds a punishing life," said Greg, sitting beside her on the hard plastic of the bench seat. The cushions had all been stowed for the night, and Vere hadn't bothered to get them out yet.

"Shall I get you a coffee?" she asked. She was so used to serving by now it was almost second nature, although he was perfectly capable of getting his own coffee.

Greg shook his head. "I've had a lot of coffee."

After a moment she said, pointing, "There's an ice pick on the speedboat cover. I think it's from the bar, but there's no reason for it to be up here."

Greg got up, strolled over to where the speedboat was tied down and covered with a white tarpaulin, and reached down to pick something up. Tossing it in his hand, he came back to her. "Maybe what was used to dislodge the panels in the ceiling," he said mildly.

"Aren't you going to fingerprint it?" she asked stupidly. Her fingerprints found on the handle would not be incriminating, since she used the ice pick every day, but still her heart was thumping with relief at the sight of his big hand enclosing the red plastic handle.

Greg shook his head. "The chances of the perp's fingerprints being on record are pretty slim. If it wasn't a kid it was someone from another yacht, or an inside job."

Her eyes slithered uneasily away from his in an involuntary movement that shocked her. She wondered if he read guilt in the action. She certainly *felt* guilty. "How do you know?"

"Somebody was looking for something, and it wasn't video recorders, was it?"

"What was it?"

He shrugged.

"What makes it an inside job, then?"

He held up the ice pick. "Somebody who comes to search a place doesn't often count on finding a tool just to hand. So it's someone who knows the yacht a bit."

Almost idly she wondered what his real reasons were. But she only laughed. "I watch too much television, I guess. I was very careful not to touch it." Even now she wasn't sure why. She had come up with every intention of finding the pick and restoring it to the bar. But when she saw it lying there, she had simply been unable to. She just kept thinking that if by some chance it was discovered that she had removed evidence, she would be incriminated.

"I know you were," Greg said, so matter-of-factly that she nearly missed it.

"Yes, I . . . what do you mean?"

He grinned the grin that didn't reach his eyes. "I was sitting over there, watching you." His nod indicated the shadowed niche behind the lifeboat.

She couldn't contain a gasp. "Why?"

He shook his head and sat beside her again. "We found the ice pick there last night. If it was an inside job, it was possible someone might try to retrieve it. Nobody came up except you, and you didn't touch it. Of course, you could just be very, very smart."

A breeze blew across them suddenly, and she shivered violently at her near escape. What angel had stopped her picking up the ice pick? She gazed at him.

"See, there's every reason for your prints to be on this thing, isn't there?"

She shrugged, trying to appear unruffled. "I guess so, if by that you mean I use it a lot."

Greg leaned back and examined his nails. "Yeah, every reason. I watched you almost pick it up three times, and then tell yourself that. You left it. That was very smart. I

admire that kind of cool." He nodded, leaned back and put
one foot up on the bench beside him.

She had to act as if she didn't know what he was talking
about. She looked at him absently, and then at the coffee
between her hands as though his statement had no impact.

"I'm glad you came up," she said. She looked up at him,
letting her fear show. "Greg, was—did the intruder..." she
faded out and dropped her gaze.

"What is it?"

"I'm pretty sure somebody searched my cabin last night,"
she said. "They went through my passport and papers, and
all my clothes. Nobody else has mentioned that their stuff
was searched. What were they looking for, Greg, and why
did they think I might have it?"

She said nothing to Cass about any of this, knowing he
would be adamant she should leave *Phoenix*. But again,
when nothing sinister happened after that conversation with
Greg, she grew confident again.

The green cat followed them up to Saint Lucia, where they
were to drop all their guests except Portia. When they were
nearly there, Hugo got a phone call from Bill Harwood. He
would be arriving with George Pagliatis, *Phoenix*'s owner.
Phoenix was to wait in Saint Lucia until they came.

Hugo passed this information on to the crew. "Right,"
he said, "this is the first time we've had George aboard, so
let's look lively, all right? I don't want him thinking I've
hired the Goon Squad." Hugo was English and often made
comments incomprehensible to them.

"What the heck is the Goon Squad?" Debbie asked.

"A bunch of goons," said Hugo, with a sigh. He looked
around for an eye with whom to share the joke, but there
was no response. "Never mind."

They went into Marigot Bay to wait for the owner's arrival. It was a spectacularly beautiful little bay, if a little
overcrowded with ships—a well-protected anchorage sur-

rounded by green hills, with a couple of boutiques that Vere
and the other female crew liked very much. And although
Portia's taste and budget ran more to the exclusive boutiques in places like Mustique, even she was looking forward to visiting the batik shop on the hill.

Vere hadn't seen Cass since the night aboard *Cat's
Whiskers*. She missed him, and she was nervous and wanted
his advice, but she wouldn't tell him yet what had happened. Now, with the owner coming on board, she had a
plan, and its execution required that she be aboard.

Vagabond arrived in Marigot Bay the morning after
Phoenix and *Cat's Whiskers*. "There's your boyfriend," Liz
said to Vere, as they watched the burgundy sailboat ma-
noeuvre and cast anchor not far away. It was Cass on deck,
she saw. She wondered when he had switched boats. There
was a light rain falling. He was wearing swim trunks, and his
hair and skin were getting wet as he worked. "Boy, is he
sexy," said Liz appreciatively as they watched.

Cass waved then, and suddenly Vere was desperate to see
him, to be with him. She had missed him more than she let
herself know.

Since the only guest aboard *Phoenix* now was Portia, Vere
got the night off, and Cass picked her up for dinner aboard
Vagabond. The first thing he did when they had climbed
down the companionway was envelop her in a passionate,
trembling embrace and kiss her with a ferocious need that
set her alight.

"I've missed you!" he whispered urgently, pulling open
the collar of her shirt and bending to kiss the pulse at her
throat. "I've never been so scared in my life as I've been
these past few days!"

Vere didn't answer. Cass's passion, as always, communi-
cated directly with her body. If she were blind and deaf she
would know him in a dark room. She had never in her life
felt sexually starved before, but she felt it now. Where had

he been? her body demanded, climbing inside his arms and gluing herself against him.

Whatever else he had been going to say was simply stopped in his throat by the clamour of her response. He drew back once to look down at her face, then kissed her again. She leaned back and felt herself supported by the companionway ladder. Her hands ran over his back, his hips, into his hair, then down again to pull up his shirt and slide her arms into the enclosed body heat against his back, his chest.

The springing hair on his chest scorched her fingertips with little puffing flames; the skin on his back, so smooth, so firm, would have been too hot to touch, except that she was already burning. Distantly she remembered the old fairy tale that said God had made humankind of earth, and another species of fire. She had been mistaken in thinking herself earth. She was one of the race of fire creatures, and her flames licked over his skin, drawing him into her core heat, where the temperature must consume them.

Somehow his shirt was off, his skin directly accessible, and she tore her mouth from his and laid a line of flame down the curve of his throat, across his shoulder, setting a little forest fire again in the mat of hair on his upper chest. Her mouth found a small, hard bud, and her tongue explored it, while above her Cass gasped, and his hands bruised her.

His own mouth was against the back of her neck as he swept the fall of her hair to one side; but as her mouth moved down his chest and he could no longer reach her, he lifted her hand and pressed a kiss into the very centre of the palm. The kiss spiraled out, a cooling, liquid shiver that ran along her arm toward the fire, and exploded when it met the central flame, so that she, too, moaned.

He was wearing shorts. Her hands ran over the fabric with a curious lack of comprehension, tugging ineptly at it, as though it should disappear because she willed it. Through the fabric she found the hard flesh that she wanted, and she pressed it greedily, so that his throat arched, his head went back, and he grunted in surprise and desire.

Her hands blindly found the buttons that would release his flesh to her, and then it was there, hot and urgent in her hands, rising from his body toward her, everything she wanted. For a moment, as she knelt, her long hair swirled and caught like a flag on a stanchion, but she swept it aside, and then the universe was only his flesh and her mouth.

He grasped the two sides of the companionway above her head and said something, but now she understood nothing but the language of the body. This was his centre, she had found it, and nothing else meant anything. Her mouth felt swollen, engorged, stretched to its limits and more; and the rhythmic pulsing she set up came from some music within that was both her and not her.

He was helpless, and that was as it should be, for the power of the feminine sweeps all before it. When she grunted in satisfaction with her task, he moaned in a response he could not control. Her hands gripped the bones of his lean, masculine hips and led him into the dance that he was in a fever pitch to join, and he cried his pleasure openly to the stars above his head while the dance had its way with them.

He lost the rhythm then, and found another, broken and wild, unpredictable, indescribably passionate—long, and short, and long again. He sobbed once, twice, and called her name; and she tasted the sea.

Chapter 17

They lay lazily on the cushions of the aft deck, eating and watching the stars. The faint sound of music floated to them over the water from one of the hotels, and the breeze was cool and soft. They had eaten, and made love again, and now were eating again.

"It's significant," Cass was telling her, "that except for your cousin, Harwood had apparently let his regular crew go and hired a bunch of ruffians in Venezuela to staff the yacht. He's on record as saying that the crew preferred to be left in the Caribbean, since with winter coming on they'd be more likely to pick up new jobs there than in the Med. So he sailed down to La Guaira and picked up what crew he could for a one-way trip, and since all their papers went down with the ship, he couldn't give anything except their first names. But we've heard since from some of the crew that they weren't given the choice. They were fired."

"So that means he had the crew he wanted," she said, popping another delicious little snack into her mouth. Cass had said they were just deep-fried breaded courgette balls, and his secret was olive oil. They tasted surprisingly succulent. She munched thoughtfully.

"And the crew he wanted was men who probably didn't have passports, wanted to get out of South America and were willing to do anything." He touched her gently. "People whom no one was likely to miss."

Vere shivered. "You're saying he planned to kill them all from the beginning. He went to sea knowing they were going to die."

"Almost certainly."

"But then, why Cilla? She wasn't someone no one would miss! It doesn't make sense . . . unless—do you think she might have found something out? That he took her along to make sure she never told what she knew?"

"Maybe he didn't plan to kill her at all." He spoke tentatively, as though afraid of hurting her. "You've told me you think Cilla and Harwood were lovers. The most likely explanation seems to me that she was party to the fraud. And something went wrong."

That silenced her for a moment, not because it was impossible, but because she had to stop to try and put herself in Cilla's place. Cilla was wild, unpredictable, and had entirely her own system of morals. She had certainly never seen any morality in money.

Vere said slowly, "I think Cilla assumed that anyone who had money—whether it was rich men or multinational corporations—had done something immoral or worse to get it." She shook her head. "I just can't say. But I can tell you one thing—insurance fraud I can maybe imagine her going along with. Just for the hell of it, if nothing else. But no way would she conspire with someone who had murder in mind."

She was trembling a little with the ugliness of it, and he stroked her in silence until she found her peace again and her distance from the distressing image of Cilla and the crew's last moments.

"So what really happened?" she asked. "What do you think?"

Cass lay back, folded his arms under his head, and looked up at the stars. "We know," he said, in a rather distant voice that only meant he was putting things together as he spoke, "that Harwood was in trouble financially, like a lot of other businessmen who'd thought the money would never stop rolling in in the eighties. We know he'd been expanding to try for international markets in a big way, and that the expansion was ill-conceived and was faltering. He pulled back pretty quickly, but not before he'd taken bigger losses than he could afford.

"He also had a sizable mortgage on *Incitatus*, and he wasn't quite in that league in the first place, though maybe he thought that he'd get big enough to match it. When the recession hit, he put the yacht on the market. But he couldn't sell it.

"So then he planned an insurance scam. He faked the buyer in Majorca—we've never been able to find any evidence of it—and that gave him an excuse to fire his crew and pick up the kind of men he did. What we didn't realize until your meeting with him was that Harry Bridges was in on it. Harwood pretended to fire Bridges along with the rest, but Bridges in fact was aboard when *Incitatus* sailed."

"Ahh," said Vere. "Of course."

"They got a few hundred miles out in the Atlantic, and Harwood got into the dinghy and pushed off." He paused and reached an arm around her shoulder comfortingly. "I guess after somehow disposing of the crew, except for Bridges and perhaps another man. We've got someone trying to track him down. Then Bridges faked a distress call, saying there was a fire aboard, and an hour later another, saying there had been an explosion and they were having to abandon ship. Then he sailed it down to Honduras or someplace where they don't ask too many questions. Probably at some point they threw the crew's belongings overboard, and that's how Cilla's case got washed up on Glass Beach.

"Harwood was picked up in the dinghy twelve hours later—he probably dumped his EPIRB and then didn't fire any flares until he thought it was safe to be found—and told his story about dead batteries and having had to bury his crew at sea."

"And said Cilla had panicked."

"Yes. *Incitatus* was in Honduras getting a refit and a new name, while Harwood waited for the insurance money to be paid. But it didn't get paid, and he must have been short of cash—after all, the refit must have cost a couple of million. Whether he only brought *Phoenix* into circulation because Seaworthy had announced they were satisfied and he thought it was safe, or whether he was so desperate for cash that he had to run the risk and try to sell it, doesn't really matter."

"So he was going to get double his money," Vere said. "He'd get the insurance money and the purchase price as well."

"Covering his risk if the company didn't pay out on the insurance. We should have suspected that, but what the company believed, after an investigation of Harwood's financial status, was that like a lot of others, he had simply scuttled the yacht to collect the premium because it wouldn't sell." He was quiet for a moment, thinking. "I had always been of the opinion that Cilla wasn't dead, but no one was taking that seriously, and I had to admit myself that my theory had no logical base. It was only when you turned up—apparently Cilla, and safe and healthy—that they seriously began to examine other possibilities. From the first, Seaworthy had assumed he'd sent everyone to the bottom with the yacht to make his story watertight. But if he hadn't killed Cilla, why pretend she had died?"

Vere's eyes were wet, and he put his thumb on her cheek and stroked a tear carefully away. "I guess you loved her very much," he said.

"We were really close," she said. "And since I've been on that yacht I've felt her presence, and it's reminded me of what we used to have. I miss her so much!"

"You never thought, when you came down here to investigate, that she was alive?" he asked.

"No, never. You see, she—she said goodbye to me. I woke up in the night knowing she was dying. And then, there was never another word from her until the anniversary, and that was in a dream. It wasn't the same at all. It's hard to describe, but the... connection was different."

They were silent again and Vere rolled over to rest on his arm, looking up. "There's the Southern Cross," she said, feeling suddenly close to Cilla, who must have looked up into the Caribbean night sky many times. She said, "Why did you think she was alive?"

Cass heaved a sigh. "I can't tell you that now. One day, I'll tell you why, but don't ask me now."

"Was there any evidence that pointed that way? Can I ask that?"

"There was no evidence. It was just something I believed."

She moved till she was on his chest, and they lay in the comfort of each other's arms for so long that she thought he might have fallen asleep. "Cass?" she whispered softly.

"I'm awake," he said, and breathed as though he had come to a decision. "Look, there's something I'm going to do, and I want you off the yacht before I do it. It isn't safe. If I'm caught, you'll be suspected immediately. How soon can you quit your job without it attracting attention?"

Vere rolled over and looked at him with her eyebrows up. "What are you going to do?"

He laughed a little, and stroked her back. "I'm afraid to tell you. I never know what you'll do."

Since Vere had never been considered unpredictable be
fore, this was charming in its novelty. She was silent for
moment, wondering just how much the past few month
had changed her.

"I have a plan, too," she said. "And it means staying o
board *Phoenix*. Shall I tell you mine and you tell me your
and then we can decide which is better? Or maybe do both.

He shook his head, grinning in resignation. "I can
imagine why your business failed," he observed.

"My partners forced it," she said; and that was all it wa
now. Not a huge and painful betrayal anymore, but just tw
weaklings who'd lacked the courage to carry on. "Neve
mind that—do you want to hear my plan?"

He stroked the hair away from her ear as she lay proppe
on her elbows at an angle to him, and bent up and kissed he
neck. "Go ahead," he said.

"I thought I could find a way to sabotage the engines, s
that Hugo would have to order another part. The—" Sh
broke off because he had caught his breath and now la
there laughing gently. She reached for the remains of a drink
in which the ice had long ago melted. "What do yo
think?"

"I think I'll be a fool if I ever imagine I can outwit you,"
he said. He took the last cold savoury from the plate and la
back, chewing. "Right. Well, we have the same idea, Vere
so we only get one choice. My idea is to scuba over to
Phoenix one night and shove something up the seawater in
take. That should ruin something or other in the strainer or
the impeller with a little luck."

Vere laughed in surprised delight. "Really? We had the
same idea?"

"Not quite," said Cass. His hand closed on her shoul
der. "My idea is that you should be long gone before I do
it."

"But what good would that do? I have to be aboard for
it to work."

"Why do you have to be aboard?"

"But what's the point otherwise? The whole point is that George is going to be on board, isn't it?"

"Is it? What are you talking about?"

"Well, what is the point of your sabotaging the yacht, then?"

"That a part will have to be ordered, and that we can have a tail on it and see who picks it up this time," Cass said reasonably.

"Ohh!" she breathed. "Oh, yes! But look—don't you see there's another reason for doing the same thing? George is the owner—or at least, they're pretending he's the owner. He's the man Hugo had to phone in order to get the oil sensor ordered. We've just heard he's coming aboard soon with Harwood. Either he'll bring the right yard number aboard with him, or else he's going to have to call somewhere to get it. With a little luck I can be listening in when he does it. If it's *Incitatus*'s number, we've got them."

His stroking hand was stilled. "Ah. That's ingenious." He thought for a moment. "But don't you think it's too dangerous, especially considering what your chances are of being able to overhear the conversation and get the number?"

"It's only dangerous if you're caught with your arm right in the intake and they realize it's sabotage," she said. "Who's going to connect me with the problem otherwise? And I have faith in you. I've never heard of *Phoenix* having an underwater burglar alarm, so why should you get caught?"

She was very glad she hadn't told him of the search of her things, or how Greg had suspected her, or the flippers she had left behind.

His hand tightened on her again. "I want you out of there, Vere. I haven't worried so much with Harwood absent, but now that he's coming aboard again, you've got to leave. The man has already killed your cousin, as far as we know. He's not going to balk at another killing if he feels threatened. Let me handle it now. If you quit, we can put someone of our own on *Phoenix* in your place."

"If she gets hired. What if they decide not to replace me? They don't have many guests at the moment."

"We'll be tracking the part."

"And that could easily fail. I'm right there, Cass. I'm in an ideal position, and it would be terrible to give up that advantage until we're sure of not needing it anymore. Anyway, you're only working for the insurance company, aren't you? For me, this is personal. She was my cousin."

"Vere—"

"You can't stop me. If you try, I'll just do it all on my own," she said.

George Pagliatis and Bill Harwood arrived the next day, a Friday, with Noah in attendance. They told Hugo to prepare for departure Saturday; they wanted to sail to Mayreau, a tiny island in the Southern Grenadines. Hugo passed the message on to the crew, with the information that they would be moving quickly; and Alice and Vere went ashore to stock up on a few last-minute supplies in the small supermarket.

Vere waved to Cass from the deck as they climbed into the tender, and Cass followed them in. She managed, with Alice's goodwill, to get ten minutes alone with him.

He swore when he heard the news. "How fast?" he wondered; but he answered his own question. *Phoenix* could make twelve knots when pushed; in *Vagabond* he could barely go half as fast. He had always kept close to *Phoenix* by the simple means of traveling longer hours, counting on *Phoenix* rarely sailing more than a few hours at a time. If they were in a hurry, it would mean sailing longer hours, and if they did that, they would get well ahead of him. "Right," he said. "*Cat's Whiskers* will set off today. If you get a clue what your first port of call is going to be, try and let me know."

"All right."

He was frowning in thought. "What the hell's in Mayreau, anyway?" Mayreau was a tiny, very poor island with one small village, two bars, several mules and a truck. Vere had been there twice before, and the two big draws were the local hooch served in the rum punch in Dennis's bar, with a kick like one of the mules, and an incredible view from the top of the hill on which the village sat. Half of the island was unpopulated palm forest surrounded by stunningly unspoiled white beaches.

"They're thinking of building a hotel there, and George doesn't have time for a leisurely sail," Vere said. "Or that's what they're saying. Do you think you should try the . . . um . . . tonight?"

"Yes," said Cass. He looked down at her, his hand involuntarily clenching her upper arm. "I'm going to have to discuss this with Barry." Barry was the name of the man on *Cat's Whiskers,* and that was all Vere knew about him. "I may not be able to let you know in advance what we decide."

"That doesn't matter."

He shook his head. "I don't like this. I wish you'd come off the yacht. I don't want you at sea with that man."

"We've had all that," Vere pointed out calmly. "Just do what you have to do. I'll be all right."

"If you discover some reason why we shouldn't make the attempt tonight, call me and say you can't see me tonight, all right? If you can't call, come on deck and wave to me."

His anxiety infected her in spite of herself, and she spent the afternoon full of nerves. It didn't help that when she was summoned to the lower saloon to get drinks, Bill Harwood had been told about the break-in and was standing at one end of the room with Greg staring up at the ceiling tiles.

"Your cabin was searched?" Harwood asked Vere with a look of frowning intensity that bespoke real worry.

She glanced at Greg in hastily suppressed surprise. Hadn't he told Harwood he had been searching her cabin himself? Hadn't it been done under Harwood's orders?

"Yes, that's right. Nothing was taken."

"Anything they might have been interested in?"

His gaze pierced her, and she thought, I wonder what you think I have that somebody might want? "I haven't any very valuable jewellery or anything," she said aloud. Did he think she might be Cilla after all? Or did he guess something like the truth and wonder what evidence she might have gathered against him, that might now have been stolen by an enemy? That thought scared her, because of what it said about his motives for keeping her aboard.

"Any reason you can think of for being singled out like that?" Harwood pursued.

How dangerous would it be to worry him now? She decided to risk it. "I don't think they did more than glance at my toilet case—you know, where I keep my makeup and jewellery. So I don't think they were really after valuables. They looked at my passport and my papers, mostly. Or at least, that's what I noticed. It was easy to see they were out of order."

That was a lie, and she felt Greg watching her. So he knew he hadn't left her papers in disorder. Vere's heart began beating double-time.

"Maybe—" Vere paused as she brought them their drinks. They both looked at her. "Maybe they just didn't know where the thing they were looking for was. Maybe they just had to start at random. What were they looking for?"

Harwood was sufficiently preoccupied to answer. "That's the question," he said, taking a long pull of his whiskey and water. She almost smiled—he was really worried. The thought of what the searcher might have been after scared him.

Of course, if she had any sense, it should scare her, too, she reminded herself. What had Greg been looking for, and why hadn't he told Harwood that he hadn't found it?

At nine-thirty next morning they felt the throb of the engines starting. Vere, who hated the tiny laundry room, was at the ironing board in the galley. She heard Hugo giving the orders for the raising of the anchor. For a few minutes the yacht hummed with the familiar sounds of departure, then suddenly there was the noise of beeping, and then an alarm. She heard Hugo swear, and the engines died. Vere bent her head to hide a triumphant smile and ironed with determined concentration.

Half an hour later the yacht had still not moved, and there had been a lot of running around by Hugo and Gordon and the deckhands. When Gordon came into the wheelhouse to report, Vere was still ironing.

"You were right," Gordon was saying. "A big plastic bag, a real solid mass."

"Right. What's gone?"

"The impeller for sure, maybe a couple of seals. Mark's working on it. Jonathan's cleaning the intake."

"Well, tell him to get a move on."

"Thing is, Hugo—" Gordon scratched his ear uncomfortably.

Hugo just looked at him. "What?"

"We don't seem to have a replacement impeller in the store."

"There's a replacement for every part," Hugo said firmly. "It must have been overlooked. Look again."

"Yeah—thing is, we found the right box, clearly labeled. Here it is." There was a moment's silence, and then Hugo grunted. "That's the way we found it—empty."

Hugo cursed for a few seconds with great colour and inventiveness, so that Vere almost laughed. "Buggeration!" he finished up. "And of course they're in a hurry!"

Gordon made a sympathetic noise. "Well, as of now we have no seawater cooling system."

Vere felt like cheering. So Cass had succeeded! And even more thoroughly than he could have hoped—what a fabulous piece of luck that there was no replacement part on board! She knew from the incident of the oil-pressure sensor that replacement parts were carried on board so that immediate repairs could be made, and the order had only been to replace the spare part. But with no part to make immediate repairs with...could they travel without a seawater cooling system?

On the heels of this came the conviction that it was too good to be luck. Yet how could he have managed... She shook her head. Surely he would not have taken such a risk, coming aboard to rob the stores *and* shoving a plastic bag into the cooling intake!

"Right," said Hugo. He had been tinkering with something, and now he wiped his hands. "Guess I'd better go talk to the bosses. Where are they? On deck? In the saloon?"

Quietly Vere picked up a pile of table linen and went through into the main saloon. The main saloon was at its best in the mornings: the sun slanting through the greenery in the glassed-in aft deck made everything seem fresh, like an early summer forest after rain. Harwood and George Pagliatis were still sitting over the remains of breakfast, arguing mildly over some papers. When Hugo appeared Vere was at the linen drawers, putting in freshly laundered tablecloths and napkins.

She paid no apparent attention as he approached the table, absorbed in her task of laying everything inside without a wrinkle.

"So what the hell does it mean?" Harwood demanded when Hugo had explained the problem.

"We can't move until a replacement part comes," Hugo said.

There was a lot of yelling, but it was certainly not Hugo's fault, and he wasn't taking the blame.

"Have you ordered the part? How long will it take to get here?" Harwood demanded, and Vere felt rather than saw Hugo look in George's direction.

"I haven't ordered the part because of the problem with the yard number of the ship," he said. "I'm here to ask George if he'll get on the phone to Portsmouth. It's already two-thirty in the afternoon there and if we don't hurry they won't get it off tonight."

Harwood swore crudely, which was so much his habit that all the crew were by now used to it. It expressed no great rage, only a kind of exasperation, and Vere sometimes wondered what language he might have recourse to if he were really furious. Hugo, having said his piece, left them in silence.

There was a briefcase on the table between the two men, full of the plans they had been discussing. It was George's briefcase; she was sure the number must be in there. Vere pulled several tablecloths out of the drawer and had started to refold one when Harwood suddenly stood up. "Right," he said, and headed toward the stairs.

With stunning certainty it crashed home to Vere that it was not *George,* but *Harwood* who was going to see to this. Of course George's putative ownership of *Phoenix* was all pretence! George was leaning back in his chair, lighting a cigarette, and of course Harwood also must have the yacht's yard number... and he was going to get it now!

She refolded the tablecloth with more speed than accuracy, shoved everything back into the drawer, and went through to the galley again. Lifting a pile of sheets, she went lightly down the companionway to the linen cupboard in the corridor beside the master stateroom.

She quickly pulled out matching pairs of sheets with pillow slips, preparatory to changing the beds. Then, gathering up one of the piles she had made, she stepped to the door of the master stateroom, tapped lightly, and her heart beating louder than she had ever felt it, entered with the calm certainty of one who expected the room to be empty.

He called out as the door opened. "Oh, sorry!" said Vere, immediately backing out and closing the door again. But not before she had taken in the scene in one glance. He was sitting on the big double bed, with papers in his hand. In the beautifully polished built-in cabinets that ran around two sides of the stateroom from the bed, the lowest drawer in the little chest immediately beside the bed was open. A key ring protruded from its lock.

She bent to set the sheets beside the door, as she would have done with any occupied stateroom; then picked up a second pile of sheets and continued to the next stateroom. She tapped and entered just as Harwood came out of his stateroom behind her, and leaving the door open she stepped across to each of the two single beds and dropped a little pile of clean bedding on it.

When she turned, he was standing in the corridor, gazing at her, the keys jingling in his palm. She forced herself to smile helpfully. "Is there anything you want?" she asked, coming out of the room. He was a big man, and he made no room for her; she was almost touching him as she closed the door. Still he stared at her.

She tried to imagine how she would react to this if she were just what she had told him she was, but he was a frightening man, and close to his cold malevolence seemed a physical thing. It was almost as if, she told herself wildly, he were not really human. She edged away from him in silence and bent to pick up another pile of sheets.

When he walked off without a word, her knees were so weak she had to kneel on the floor to recover. After that, how could she follow him upstairs and try to eavesdrop on his phone conversation?

Yet it must be done. This was the chance Cass had given her, the chance she had insisted on having. Fear must not overcome her now.

She grabbed up a pair of pillow slips that were slightly creased and dashed back up the companionway to the galley. The iron and ironing board were where she had left them—but the door to the wheelhouse was closed. Behind the door she heard Harwood's voice, loud and contemptuous but the words inaudible.

Liz was nowhere to be seen, the crew mess was empty. Everybody was down in the engine room, feeding on the disaster. Vere lifted the ironing board as close as possible to the closed sliding door, then crept the remaining distance and gently, gently pushed at the door.

It moved sideways under her fingers. The latch hadn't caught! Oh, the gods were with her today! Silently, with incredible slowness, she edged the door open till there was a space no wider than a quarter of an inch between the door and the jamb. She bent and pressed her ear to the space.

"BXF359," she heard him say. "Have you got it now? Right. We'll expect to see replacements here tomorrow."

Her heart soaring with relief and a feeling of something like divine intervention, she stepped noiselessly back from the door, snatched up the pillowcases again, and ran lightly down the companionway, repeating the number to herself. On the level below, she returned to the stateroom and began to strip the beds, singing a tuneless song.

She felt Harwood's passing in the corridor outside, but ignored it until she heard his stateroom door close. Then she hugged a pillow and danced around the room. He was in there carefully locking away his dirty secret, but she had it already!

Chapter 18

"Terrific," said Cass, with an admiring smile that warmed her to the core. He shook his head. "You were right. I was wrong. I'll fax it to Toronto tonight."

They were sitting in the cockpit of *Vagabond* late in the afternoon, enjoying a drink and waiting for the clouds overhead to move on. It was warm and close but not unpleasant.

"What will happen then?"

"I'm not sure. The first step will be to match it up at the builder's yard. After we have that as evidence, it'll be a police matter. We'll keep the tail on the part, because he's too slippery for us to chance holding him with only one hand."

"Wasn't it a stroke of luck that the part was missing?"

"Very lucky," said Cass; at which something clicked in her head. She eyed him suspiciously.

"How did you do it? Did you come aboard yourself?"

He smiled lazily. "It was easier to bribe one of the deckhands."

Her mouth fell open, though it shouldn't have surprised her. "What did you tell him?"

"I didn't speak to him, of course—it would have put you at risk. Barry told him he wanted to get a deal clinched for Mayreau before Harwood appeared on the scene. Along with a substantial offer of money, there was the pleasant fact that Barry's own development plans were more environmentally friendly than the Harwood-Pagliatis one."

Vere laughed. "You've really got it all in hand, eh?"

"I think so." He stroked a strand of hair off her forehead and leaned to kiss her lightly. "*Now* will you quit that job?"

"Yes," she said. "What then?"

"Then we sail away for a year and a day," he replied, "and then we go home and get married. How many children do you want?"

She swallowed, gazing at him. "But...you—I mean..." She stopped speaking, because she simply didn't know how to put it.

Cass smiled a slow, tender smile and stroked her cheek. "It's all right," he said. "I'm going too fast. But you'll get used to the idea."

It wasn't the speed that threw her. She said, "I'm so confused. First I thought you were in love with Cilla, and then you admitted you'd only made that up and now . . . do you love me?"

"Very, very much," he assured her, and the look in his eyes told her that it was the truth. "Desperately."

"But—when did you fall in love with me, then?"

Cass looked away for a moment, then into her eyes again. "Don't ask me that now," he pleaded. "Just get used to the idea that I love you, and think about falling in love with me." He lifted her hand and kissed it. "I've got months of sabbatical to go. We'll paint the boat pea-green and lay in some honey." He smiled into her eyes then, but behind the smile was an intensity that shook her. "Will you come?"

"What will we do?" she asked.

"We'll find every beautiful, empty bay that's left between here and Venezuela. We'll make love on sandy beaches under the stars. We'll eat as much lobster as you can eat. If you like, we'll join a convoy of friends and sail to Australia. And I will make you love me."

She smiled from her heart into his eyes. "I don't think you can do that," she said softly.

He dropped his eyes and took a breath. "No?" he asked. Still holding her hand, he drew absent circles on her palm. "You're sure of that?"

"I'm already in love," said Vere. "Very, very deeply."

"Ah" was all the sound he made.

"With you," she said.

"'Oh, lovely Pussy! Oh Pussy, my love, what a beautiful Pussy you are, you are,'" Cass whispered in her ear, stroking the length of her flank and her back with a possessive touch that made her shiver.

She rolled over in sudden enlightenment. "Is *that* what it's from! I wondered what you meant about painting the boat green!"

"Not green. Pea green. Are you going to get off that yacht now?" He bent and kissed her breast.

"Yes. I'll tell Hugo tonight, and see how much notice he needs."

"Don't offer him notice. Just tell him you're leaving. Go back and pack, and I'll pick you up as soon as you're ready."

"We don't want Harwood to be suspicious, do we? If I leave in such a rush and he suspects I know something, he might destroy the evidence."

"He can't destroy the evidence unless he sinks *Phoenix*."

"Well, and what if he did that? It's not impossible. We'd never get him."

"I want you out of that man's reach." He kissed her. "I want to marry you before you change your mind. Where do you want to get married?" he asked, as though what he had said had sidetracked him.

"At home," she said. "I'm the only one they've got now. It would be horrible to get married without Alexa and Robert there. I want Robert to give me away."

"Right. You get off that yacht, and we'll fly up on Saturday and arrange it."

She thought a moment. "Can we wait until we've sorted things out a bit more? I'd like to go home when I can tell them not just what happened to Cilla but that Bill Harwood is going to pay for it. I don't want them waiting in suspense to see if he's going to get away with it."

"At that rate we'll be here two years. By the time the case gets through the courts, with an appeal or two—"

"When we know he's been charged and will stand trial," Vere interrupted. "That's all I mean. If we don't get a conviction, that's different."

Cass grinned. "I'll phone Ben in the morning."

"Who's Ben?"

"My friend Ben Glass is the Crown Prosecutor in Toronto. If he argues the case himself, Harwood is sunk. Assuming we can get him tried in Ontario."

"Can you do that? Isn't that interfering with the course of justice or something?"

"Ben Glass prosecuting William G. Harwood would be the purest form of justice you could find," said Cass.

"No problem," said Hugo. "You'll be going aboard *Vagabond,* will you?"

She couldn't suppress the smile. "Yeah," she said, suddenly shy.

"I'd appreciate it if you'd stay over tomorrow. I've given Debbie and Alice the afternoon off."

She couldn't argue with that, nor did she want to. George Pagliatis had chartered a small seaplane and would be flying down to Mayreau; but Bill Harwood would stay aboard *Phoenix*, and he was restless and irritable and making everyone's life miserable. Debbie and Alice had a right to some time off. Vere had had her share of time off lately while they covered for her.

In the event, Portia went ashore with them, saying there was a batik dress she had ordered that might be ready now that they'd spent an extra two days in port. But Vere suspected she just wanted to get out of Harwood's way. And Gordon and the deckhands, having done as much as they could without the replacement pump, went as well.

So there wasn't much to do. Harwood had her chasing back and forth with drinks for a while, but then he fell asleep in the sun while Noah sat impassively on guard.

Vere did her packing and then went into the galley to make tea. Hugo liked his afternoon tea, and it was only on the hottest, busiest days that he exchanged it for beer.

"Tea!" she sang when it was ready, and poured a glass of orange juice for herself. Hugo came in from the wheelhouse, an empty cardboard box in his hand. He tossed it on the table, sat down and picked up the teapot. As he poured, Vere absently picked up the box.

"Is this the box that had no part in it?" she asked.

"That's it, damn their eyes. I've had Mark and Gordon going through every box in the store, checking for any other empties."

"How could it have happened?" she said.

He drank deeply and shook his head. "Don't know, really. Could be a simple mistake, could be—some kind of scam at the factory, somebody ripping off parts and selling them privately."

She was only glancing idly at the box, with its colourful print detailing the manufacturer's name and the item, but suddenly her hand clenched and she looked closer. Her heart and her breathing both stopped together, and she said breathlessly, "Hugo, what's this?"

"What's what?" he asked, taking it from her and glancing at it. "That number? It's the manufacturer's part number. Why?"

There was no why, and she didn't answer, but now her heart was choking her. In small black print, the little number read BFX359.

The number she had heard Harwood say over the phone. The number Cass's people were checking, to see if it matched *Incitatus*'s yard number.

Chapter 19

She didn't stop to think. It wasn't like her to be impulsive, but she was suddenly overwhelmed with determination. She finished her orange juice, then interrupted whatever Hugo was saying to excuse herself. She walked out into the saloon, through greenery of the aft deck and outside to look over onto the deck below. Harwood still lay sleeping in the sun beside the Jacuzzi, and it gave her some satisfaction to know that he would have a bad and painful sunburn by now. Noah, hearing her footsteps, glanced up from his book and shook his head to indicate he needed nothing. There were a couple of unopened bottles of beer in the ice bucket beside him, and the plate of snacks she had taken down earlier was mostly untouched.

She smiled and nodded and turned back inside, where she went lightly down the staircase. Pausing to take some fresh towels from the linen cupboard, she opened the door and stepped inside the master stateroom.

The bed and the top of the built-in unit were clear. She stepped over to the little chest of drawers beside the bed and tried the bottom one, but she had known before she started that it would be locked. It was, she noted, the only drawer with a lock. She pulled open the top one—no keys. Quickly and competently she searched all the likely places in the room where Harwood might think it safe to leave his keys, but she didn't find them. She searched the bathroom and his shower bag—still nothing. Probably they were in his shorts pocket on deck.

She knew the evidence to incriminate him was in that little bottom drawer. Once she had her hands on it, he was powerless, wasn't he? So she need not worry about leaving signs behind of what she had done—by the time the break-in was discovered—the moment the break-in *happened,* she told herself—it was already too late for Bill Harwood.

She left the stateroom and jogged along to the engine room. Evidence of the work that was going on to repair the engine was everywhere, but it didn't take her long to see that what she wanted was the open toolbox. She bent and after a few moments' search extracted a small, flat screwdriver, then turned and left again.

Back in Harwood's stateroom, she knelt in front of the little drawer and slipped the screwdriver into the space above the lock. At first she tried to catch the top of the bolt and push it down, but it was too good a lock. Finally, forgetting the length of time she had taken and the danger inherent in the possibility that what she was looking for wasn't really inside, she forced the screwdriver well into the space and simply pushed it up so that something had to give.

It was the wood that gave, and it gave with a loud crack that startled her, making her momentarily aware of her surroundings. But the heat was on her now, and hearing no response, no footsteps, she bent to her task. It was now or never.

After a few moments, she had the shattered drawer open. Forgetting to breathe, she reached down for the papers she saw there and drew them out.

As she lifted them, she saw there was more than paper in the drawer. Underneath, there was the familiar colour and shape of a Canadian passport. But she knew Hugo had all their passports, because he had had to check them all out with Immigration two days ago, and then in again when the delay occurred.

With trembling fingers, Vere set down the papers and reached for the passport. Somehow she knew, before she opened it. But still it was a terrible, a horrifying shock to see Cilla's face looking up at her. Her eyes clouded with tears. Had she been hoping, in spite of everything, that Cilla had died an ordinary death? Vere gave a little sob and wiped her eyes with the back of her hand.

The passport had been counted lost with *Incitatus*. Whatever the other papers held, here in her hand was surely indisputable proof that *Incitatus* had not gone down. Vere shoved the passport into the pocket of her shorts, and suddenly becoming aware of the passage of precious minutes, reached again for the two sheets of paper she had laid down.

She saw that the top one was an official document, and read the name *Incitatus;* then, behind her, there was a soft sound. She whirled.

"What the hey are you doing?" Greg asked, as if he really wanted to know.

Vere scrambled to her feet, facing him. She was closer to the bathroom than he to her, and with no more than a second's hesitation she dashed inside and out the other door, leading to the corridor. At the companionway she went down, and was running toward the aft deck when she realized that this was the Jacuzzi deck and Noah and Harwood must be there. As she altered her course to go up the main staircase, she heard the sliding door move: Greg had called Noah on the radios they always carried.

On the deck above, the saloon was empty, and she ran through it, through the glassed-in aft deck, tore open the sliding door and out onto the short open deck. There, where a few days ago she had jumped, she suddenly paused for a fatal second—would the water destroy the precious documents she carried if she swam for it? Would he get away with it after all?

"Cass!" she screamed once, and then turned to face Greg as he came to get her.

"Who are you?" Bill Harwood demanded again, in a voice harsh with anger. They faced her in a semicircle—Noah and Greg and Harwood, and there was no chance to run now.

"I am Cilla Fairweather," Vere said at last. "You thought you killed me, didn't you? But you were wrong. I survived."

Harwood swore grotesquely. "Cilla Fairweather is dead. I saw her die." Then, as if he had suddenly reminded himself of the story, "She went down on *Incitatus*."

She smiled at him. "But *Incitatus* never went down, Mr. Harwood, don't you remember? Harry sailed it south. And I didn't die. You thought you'd killed me, didn't you? But you didn't succeed."

She saw the first flicker of doubt enter his eyes. He swore again, a crude but unimaginative invention that turned her stomach, the import of which was that she was lying.

Noah and Greg exchanged glances. "Somebody aboard," said Noah.

"Dammit, I told him to stay there till I called!" Harwood exploded. "Get him—"

Noah shook his head. "I don't think it's the captain, Mr. Harwood." Harwood had sent Hugo ashore on a fool's errand. They were alone on the ship.

Harwood started to speak, but Noah waved him imperatively to silence. He and Greg stood immobile, listening for a repeat of the sound that had warned them of someone's presence on the yacht, something that would give them a bearing.

"*Incitatus* never went down," Vere said loudly, trying to make some covering noise. She stamped a couple of times with her foot, making the deck ring hollowly. "We're standing on it now, aren't we, Mr. Harwood, so it could hardly be said to have suffered either fire or sinking, though I must say the new decorations haven't improved it. Gold-plated taps!"

"Shut up," Harwood said, with quiet menace, and in his hand there was suddenly a small but effective-looking gun, and it was pointing her way. Vere choked, swallowed and said no more.

"Get in here with your hands up, or the girl gets it through the head," Harwood said, in the same level voice.

"Never mind me! Go get the police!" Vere called quickly, but too late. A tall, muscular figure, still beaded with water and nearly naked, unfolded itself from behind a sofa across the saloon and approached, his hands loosely at his sides, palms out to show they were empty.

They all gasped. No one had expected him to be so close. "Who the hell are you?" Harwood demanded hoarsely.

"My name's Conway, Harwood," he said, nodding as if this were a business meeting. "We haven't met, but I feel I know you very well. I'm a lawyer for Seaworthy investigating the fraudulent *Incitatus* claim."

Greg shook his head. "I'm in security, Mr. Harwood. If you were looking for someone to act as your hit man, you should have specified. It's not a risk I'm prepared to take."

"Look," Harwood said persuasively. "There's a lot at stake here. All right, a million. That's half a million each. You'll be set up for life. You'll never get a chance like this again."

"It can't be done. People will miss them. Everyone knows the girl was—"

"He owns a boat, doesn't he? Take it out and scuttle it. They'll be called lost at sea."

"How are we going to get them off the yacht without the whole harbour seeing? It's broad daylight." Greg was speaking in a calm, reasoning tone, and it seemed clear he felt Harwood was in the grip of the irrational. Vere agreed. Harwood's eyes were alternately wide and narrow, and he kept moving the gun between her and Cass as though at any moment he might forget common sense and simply shoot, on the cornered-rat principle. She was terrified. Her sweat was cold on her skin. She thought that this was perhaps the last sight Cilla had seen in life—Harwood with a gun, and she marveled at the calmness of that goodbye. How brave her cousin had been.

"You haven't said anything," Harwood said suddenly, turning to Noah. The black bodyguard glanced at Greg and spread his hands.

"I've been thinking of ways and means, Mr. Harwood. It might be possible. But it'll take a lot of thinking and planning. We can't just go at it like a battlefield attack." He turned to Greg. "I think it could be done."

Greg seemed to waver, and then find his resolve again. "I don't see how. It's just going to be you and me taking the rap and him getting off. What good's a million when you're on the inside for murder? Where I come from, that's life, and no parole for twenty-five."

"I think it could be done. First off, we have to get these two below and locked up. You're right, we can't take them off the yacht in daylight. But the longer we stand here, the more chance there is of something going wrong. Like the crew coming back." Casually he reached behind his back and pulled his gun. "Look, Mr. Harwood," he said. "Why don't you let me handle this? You can put your gun away now. I'll get these two secure, and then we can discuss it."

There was a terrible pause, while she wondered whether Harwood would simply shoot Cass in his fear. Then he smiled briefly, dropped his gun hand, and slid the little revolver into his shorts pocket. Beside her there was a sudden whirl of motion, and then Cass was moving across the space that separated him from Harwood in a curious kind of dance and his leg went up and Harwood went down with a crash and lay unmoving. It happened too fast for reaction, and she simply stood gawking when she might have acted.

"Run!" Cass called over his shoulder to Vere, turning to face Noah and his gun, his hands moving gently in a way she had seen only in movies. "He won't shoot, not here in port. Get the cops!"

Greg reached the door before her. "No, don't bother getting the cops," he said slowly. "They're—uh, already here." He pulled out a wallet from his back pocket and flashed it with practised ease. "Staff Sgt. Greg Reynolds, RCMP," he said. "This over here is my friend Sgt. Noah Williamson, Eastern Caribbean Police."

Noah looked down at where Harwood lay beached and unmoving. He belched delicately. "You're pretty fast," he observed to Cass. "You haven't killed him, have you?"

"What are you, a Ninja Turtle?" Vere asked. She was giddy with excitement and fatigue. The yacht was full of policemen, summoned by Noah and Greg, and Cass and Vere were sitting in the crew mess over coffee. The waiting seemed interminable.

"That sounds like the confession of a misspent youth," said Cass.

"I admit we had a computer game that I liked a lot," Vere said. "Was it karate?"

"Yes." He drank deeply and refilled his cup.

"Are you a black belt?"

"Yes."

"Didn't I hear somewhere that you can't take on a gun with karate?"

He smiled. "That's why I waited till he put the gun away."

"But Noah had a gun."

"I didn't think Noah was stupid enough to shoot. Harwood was another matter. He was crazy enough to do anything." He reached out and wrapped his hand around her upper arm. "You took too big a risk," he said. "He might have killed you." Vere was going to reply with something flippant, but the look in his eyes stopped her.

The door from the saloon opened and Greg walked in. "All right, you two can go now."

Cass asked him what had been done. "Harwood's on his way to prison here. We'll ask for extradition, of course, but there's no knowing if we'll get it. They may want to try him here." He looked at Vere. "You've been very helpful, but I wish we could have got him back to Canada before making the arrest."

"There are good grounds for trial in Canada," Cass pointed out. "You may get your extradition."

Vere was looking at Greg, and he raised his eyebrows at her. "Did you know who I was when we were on the plane?" she asked.

His eyelashes dropped over his eyes briefly, and then he gazed at her. "I don't think I can answer that," he said.

"Were you investigating the *Incitatus* fraud?" she pursued. "Or is Harwood involved in something else, too?"

"I wouldn't want to jeopardize the case by answering that question just at the moment."

"You can't have thought I was Cilla," she said. Greg just looked interested, and with a shake of her head she gave up. Mounties were Mounties, she reminded herself.

Cass stood up. "Are you packed?" he asked Vere. "I want to get you off this boat before you set any more bombs off."

They flew to Canada to give the news to Alexa and Robert, and to get married. But Alexa wouldn't hear of the quick ceremony that Cass wanted. She wanted a big wedding, and she would arrange it all. "You go and have your sail," she ordered them. "Be back in three months for the final dress fittings."

So they returned to *Vagabond,* to sail away for a year and a day and to dance by the light of the moon. From time to time they received news from home. Because the murders and the insurance fraud had been committed in international waters and primarily against Canadians, and because the accused and most of the witnesses would be Canadian, the Saint Lucian authorities did eventually agree to Bill Harwood's extradition for trial to Canada.

The case hit the papers with a loud splash, and it was another reason, if they needed one, for Cass and Vere to be unreachable. One reporter did track them down, finding them when they stopped in Bequia for supplies, and they gave her a brief interview that was reprinted everywhere. From her they learned that Harry Bridges was also under arrest in Toronto, and that he had named another man, one of the men without passports taken on in La Guaira, who had been the lucky one chosen to survive and help Bridges take the yacht to Honduras. This man was still being sought.

"If Ben can't get a conviction with all this," Cass said, "he'd better resign."

One cloudy afternoon, six weeks later, they lay at harbour in the small, empty, emerald bay in Martinique, with the canopy up, waiting for the rain. Cass had his knee bent up, and Vere was stretched along the bench, lying against his chest.

"Cass," she began softly.

"Mmm, my love?"

"When did it stop being a lie and turn into the truth?"

His large hand caressed her bare shoulder firmly. "When did what stop being a lie?"

"When you told me you loved me, thinking I was Cilla— when did that—change into the truth?"

"It was never a lie." Cass looked up as the first drops of rain began to spatter the awning above them. Then he was silent, as if assessing something. "All right," he said, "you're going to know sometime. I suppose—" He sat forward and swung down his leg. His elbows resting on his knees, he looked down at his hands, hesitant and unsure, and Vere's heart started to beat painfully. What was the secret he didn't want to tell her?

After a moment he got up and disappeared down the companionway. He was gone only a minute. When he returned, he was carrying the photo that she had seen at his bedside months ago. He sat again beside her, looking down at the pictured face with its faint water stains and the inscription, "Lots of love, Cilla," and briefly, almost absently, he stroked the length of the nose. Then, as if coming to resolution, he looked up at her.

"The *Incitatus* disaster was just another case for me at the beginning," he said. "It's not my area, but we're not a big firm, and somehow—I think one of my partners was on holiday—it came to me, and once I'd taken it on I didn't bother to pass it on." He looked back at the photo between his hands. "This picture was washed up a few months after the incident and a copy was eventually forwarded to me, but it didn't pass through my hands. My secretary just put it straight into the file."

His eyes had taken on a distant look. "I remember the day I opened the file, and this face was looking up at me and it was as if I'd ... I can't describe it." He smiled at her, but not with any apology for looking a fool. "If you'd asked me before that moment whether a man could fall in love with a photograph, I'd have said only in Victorian novels. But that's what I did. It was a sense of recognition so deep it lacks words to describe it."

He set down the photo on the seat beside him and leaned back. The rain was getting stronger now, and the tattoo on the awning had thickened into real drumbeats. Behind them water was collecting on the deck and running down toward the gunwales.

"Then I read the covering letter that had come with it, that explained who it was. The woman who'd died. And I was swept with the utter and certain conviction that it was not true. I loved this woman, and she could not be dead. That was all. I knew it. There was nothing rational about it, but it was pure conviction nonetheless. She was not dead. I will never forget that moment—of knowing, of joy, of determination. It sounds insane, I guess. I knew that if I told people they would think I'd gone crazy. But it was the most real moment I've ever experienced. It was like clouds parting and allowing a glimpse of the truth."

He paused for thought and looked deep into her eyes. "I'm sorry to tell you this now, because this picture is your cousin and it's you I love, and I have no explanation for that." He picked up the picture again.

She sat wordless, breathless, unable to move.

"I knew I had to find this woman, that it was up to me, since I was the only person who knew, or believed, that she was alive. I told you I had a sabbatical planned. In that moment—it all happened at once, Vere, much faster than it takes to tell, I've rarely had such a moment of understanding in my life—I knew that I would sail down here and spend my sabbatical looking for the woman in the photo. I told the client that I thought they had firmer grounds for suspicion in the case than they knew, and told them what I planned. They offered me the support of the man they had down here already investigating." He set the photo down and turned to her.

"So I came, and then one day there you were. I knew it was you. There was the same sense of recognition as I'd felt with the photo. And I believed so firmly that you were the woman in the picture that I couldn't hear you when you said you were someone else. I'm sorry. I doubted you for the longest time. I knew it was you I loved, and so I imagined that you were Cilla Fairweather and involved in the fraud. I couldn't stop the investigation, but I felt that if—well, I thought I could get you clear, if you let me."

He took her face between his hands and saw the tears on her cheeks, and his own eyes were suddenly damp. Gently he leaned forward and kissed the tears on one cheek and then the other. "Don't ever think it isn't you that I love," he said. "I have no explanation for the photo, but I know that it was you from the beginning. Please trust me. It was you. Can you believe that?"

Overhead now, the rain was a thunder and a torrent, matching the mighty beating of her heart. Reaching across him, she picked up the photo and looked down at it, remembering again that day, and the cousins' joy in each other's company. Her tears flowed for happiness and for grief together, and she smiled up at him.

"I remember the day this was taken," she said. "We were at the cottage, and I'd just graduated and Cilla had just taken a job on a boat, and it was our last summer together. We took the camera out one day and took pictures, and when we got them developed, Cilla asked me to get a blowup of this one and send it to her.

"So I did. Before I sent it, I wrote on it, what you see here, 'Lots of love, Cilla,' and then I signed it with our secret signature. See this little squiggle here underneath? That's my version of it. Cilla's was the mirror image. We invented it as children, our secret code. I put it on here as a kind of—reminder of the childhood that was gone, but the friendship that wasn't. I didn't know it until I saw this, but she must have carried it with her ever since. I always carried a photo of her with me, too," she said. "Somehow it made the connection stronger when we were apart. So I should have known she would have kept this."

She turned to him, smiling at the look that was coming over his face. "It wasn't a photo Cilla had given to someone else, the way you all thought. It was one I gave to her."

She wiped her tears as he gripped her shoulders and drew her toward him. "So you were right, you see. It was me all along."

Then he kissed her, and the tenderness of his passion was ice and fire on her flesh.

Epilogue

"She's alive?" Vere cried, in a high, incredulous voice. "Cass, she's really alive?"

"She's been found in a hospital. Would you like to read it?"

Somehow she turned up on the doorstep of a Miami hospital, and she's been in a coma there ever since. She had no identification, and no one has known who she was until a nurse saw your picture in a story about the *Incitatus* fraud.

"Oh, thank God! Thank God! Oh, Cass! Can we go home right now?"

"The coma has been getting progressively lighter for several months, according to the Miami hospital," said Alexa. "Since we've got her back here, she seems to be responding to the voices of people she knows, and we've got as many people as possible coming to speak to her, because they think that might draw her out of it. The doctors say there's been observable progress, but she still hasn't opened her eyes." She stopped at the door and turned to Vere, momentarily blocking her way. "She doesn't look very good," she said. "It's a shock at first. But she's physically all right, they think."

She turned and pushed open the door. Vere walked in. Alexa and Cass exchanged a look and remained outside, but she was scarcely aware of that. Slowly she approached the hospital bed, its chrome sides drawn up like a child's crib, and looked down at its tiny occupant.

Cilla had lost so much weight she almost looked like a child, and there was an ugly, puckered scar at her left temple. But all Vere could see was that it was Cilla.

"Silly?" she whispered, using the old childish code by instinct, the name only the cousins knew. Her voice was a breath, a whisper. She cleared her throat, which was choked with emotion. "Silly? Guess who?"

The body on the bed stirred, and then, inside her own mind, Vere felt a sense of terrible effort, of pulling upward through layers of...something, of a struggle to the light. She joined in the struggle, pulling Cilla's spirit up from the depths, calling her, urging her, pleading, praying, and then, so suddenly she started, it was done. The effort was over. She was ashore. Cilla opened her eyes and looked straight into Vere's.

"Verily?" she whispered, her voice croaking with disuse. "Where have I been?"

"It was the life jacket that saved me, I guess," said Cilla. "In the first few minutes. I had that on prior to getting into the life raft, and then it turned out the other two were... weren't going to survive. I refused to get in unless Bill threw his gun over and let the other two get in. I could see he was prepared to kill all three of us, then, so I jumped into the water. He shot me." Her hand went up to her forehead. "What happened?"

"They say it caught you at an angle and ricocheted off your skull."

"I thought I was dead."

"I know you did. I heard you say goodbye," Vere said.

"Not then. I was unconscious, but then I woke up again, I guess not very long afterward, or the sharks would have had me. Anyway, I've got some guardian angel, because what woke me was being bumped by a long wooden crate. Almost as good as a raft. I climbed on it, but I was sure I was... I could see blood all over my hair and clothes and my head felt as if it had been split in two. But I was grateful to die out of the water. I didn't want a shark to find me and go that way." She smiled at her cousin. "That's when I said goodbye. And it's the last I remember of anything much. I vaguely remember trying to talk to you across a huge distance. I knew something was wrong, I knew I had something to tell you, but I didn't know what."

"Yeah, I got those messages, too. But I thought they were—" She blinked back the sudden tears. "It was the anniversary of when you were lost."

"The *anniversary?* Have I been here a *year?*"

"You were in on the plot at the beginning?"

"Oh, yeah. Half a million, he was going to give me." Cilla sighed, as though she regretted the loss, and Vere laughed.

"But it was dishonest," she protested.

"It was just money," Cilla said.

"The insurance company was going to be taken for a pretty heavy ride."

Cilla stopped smiling. "Insurance companies are maybe the worst of all. Don't you remember what the insurance company pulled when Uncle David and Aunt Morgana got killed?''

Vere said nothing.

"I figured any scam against an insurance company was just beating them at their own game. And I thought it wouldn't hurt them to invest a little in your company. If they'd paid up like honest men in the beginning, you'd have had a much better start to your business than you did.''

Cilla said, "Your friend Greg says they've found out how I got to that hospital. Somebody just got an anonymous phone call. Apparently there *was* a ship in the vicinity when the distress call went out, but it didn't answer 'for reasons of its own.' After the second call, they sailed that way, but saw no sign of any sinking ship. Then they found me, floating on that crate. I went into a coma after they got me aboard—I don't remember any of it. They were on their way to Miami. They dropped me at a hospital there.''

"Why on earth didn't they say anything before this?'' Vere demanded.

"They didn't answer that, but your friend Greg thinks it's probably because they were running something very illegal.''

Vere's mouth opened as the last piece fell into place. "But that's the story I told Harry Bridges! And I thought I was getting it from an old TV show!''

"They say there's nothing to stop you getting better very quickly now. All you have to do is eat and exercise and you'll be fine.''

"Mmm.''

"Do you mind making a little push? We're putting off the wedding till September, and I'd kind of like you to be my maid of honour.''

Cilla grinned at them. "Marriage,'' she observed, shaking her head. "It's a very patriarchal institution, you know.

Invented by men to give them exclusive rights with a woman."

Cass grinned at her, reached one strong arm around Vere and pulled her close and safe against his side. "I believe it," he told Cilla. "I believe it."

* * * * *

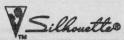

Take 4 bestselling love stories FREE

Plus get a FREE surprise gift!

HE'S AN

AMERICAN HERO

Men of mettle. Men of integrity. Real men who know the real meaning of love. Each month, Intimate Moments salutes these true American Heroes.

For July: THAT SAME OLD FEELING,
by Judith Duncan.
Chase McCall had come home a new man. Yet old lover Devon Manyfeathers soon stirred familiar feelings—and renewed desire.

For August: MICHAEL'S GIFT,
by Marilyn Pappano.
Michael Bennett knew his visions prophesied certain death. Yet he would move the high heavens to change beautiful Valery Navarre's fate.

For September: DEFENDER,
by Kathleen Eagle.
Gideon Defender had reformed his bad-boy ways to become a leader among his people. Yet one habit—loving Raina McKenny—had never died, especially after Gideon learned she'd returned home.

AMERICAN HEROES: Men who give all they've got for their country, their work—the women they love.

Only from

ROMANTIC TRADITIONS

Barbara Faith heats up ROMANTIC TRADITIONS in July with DESERT MAN, IM #578, featuring the forever-sultry sheikh plot line.

Josie McCall knew better than to get involved with Sheikh Kumar Ben Ari. Worlds apart in thought and custom, both suspected their love was destined for failure. Then a tribal war began, and Josie faced the grim possibility of losing her desert lover—for good.

October 1994 will feature Justine Davis's LEFT AT THE ALTAR, her timely take on the classic story line of the same name. And remember, ROMANTIC TRADITIONS will continue to bring you the best-loved plot lines from your most-cherished authors, so don't miss any of them— only in **INTIMATE MOMENTS®** *Silhouette®*

Return to Southern Alberta's rustic ranch land as Judith Duncan's Wide Open Spaces miniseries continues in July with THAT SAME OLD FEELING, IM#577.

Chase McCall had come home a new man. Yet painful memories—and an old but familiar lover—awaited his return. Devon Manyfeathers had refused him once, but one look into her soulful brown eyes had Chance focusing on forever.

And there will be more McCalls to meet in future months, as they learn love's lessons in the wide open spaces of Western Canada.

To order your copy of *That Same Old Feeling*, or the first Wide Open Spaces title, *Beyond All Reason* (IM #536), please send your name, address, zip or postal code, along with a check or money order (please do not send cash) for $3.50 ($3.99 in Canada) for each book ordered, plus 75¢ postage and handling ($1.00 in Canada), payable to Silhouette Books, to:

In the U.S.	In Canada
3010 Walden Ave.	P. O. Box 636
P. O. Box 9077	Fort Erie, Ontario
Buffalo, NY 14269-9077	L2A 5X3

Please specify book title(s), line and number with your order.
Canadian residents add applicable federal and provincial taxes.   WIDE2